The Author

MARGARET LAURENCE was born in Neepawa, Manitoba, in 1926. Upon graduation from Winnipeg's United College in 1947, she took a job as a reporter for the *Winnipeg Citizen*.

From 1950 until 1957 Laurence lived in Africa, the first two years in Somalia, the next five in Ghana, where her husband, a civil engineer, was working. She translated Somali poetry and prose during this time, and began her career as a fiction writer with stories set in Africa.

When Laurence returned to Canada in 1957, she settled in Vancouver, where she devoted herself to fiction with a Ghanaian setting: in her first novel, *This Side Jordan*, and in her first collection of short fiction, *The Tomorrow-Tamer*. Her two years in Somalia were the subject of her memoir, *The Prophet's Camel Bell*.

Separating from her husband in 1962, Laurence moved to England, which became her home for a decade, the time she devoted to the creation of five books about the fictional town of Manawaka, patterned after her birthplace, and its people: *The Stone Angel*, *A Jest of God*, *The Fire-Dwellers*, *A Bird in the House*, and *The Diviners*.

Laurence settled in Lakefield, Ontario, in 1974. She complemented her fiction with essays, book reviews, and four children's books. Her many honours include two Governor General's Awards for Fiction and more than a dozen honorary degrees.

Margaret Laurence died in Lakefield, Ontario, in 1987.

MARGARET LAURENCE

This Side Jordan

With an Afterword by George Woodcock

M&S

This book was originally published by
Macmillan and Company Limited in 1960

The characters and events in this novel are fictitious.
Any resemblance they have to people and events
in life is purely coincidental

Canadian Cataloguing in Publication Data

Laurence, Margaret, 1926–1987.
This side Jordan

(New Canadian library)
Bibliography: p.
ISBN 0-7710-9967-3

I. Title. II. Series.

PS8523.A86T4 1989   C813′.54   C89-093763-X
PR9199.3.L39T4 1989

Printed and bound in Canada

McClelland & Stewart Inc.
The Canadian Publishers
481 University Avenue
Toronto, Ontario
M5G 2E9

In Memory of my Mother
Margaret Campbell Wemyss

Acknowledgements

HIGHLIFE

FIRE, FIRE, FIRE – Calender and his Maringar Band
(*Decca*). CLUB GIRL – E. T. Mensah's Tempos Band
(*Decca*). ESTHER ELDER – E. T. Mensah's Tempos Band
(*Decca*). EVERYBODY LIKES SATURDAY NIGHT (*Decca*).
ALL ANGELS PRAY FOR ME (*Decca*).

AKAN DRUM PROVERBS AND DIRGES: SOURCES

'Whom Does Death Overlook' – Rattray, R. S., *Religion
and Art in Ashanti* – Published by Basel Mission, Kumasi,
1927. Reissued by Oxford University Press, 1954. 'As We
Pass Here, Hate!' – Rattray, R. S., *Religion and Art in
Ashanti*. Drummers' Group Funeral Dirge – Nketia, J. H.,
Funeral Dirges of the Akan People – Achimota, 1955.
'Thou Speeding Bird' – Meyerowitz, E. L. R., *Sacred State
of the Akan* – Faber & Faber, London, 1951. Other Akan
proverbs – Danquah, J. B., *The Akan Doctrine of God*,
Lutterworth Press, London, 1944.

'Until the Lord have given your brethren rest, as he hath given you, and they also have possessed the land which the Lord your God giveth them; then ye shall return unto the land of your possession, and enjoy it, which Moses the Lord's servant gave you on this side Jordan toward the sunrising.'

(Joshua I:15)

The Day Will Come
Authority Is Never Loved
Flee, Oh Ye Powers Of Darkness
Rise Up, Ghana

(Slogans from African 'mammy-lorries')

'Oh God, there is something above, let it reach me.'

(Akan proverb)

★ I ★

THE SIX BOYS were playing the Fire Highlife, playing it with a beat urgent as love. And Johnnie Kestoe, who didn't like Africans, was dancing the highlife with an African girl.

Charity's scarlet smile mocked his attempts to rotate his shoulders and wriggle his European hips to the music. Her own fleshy hips and buttocks swayed easily, and her big young breasts, unspoiled by children and only lightly held by her pink blouse, rose and fell as though the music were her breath. Johnnie grinned awkwardly at her, then he jerked his head away.

> '*Fiyah, fiyah, fiyah, fiyah-ma,*
> *Fiyah deah come — baby!*
> *Fiyah, fiyah, fiyah, fiyah-ma,*
> *Fiyah deah come — ah ah!*
> *I went to see my lovely boy,*
> *Lovely boy I love so well——*'

At one of the tables around the outdoor dance floor, a young European woman watched thoughtfully. At another table an African man watched, then turned away and spat. Both were angry, and with the same person.

Music was the clothing of West African highlife, but rhythm its blood and bone. This music was sophisticated.

I

It was modern. It was new. To hell with the ritual tribal dance, the drums with voices ancient as the forest.

The torn leaves of the palm trees shivered in the wind and the strings of fairy lights glittered like glass beads in the musty courtyard.

The dancers themselves did not analyse the highlife any more than they analysed the force that had brought them all together here, to a nightclub called 'Weekend In Wyoming', the wealthy and the struggling, the owners of chauffeur-driven Jaguars and the riders of bicycles.

They were bound together, nevertheless, by the music and their need of it. Africa has danced pain and love since the first man was born from its red soil. But the ancient drums could no longer summon the people who danced here. The highlife was their music. For they, too, were modern. They, too, were new.

And yet the old rhythms still beat strongly in this highlife in the centre of Accra, amid the taxi horns, just as a few miles away, in Jamestown or Labadi, they pulsed through the drums while the fetish priestess with ash-smeared cheeks whirled to express the unutterable, and the drummer's eyes grew glassy and still, his soul drugged more powerfully than the body could be.

Into the brash contemporary patterns of this Africa's fabric were woven symbols old as the sun-king, old as the oldest continent.

Johnnie Kestoe was thin in a sharp, almost metallic way, like a man made of netted wire upon which flesh has been inadequately spread. He had the extreme whiteness of skin that sometimes accompanies dark hair, and although he was not tall, the thrusting energy with which he invariably moved gave him a passable substitute for height.

He held the brown girl's hand tightly, their gearfingers meshed to synchronize their separateness. His other hand rested on her shoulder; his fingertips received the tremor of her upstretching muscles, the delicate levering of bones, and he was guided by her through the highlife's gradual frenzy.

The music was languid on the surface. The main beat was lazy and casual. Then the second and third rhythms — the racing inner pulse, the staccato heartbeat in the slow flesh.

Oppressive and stifling, the air seemed to be hung with hot unshed rain, and the leaves of the palm trees crackled like breeze-fanned flames. But the African dancers were unaffected by the heat. They moved to the new-old drumcall as though it were their only purpose.

Johnnie was still new enough to want to stare at them. He looked forward to the time when he would be as blasé as the other Europeans in the Firm: that attitude marked the men of experience from the green boys.

A fat old mammy, purple-swathed, enormous of buttock, squealed with laughter as she bounced her melon breasts up and down. And the young man with her laughed too, perhaps at himself.

Around the edge of the dance floor, in a huge shuffling circle, African couples danced without touching one another. The rhythms of the highlife seemed to make each body an extension of the other, of every other. To Johnnie's mind there was something weird about it, like a sexual experience with more than two. But his arms tightened around the girl. Her moist skin and the smooth-oiled twisting of her body caused in him an itch of curiosity.

And over there was his wife, sitting with the others, seeing him make a fool of himself.

The touch of the highlife was growing more rough and demanding, as though building to an unimaginable climax.

3

The climax was never reached. The music stopped — more than stopped. It went out like a puffed-at match. It broke with the suddenness of cracked china into silence. The vibrant bodies sagged, ceased, turned to clay. The women who had danced so magnificently, flames of the forest, clumped off the dancefloor heavily, clumsily, shoulders stooping, bellies protruding. Human voices began, chattering nonsense, trivial noises in the night.

Johnnie drew away from the girl and looked at her. The brown girl, still laughing, leaned against him, her breasts brushing his arm.

She was drunk. He hadn't noticed before. She giggled, and her head, bent close to him, reeked of the penny perfume the native markets hawked. She wore a headscarf, and it was disarranged, ridiculously askew. Sweat lay wetly between breasts that were partly exposed by her wilted pink drawstring blouse.

Johnnie dropped the girl's hand and walked away from her, feeling a vague sense of righteousness as he did so. The curious itch of desire had gone out with the music. Like sweat in the hot night, the excitement had turned to chill.

In that gutterstreet of his childhood there had co-existed, but not peacefully, some Jamaicans. Children learned young there. Stick, stone, shod foot in belly, knee in crotch, and — when you had filched enough from shop or barrow to earn one — knife. The streetchildren's creed, more powerful and obeyed than that of the Apostles, did not admit the brotherhood even of siblings, but even in anarchy there must be some order. All despised all, but some were despised more than others. Those London Irish were low in the social scale, but lower still were the Jamaicans, blacks, heathens. They lived cheaper than anyone else could, a dozen to a room, big-muscled men with a crazy fear of being deported. A

4

slow-witted Irishman, a halfman with a bone disease, a limping clown who went by the name of Dennis Kestoe and who earned his two quid a week slopping out the Men's lavatories in the tube stations with bucket and rag — he lost his job to a man-ape Jamaican who, being whole of bone, could swab down twice as many urinals in a given time. The Irishman's son was ten, and small, but he had his blade-friend. The buttocks of the Jamaican's son bled profusely like life turned to mere meat, and the nigger, who was thirteen and a head taller, bawled like a raped nun, each huge tremulous tear setting off an orgasm of laughter in the bitter Irish bellies of young bystanders. But the big Jamaican had caught them at it, and the others fled girlish into the night. In a fury of paternal tenderness, the Jamaican had hit with his clenched fist, and when the white boy had finished spitting blood into the gutter, the black man had picked him up and he could feel the big dark body trembling. He had spat again, in loathing, and the black father dropped him abruptly onto the cobblestones. The boy, crouching, terrified, had hissed — 'bastard, bastard, black black bastard——'.

Johnnie straightened his bony shoulders and shook back the hair from his forehead. He was tight, or he would never have danced with a black woman. He wondered if there would be any lifted eyebrows.

And then, there was Bedford, standing beside him, looking embarrassed.

'I think you should know,' Bedford said. 'Bags of umbrage being taken.'

'James?'

'Yes. I thought I'd just have a word with you, you know, so you could think up something soothing to say.'

Shame made Johnnie aggressive.

'What business is it of James'? I'll dance with whoever I——'

Bedford gnawed at the grey moustache that sprouted like a clump of elephant grass under his nose. His handsome red-veined face looked vaguely troubled.

'Don't upset yourself,' he said with gigantic calm. 'Bad for the blood-pressure. Does no one any good. I've been knocking around the East half my life. Don't take it amiss if I pass on a friendly word or two——'

'Sorry,' Johnnie mumbled. 'You've been very good. You mustn't think I don't appreciate——'

'A chap is seen with an African woman, and soon his own servants or clerks get cheeky — won't work — laugh behind his back. Even your little flurry tonight — your own boys will know by morning. Bush telegraph. It doesn't do. That's what upsets James, you know. God knows there's no love lost between James and me, but I will say this for him — he won't stand for any nonsense.'

'It won't happen again,' Johnnie said. 'I don't know why the hell I did it. I don't like Africans any better than you do.'

The grim humour of exile showed in Bedford's grey eyes.

'You couldn't possibly dislike them half as much as I do, old boy. You haven't been here long enough.'

Johnnie made a half-hearted attempt to neaten his hair, dishevelled and sweat-damp. His fingers came away smelling sour. Sweat had seeped coldly through his white drill dinner jacket, and he shivered a little in the sultry air.

The occupants of the table did not look up as the two men slid into chairs. Cora Thayer, who could never sit still, was picking at her nail varnish with agitated skeletal fingers, peeling away shreds like red scabs. Beside her, Helen Cunningham, Bedford's wife, fixed blue amused eyes on the middle distance. Miranda Kestoe leaned forward, listening to James Thayer holding forth about Africa.

Johnnie sat back in the flimsy canvas chair. One thing about the Squire — he had been here a long time, and he knew.

'When I first came here,' James was saying, 'insolence was practically unheard of. Even today, the bush African is all right. If his belly's full, that's all he's worried about. But when they move to the cities — look at them! They get cheeky as the devil, and every boat-boy thinks he has a right to a Jaguar. That's Free-Dom for you.'

James was frail and gnomelike, with tufts of grey hair circling a crown so bare it seemed tonsured. The skin of his face was soft and creased like a piece of chamois. He looked unprepossessing enough — a hearth-dweller, waking only to mourn fretfully the dead years, the better years when things were done in the right way. But the gentle whining voice could snap and snarl when it had to, and the eyes, so nostalgic after the first sundowner, were shrewd and uncompromising by day. Allkirk, Moore & Bright thought enough of him to keep him on for thirty years and to make him, finally, manager of the all-important Textile Branch.

'I don't dislike Africans,' James went on, 'but they're children, and if we forget that fact, we're liable to wrong both ourselves and them.'

He turned to Johnnie.

'Don't you agree?'

'Do you mean — politically?' Johnnie asked.

'Oh yes — that,' James said, 'and other things.'

Johnnie felt fresh rivers of sweat pouring from him.

'An hour ago I might not have known what you meant,' he said, 'but now I know.'

'Good,' James said quietly. 'I rather thought you would.'

7

Expertly, Bedford and Helen took over the conversation and began recounting anecdotes about their servants. Relieved that he had been let off so easily, Johnnie turned to his wife.

Miranda — his affectionate, well-mannered Miranda — was looking at him as though she detested him. He hadn't thought she would be this angry. He was startled, but he found himself, as well, admiring the look of her. Her face wore a haughtiness that suited it. She wasn't pretty. He wouldn't have married a pretty girl. Her face was thin, almost whittled down to its bones. The skull of her was more beautiful than the flesh. Fine-shaped as glass, but strong, her bones were the bones of Deirdre, that long-dead queen the poem said no man now can ever dream to be her lover.

He leaned close to her so no one else could hear.

'Manda — I'm sorry.'

She looked away.

'For what?'

'For dancing with that whore — for whatever made you angry.'

'You don't have to apologize. Not for that. Did you think I cared that you danced with an African girl? The only thing I minded was that you — you thought there was something dirty in doing it. That's all.'

'Oh Christ,' Johnnie said, angry now, too, 'so that's it. What's the use of discussing it? Ever since you got pregnant, you've been so damned unreasonable——'

'Of course,' she said furiously, 'blame everything on that.'

But now he had made her conscious of the smock billowing unprettily around her. She smoothed at it and adjusted the collar. Johnnie watched. As though a twist and a tug here and there could make a piece of cloth conceal more effectively the mound that had once been a body belonging to her, and

8

to him. Now it belonged to neither of them, but only to the half-formed sluglike thing inside her, straining food from her blood.

'Day after day,' Bedford was saying, his moustache quivering with laughter, 'the wretched cook kept saying to Helen, "Madam, my belly humbug me." She got herself all worked up about it. Expected him to conk out with peritonitis any moment. But d'you know what it was? The stupid oaf was constipated.'

'So I gave him some mag.sulph. in a bottle,' Helen said, 'and told him to take a dose at night. The next morning I thought he looked a bit wan, so I asked him. He said, "Madam, medicine he be fine too much." It turned out he'd taken the whole bottleful.'

Helen was like a Viking woman, big-boned and about five-foot-ten. She always looked sluttish in the daytime, but in the evening she shed her untidy daytime self. Tonight she wore a green cocktail frock with a white Kashmir shawl. Her hair, genuine blonde, yellow as sunflowers, was brushed back and held with fancy jade combs that might have been the loot of a seafaring ancestor.

'Speaking of the well-known African cluelessness,' Bedford said, 'the other day I found one of my clerks reading a speech of Nkrumah's. So I said to him, "Now, Quansah, tell me truthfully — what the devil do you think you're going to get out of Independence?" You won't believe this, but I swear it's absolutely true. He said, "I have been told, sah, that every citizen of the new Ghana will own a car. I would like an Opel Kapitan." What can you do with a chap like that?'

Johnnie looked at Bedford appreciatively. Major (he still used the title) B. L. K. Cunningham. Johnnie always thought of Bedford as the massive knight. Once, shortly after Johnnie first met Miranda, she had dragged him to see

9

the Tower of London. He'd found only one thing interesting — a suit of armour that had been forged for some massive knight who must have seemed magically powerful to his little contemporaries, the embodiment both of their childhood's longing fantasies and of their shadow-fears. That armour was made for a man like Bedford. Too bad he had to make do with the mediocre present. But he did his best. He never walked ordinarily; he always gave the impression of being On Parade, or perhaps Inspecting The Troops. Even when sober he walked heavily, and even when drunk his steps had an odd precision. He never forgot that men like himself do not stumble or cavort: they bear themselves well under every circumstance.

'Let's talk about something different,' Cora said in her birdvoice. 'The Africans — it's always the Africans. I get so sick of them.'

'All right,' Bedford said, frowning in annoyance, 'what shall it be? Art? The theatre? Horse-breeding? Name your subject.'

But of course she could think of nothing, so they all sat without speaking. Johnnie wondered why any lemon-skinned woman would wear a urine-coloured dress. Cora had had too much tropical heat and too little sun for many years. Her hair was pale straw. Face, hair, dress — all were the same colour, the faint yellow of age, like a linen tablecloth tucked away in the bottom drawer of the sideboard for half a century. Maybe it wasn't such a bad thing that Miranda was having a baby. The childless women fared the worst here.

The music tootled and jigged forth once more, a fanfaronade of drums and braggart horns.

> '*Jaguar — Been-to——*
> *Jaguar — Fridgeful——*'

Several African boys were picking their way past the table. One of them — on impulse, or perhaps egged on by his friends — stopped beside Miranda's chair. Obviously he had not realized she was well-advanced in pregnancy. When he saw, he drew back a step and hovered there, gauche and uncertain. But he recovered himself quickly. Turning to Cora, he bowed, then spoke to James.

'May I ask your wife for this dance, please?'

Cora's face flushed damson-red. James fixed the young African with a steady unblinking stare.

'You may not,' he replied coolly. 'Madam doesn't wish to dance with you. Is that clear?'

The boy's hands clenched and unclenched. Then, astonishingly, he smiled.

'Perfectly clear, sir,' he said softly. 'I thank you.'

Johnnie felt himself bristle with resentment. The African had asked for that slap of rejection. He must have known it would happen. The boy had sought it out and courted it, merely for the gratification his own resulting hatred would give him.

James was watching Johnnie's face.

'That's precisely what I mean about the urban African,' he said.

'How could he think——?' Cora cried. 'As if I would——'

Johnnie glanced at her and looked away immediately. Her cagebird eyes had grown bright and hot with a hatred beside which the boy's seemed simple and uncomplicated. Johnnie knew it as the same he had felt with the brown girl — a disgust that beckoned almost as much as it repelled. He at least had recognized it in himself. She, plainly, did not.

Then Miranda's voice, outspoken, reassuring in its literalness and health.

'I don't see what was wrong. I thought he was very courteous.'

The other four gasped at her, unable to believe that she was not being facetious.

His heavy body slouched out full length, Victor Edusei watched the dancers. He watched Charity dancing with Johnnie Kestoe and he spat on the packed-earth floor.

When she came back he ordered another drink for her. She was drunk already, her face vacant and relaxed. But she expected it, so Victor put the glass obligingly into her hand.

'Did you enjoy it, dancing with one of our white brothers?' Victor asked.

He spoke in Twi, her language, and originally his. His eyes had a fire that made his square ugly face compelling despite itself. His voice was soft, but something in it made Charity look at him suspiciously.

'He is all right,' she said unsteadily. 'He is a nice boy.'

'A nice boy——' Victor said. 'Oh, good. Fine. I'm glad to know he is a nice boy. I wouldn't have suspected it.'

'You are jealous,' she said, with a laugh. 'He is not bad.'

She reached one hand inside her blouse to scratch her breasts.

'He is not rich,' Victor said casually. 'Be careful, Charity.'

'Richer than you.'

'That would not be difficult.'

'He is a nice boy. You're jealous, Victor.'

'You have a kind opinion of him,' Victor said brutally, 'considering that he thinks you're a whore.'

Charity slapped at his hand.

'He does not! How do you know?'

'Because——' He hesitated and then laughed. 'Never mind. Enjoy your visit in the big city, Charity. Is this better than Koforidua?'

'Even if he wants that,' she said, leaning against him, 'what do you want that's so different? A mother, I suppose?'

'My mother is like ten,' Victor replied. 'No, thanks.'

'There. You see?'

'You're drunk,' Victor was smiling, 'and all because you and your husband can't get a baby——'

Charity drew herself up. Her light blue headscarf was crooked and her tight mauve skirt was creased around her hips. But in the soft drunken face there was pain and dignity.

'Don't speak of it,' she said in a small voice. 'I beg you.'

'All right,' Victor spoke gently. 'I'm sorry. Don't dance with any more whitemen, Charity, will you?'

'Why not? I can look after myself.'

'Said the bird as she flew into the crocodile's mouth.'

'All you know how to do is talk, talk, talk!' she cried. 'I'll dance with him if I like.'

She lurched to her feet.

'See — I'm going now to dance with him again. I'll let him take me home if I want to. And that's not all I'll let him do. He liked me——'

'You're stupid, Charity,' he said in a low harsh voice, 'do you know that? You're really pleased, aren't you, that he asked you to dance? I wish you knew what it was all about. Come on, I'm taking you home now.'

'No!' she shrilled. 'No, Victor! I won't go! I'm having a good time.'

He dropped her wrist abruptly.

'Have it without me, then,' he said.

He turned to go.

'Victor——'

He looked at her. Then, suddenly, he held her tightly, his broad hands biting into her shoulders.

'All right,' he said, 'we'll stay. What's the difference? Come on — maybe another whiteman will ask you to dance, and you can tell all your friends at home. Will that make you happy? Or do you just want me to——'

Her shoulders began to lift and her hips to sway with the rhythm of the highlife. Victor's hands slid down close to her breasts.

'Is that all you want, after all?' he said. 'Just highlife?'

'Maybe,' she said. 'Maybe not.'

The tensions of Victor's big body seemed to change. Normally, he moved with a caricatured slouch. But when he danced, his body possessed an easy grace. He kept his hands close to Charity's breasts. Otherwise, their bodies hardly touched, yet they responded to each other.

It was a calypso this time.

> '*My aunt daughter Esther,*
> *Gal of dozen year old,*
> *Yet act like a woman-o——*'

When it was over, Victor half dragged her back to their table. Charity's lipstick had worn off, and the pale powder she had daubed on her mahogany skin was channelled with sweat. Her blouse was stuck with sweat to her breasts. She hobbled a little, in the high heels she was unused to wearing. But her body, ripe and supple — nothing could change that but the years she had not yet lived.

'You dance——' she began in Twi, then switched to slurred pidgin, 'fine too much.'

He looked at her for a long moment, unsmiling, his eyes stony, and he leaned close to catch her body's rank sweet

14

smell that was almost obscured by the cheap perfume with which she had drenched herself.

'That surprises you?' he said at last. 'I just didn't feel like it before, that's all. You happy now? You think I'm ugly, Charity?'

She shook her head and giggled.

'Yes,' he said. 'Most women do, until — never mind, you won't think so tomorrow.'

Her mind was too foggy to listen to him. She smiled at him prettily, in the way she had learned.

'You still want to stay?' he asked.

'No,' she said. 'I'll go now. With you.'

Both his scorn and his need showed in his eyes, but she did not see. He put one arm closely around her and bent his head to hers.

'You were right, mister whiteman,' he whispered softly in English, 'but it's not for you. No, sir. Not this time.'

'What you say, Victor?'

'What do you think?' he said. 'Only that I love you.'

'Did you say that?'

'Sure,' he said. 'Sure.'

★ 2 ★

NOT SO LONG AGO the building had been a tenement. Now it was a school. In the damp heat and corroding salt winds, it sagged, buckled, rotted and decayed a little more each year. Warped wooden shutters flapped brokenly at every window, and the discolorations of time oozed wetly from the walls. It was like an old unburied corpse. The sun and sea and wind would surely pick its bones clean one day, but the process of its decomposition was ugly and ill-smelling.

The face of the cadaver wore, ironically, daubs of shiny paint. The sign above the door, letters scarlet, read:

FUTURA ACADEMY
— THE FUTURE IS YOURS! —

And underneath, in sober, suitable, scholarly black:

J. A. MENSAH'S SECONDARY SCHOOL

In the inner courtyard, behind the main building, a few of the inheritors of this scarlet future squatted in the rusty dust playing ludo. The boys looked oddly childish in their khaki shorts, their brown limbs bony and hairless. They were absorbed utterly in their game. The dice rattled and rolled. The boys shouted, flexing their supple bodies in exaggerated attitudes of glee or disappointment.

Around them scrawny chickens squawked and pecked, and a turkey, tethered by a vine, repeated untiringly its sad demented cry. The mud compound was littered with crumpled bits of paper, blackened banana peels, mango stones with shreds of fruit clinging dirtily to them.

Residence and classroom buildings, which formed three sides of the compound square, were one-storey lean-tos built of mud and wattle. The lavatory was in the middle of the compound, four mud walls, shoulder-high and unroofed. Out of the doorway spilled scraps of newspaper, excreta-soiled. Beside the lavatory grew a tall frangipani tree whose tender scented blossoms fought a losing battle with the latrine stench.

In the Fourth Form classroom, Nathaniel Amegbe, schoolmaster, sat at his rickety desk worrying. Nathaniel spent a good part of his day worrying. He would have been lost without this time-filling occupation.

He was a short man, a little stooped despite his youth. Thickly built, he had surprising strength in his arms, and his squat neck was set bull-like on sturdy shoulders. But this strength was overshadowed by his permanent anxious frown, by the spectacles that made brown and white bulbs of his eyes, and by the way he had of opening and shutting his hands constantly when he was speaking with anyone.

As usual, Nathaniel was worrying about money. He looked again at the letter. Kwaale was not literate, so the letter had been written by a semi-literate scribe. But under the garbled flowering phrases the shrewd personality of his eldest sister showed like thorns thrusting up through a cluster of sickly-sweet cactus blossoms.

'It is with high respects that I beg advice to you, my dear Brother, of the Needful of our family. The case against

Kofi Abaku is proceeding one and half Year so far to date and Mr. Cudjoe, Barrister, begs advice for Fee it must be pay for six month Previously and soonest possible at our early Convenence. We are remembrance your Great Affection, and turusting your High Position as Schoolmaster——'

A couple of machetes and six sacks of cocoa pods had been stolen. One of the machetes had turned up in Abaku's hut. Two years and dozens of bribed witnesses later, the two families were still battling in court with unabated vigour and dwindling finances.

Kwaale wanted money. Aya wanted money. Aya's mother wanted money. The uncles wanted money. 'Your High Position as Schoolmaster——'

Nathaniel pushed his glasses up on his forehead and ran one hand across his eyes. This was his inheritance — a family. A family that grew and grew, increasing as their poverty increased and their land diminished.

He saw them suddenly as the surf, wave after wave, a tumult of outstretched hands battering endlessly at one weak island.

'You still here, man?' The voice was cocky. 'You better watch out for that sweet young wife of yours if you never go home to her.'

It was Lamptey, who taught English. He snaked into Nathaniel's classroom now, his shoulders jiggling to the tune he whistled under his breath. He was elegantly outfitted in a lavender silk shirt and fawn draped trousers.

'Where you going,' Nathaniel asked, 'dressed up like that?'

Lamptey was unmarried. He lived in the residence and was supposed to be responsible for the boys there.

18

'Oh, just out,' Lamptey grinned. 'I and some of the fellows, you know.'

'You shouldn't,' Nathaniel said half-heartedly.

'Why not? They come here to be educated, don't they?'

Nathaniel laughed and shrugged. Lamptey clapped a hand on his shoulder.

'You live too quiet. You working now, Nathaniel?'

'No. Just — thinking.'

Lamptey clicked his tongue disapprovingly, and the handsome shallow face grimaced.

'Never think, boy,' he chirped. 'If you think, you worry. And if you worry, you get bad luck. It's true. If you worry, bad luck'll land right on your shoulder like a cowbird on a cow. If anybody worries, it should be me. But do I? Not this man. And I tell you, Nathaniel, I'm broke tonight. Nothing with man — that's me, true's God.'

'You'll do all right,' Nathaniel said.

He could not keep an edge of bitterness out of his voice. Lamptey always did all right. He couldn't buy silk shirts with the money Mensah paid him. His conducted tours weren't cheap. Nathaniel wondered if Lamptey got a cut from the girls as well. Yes, of course he would.

Nathaniel knew he was a fool not to work some game like Lamptey's. New boys were always coming to Futura, fresh from the villages, eager to experience the city. Why not, then? He didn't dare. That was the truth. Lamptey could carry it off, but he, Nathaniel, would be certain to be caught. Anyway, he wasn't the type, not for Lamptey's game. Nathaniel fingered his spectacles. He wondered if the girls would laugh at him. A rage against Lamptey took hold of him. Anger flowed into his hands. Sometimes he liked Lamptey, with his boldness, his jazzy irreverence. But sometimes it would have been pure joy to grip him by the throat until the frivolous lavender shirt became only a scarecrow's rag.

'I'm going to do some work now,' Nathaniel said brusquely.

Lamptey's thin light-skinned face was a beaten copper mask with slitted eyes. Then he lifted his shoulders delicately.

'All right, all right. I got to go now anyway. My students will be waiting, eh?'

A slim hand flicked at the books on Nathaniel's desk.

'You really prepare your lectures, Nathaniel? You crazy, man?'

'It's a new course,' Nathaniel said stiffly.

Lamptey made him feel raw, a bush boy, a villager. Anger swelled again.

'What's so terrible about preparing a lecture, anyway?' he snapped. 'You ought to try it sometime.'

'What's the use?' Lamptey said candidly. 'The stuff I teach don't make sense anyway. So I just tell them to memorize everything. Nobody do it, but that's their business. You know what we took today, Nathaniel?'

'What?'

'Wordsworth.' Lamptey pulled a mock-earnest face. '"Stern Daughter of the Voice of God" — what kind of stuff is that? Some god — his voice can make a daughter? What you think of that? It's crazy, man. I tell you, it got no sense.'

Nathaniel laughed despite himself.

'So what did you tell them?'

'I told them this God is a very clever fellow, and they should memorize the poem and never mind what it means.'

He grinned.

'Kwesi said what could you expect — the whitemen don't believe in having women, anyway.'

'Kwesi will be a fine politician some day,' Nathaniel said.

'No, he won't. He's like you — too serious. You live too quiet, Nathaniel.'

'I got a wife and no money, Highlife Boy, and the baby coming.'

'How you make that pickin, Nathaniel?' Lamptey said. 'With your voice? Wha-at?'

With a shriek of laughter, he was gone, green silk tie fluttering, fine fawn trousers hugging slender hips sensuous as a cat's.

At once Nathaniel was furious at himself for having yielded to Lamptey's easy charm. That was Lamptey — you talked to him for a while, and he made you laugh, and you forgot to be on your guard. And then — was it unintentionally? — he would make you feel clumsy once more, a bush boy.

What Lamptey thought of him didn't matter. The Highlife Boy was no good as a teacher anyway. How had he ever managed to get his School Certificate?

But the boys liked Lamptey. They attended his classes. Half the time they didn't bother to attend Nathaniel's. Jacob Abraham Mensah, the headmaster, conscious only of fees, was afraid to discipline the boys in case they left, and Nathaniel did not have the knack of making students want to attend his classes.

Nathaniel glanced down at his shirt. It was mended. He had only two good enough to wear to school. Perhaps if he dressed better, he would impress the boys more.

— A silk shirt. A gabardine suit. Here endeth the first lesson. Vanity of vanities, saith the Preacher. All is vanity. Oh, Nathaniel.

— Ghana. The future is YOURS, the sign said.

Nathaniel wondered if he managed to teach these citizens of the new Ghana anything at all. He felt sometimes as though he were talking to himself. He had shaken one boy awake today, and the boy hit him, and Nathaniel, who knew he could have beaten the tall nineteen-year-old, had not dared to touch him in case Mensah found out.

Nathaniel taught History. He did not have the gift of spoken words — only of imagined words, when he made silent speeches to himself. In class he referred too often to the text, and the boys had discovered that if they all stared hard at him he would begin to stammer.

Only in one course did he hold their interest, his own fire breaking through his anxiety.

He had begun teaching African Civilizations of the Past. Victor Edusei, who was a journalist, made fun of him, claiming there were no African civilizations of the past worth mentioning. Victor was wrong. But it made no difference. They were still right to teach the course, even if every word of it was a lie.

In some way, this course was his justification.

— Nathaniel the Preacher. Nathaniel the Prophet.

— There must be pride and roots, O my people. Ghana, City of Gold, Ghana on the banks of the Niger, live in your people's faith. Ancient empire, you will rise again. And your people will laugh, easily, unafraid. They will not know the shame, as we have known it. For they will have inherited their earth. Ghana, empire of our forefathers, rise again to be a glory to your people.

When Nathaniel was eight years old, a visiting priest had come to inspect the mission school. As the man was leaving, a crowd of boys, Nathaniel among them, had surrounded him and asked for a dash. Nathaniel could still hear his own voice, whining at the whiteman.

Mastah. I beg you. One penny.

The priest's look of disgust had startled the boy and made

22

him uneasy in a way he did not then understand. The priest had hissed at them.

Beggars! Shame on you!

It was like a curse, a still-potent curse that made him search for a counteracting spell.

— Ghana, rise again, your people proud, proud and without shame. Rise up to be a glory to your people.

Quietly, with the soft bouncing catlike tread common in big men, Jacob Abraham Mensah entered Nathaniel's classroom.

Jacob Abraham's grey hair gave his massive head a distinguished appearance, which he took pains to further by wearing clothes that clearly had cost a great deal. Today he wore a grey pinstripe suit, a yellow shirt of fine poplin, a blue Paisley tie, all shouting guineas, guineas, guineas. His features were heavy, but handsome, almost Semitic. His skin was pale brown, like unpolished mahogany. Nathaniel always suspected that this lightness of skin secretly pleased him.

'Oh, Amegbe — if you could spare me a moment——'

An unnecessary politeness that always smacked of irony, Nathaniel thought. He reached up automatically and straightened his spectacles.

'Certainly, sir.'

Classes at Futura Academy were conducted in English, but the masters out of class often spoke to one another in the vernacular, Ga or Twi or Fante. But not with Jacob Abraham. With him they always spoke meticulous English.

'About that boy you mentioned — young Cobblah,' a short laugh indicated the triviality of the subject, 'he'll have to go, Amegbe. I've spoken to his father again.'

'He still won't pay?'

23

'Yes. He refuses absolutely. After all, the boy is living with his mother. His father is married again. And the mother pays five shillings here, ten bob there. It's no use. She can't or won't——'

'She can't,' Nathaniel said. 'I have seen her. She would do almost anything to educate him. I think she would even go on the streets, but I guess she is not young enough or pretty enough for that.'

'There is no need,' Jacob Abraham's voice grew hoarse with annoyance, 'there is absolutely no need to be insolent, Amegbe.'

'I'm sorry, sir.'

'School Cert. men,' Jacob Abraham said with a friendly smile, 'are more common than they were when you joined our staff. And no one is indispensable, you know.'

If Jacob Abraham sacked him, where would he go? What other school would take him?

None, obviously.

Or if one did, it would be worse than Futura Academy, difficult as that might be to imagine. Mensah's school was not rock-bottom, but it must be very close. The country swarmed with private Secondary Schools. Some of them — the mission schools and others of high quality — were government-aided. This status indicated that they had a recognized standard and had passed government inspection. Futura Academy was not on the government-accepted list.

If it had been, it would never have employed Nathaniel Amegbe.

For Nathaniel was teaching in a Secondary School having himself failed Secondary School. He had no teacher training, no School Certificate. Sometimes his lack of qualifications terrified him. He tried not to think of it.

His father had died a few weeks before Nathaniel wrote his final examinations. Victor Edusei had won a scholarship that year. But Nathaniel had failed. He knew he did not have Victor's brains. But he was not stupid, and he had worked hard. It had meant everything to him to get through.

He could remember the fear now. Overseas Cambridge School Certificate — it was like a regal title, hated and coveted. Sometimes, in the state of mind he had had then, the words took on a peculiarly evil, feminine quality — repelling him, beckoning, repelling again. He had not honestly known whether he wanted to pass or fail. He had felt the unnerving desire to fail, as though it would be a penance.

The examination room had been still, only the scritch-scratch of pens, and the priest, white skin and white robe, absentmindedly tapping his great ebony cross on the desk. Nathaniel remembered his own dry mouth, how he could not make the saliva flow, for the dry taste of fear in his mouth. He kept wanting to urinate, and finally did not care about the examination paper, as long as he could leave the room for that purpose. But when he handed his paper in and went out to the bush, nothing came.

He had not thought about it for a long time. His mind drew away, like a hand instinctively withdrawing from a flame.

He had met Mensah three years after leaving mission school. Nathaniel could still hear the deep syrupy voice — 'Failed School Certificate, eh? Never mind. These things happen. One could really say you have Secondary. You could teach History? I like to help young men. You realize, of course, that as far as salary is concerned——' Jacob Abraham had taken him because he got him cheaply.

Six years ago. He could still go back and get his School Certificate, couldn't he? But what would he and Aya live on while he studied? And he had no confidence, anyway, in his own ability. However small and grimy his niche, Nathaniel did not feel capable of leaving it now.

And yet his life here was growing insufferable. He was made to grovel apology for every insignificant remark that Mensah chose to interpret as insubordination. Nathaniel sometimes thought the headmaster kept him on only for his sport.

'I'm sorry, sir,' Nathaniel repeated, stammering a little. 'I didn't mean to be insolent. It was only that — that — Cobblah was one of the brighter ones.'

'I am not running a charity organization,' Mensah said.

'I know.'

The big man became confiding.

'You know your trouble, Amegbe? You are a dreamer, A dreamer. Unrealistic. Do you think in England a boy would be allowed to continue——? Of course not. Pay or go. Pay or go. That is the policy. But because this is the Gold Coast, we should be kind-hearted, eh? The new Ghana, eh? Well, let me tell you——'

He broke off and stared at Nathaniel.

'By the way, Amegbe — Cobblah's family comes from the same part of Asante as your own — is it so?'

Nathaniel looked at him steadily.

'Yes. But it was not that way.'

At least he did not take bribes. Perhaps Jacob Abraham would respect him more if he did.

'Naturally, naturally,' Jacob Abraham's voice was acid overlaid with oil. 'I had forgotten. You're our honest man, eh? Well, send him in to my office tomorrow, will you?'

'Yes, sir.'

The headmaster still hovered, like an absurd gigantic mud-wasp vacillating over the choice of nest.

'Another thing——' he said. 'I am asking all the masters to make suggestions about Independence Day celebrations in the school. There will be some suitable service. People will expect it. I thought we might solicit among parents to get some lasting memorial.'

Nathaniel glanced around at the shabby classroom with its unswept earth floor, its straight wooden benches shredded at the edges by pocket-knives, termites and time. On the wall hung a torn map of the world. The blackboard at the front was ridiculously small and permanently dulled by chalk.

'We need new benches,' he murmured.

Jacob Abraham Mensah laughed merrily.

'My dear chap,' he said, 'not that sort of memorial. No, no. I mean something that will make an impression. An Independence window, perhaps, or a brass plaque on the front of the building.'

The front of the building was plaster over mudbrick. The façade had been chipped by inhabitants fifty years before Futura Academy was born, stained and furrowed by rain, glued with paper bills proclaiming funeral rites or this week's dances at Teshie and Labadi, chalk-scrawled, chicken-scratched, urinated against by humans and dung-splattered by goats.

A brass plaque, thought Nathaniel with a bleak inward grin, would look wonderful on the front of the building.

'That is a fine idea,' he said soberly.

Nathaniel took the bus home. He tried to stop thinking about his talk with Mensah, but it would not go away. What hope was there now of a rise in salary? None. Nathaniel felt vulnerable and without bargaining power.

His failure at the mission school was the thing that had set the course of his life. He had never told anyone what had made him unable to write the examinations properly. He would not even think of the details in anyone's presence, as though he might blurt it all out in his anxiety not to do so.

He had been a fool to be afraid. But that was nine years ago. He was eighteen then. He had lived at mission schools since he was seven, only going back to his village in holidays. The stamp of the mission was deep on him.

His father. Kyerema, Drummer to a Chief. He who knew the speech of the Ntumpane and the Fontomfrom, the sacred talking drums. His father, with the proud face and cruel eyes of a warrior of Asante. His father, who prayed to Tano, god of the River, Lord of the Forest.

The Kyerema would not be acceptable to God. That had seemed very clear at the time. Had not the mission priests taught it? 'I, the Lord thy God, am a jealous God, visiting the iniquity of the fathers upon the children, unto the third and fourth generation of them that hate Me.' The Drummer would walk among the howling hordes of hell to all eternity, his dark eyes as haughty and unyielding as they had been in life.

Damned. The Drummer, damned. That had seemed very clear at the time. (Oh, young Nathaniel, having eaten the mission's consecrated bread, year after year, having eaten faith and fear and the threat of fire.)

He, Nathaniel, had damned his father to that eternity. The father had been damned by his son's belief.

Nathaniel had taken part in his father's funeral rites with a fervour that surprised the uncles.

— He had not forgotten the ways of his people, they said.

He had feared, himself, that he might have forgotten. But then he knew there were some things a man never

28

forgets, though they may lie untouched in the urn of his mind for years. The urn is unsealed and they are there, relics of another self, a dead world. Around Nathaniel's head was bound the 'asuani' creeper, whose name means 'tears'. The rust-hued mourning cloth, colour of Africa's earth, was twisted around his body. And the lamentation, the ancient lamentation, had risen to his throat unbidden.

— Alas, father!

And the dirges came out of the unsealed urn. At the wake-keeping, the dirges came back as though he had heard them every day of his life.

> *'Whom does death overlook?*
> *I am an orphan, and when I recall the death of my father,*
> *Water from my eyes falls upon me.*
> *When I recall the death of my mother,*
> *Water from my eyes falls upon me.*
> *We walk, we walk, O Mother Tano,*
> *We walk and it will soon be night.*
> *It is because of the sorrow of death that we walk.'*

The dirges that the women sang were as familiar to him as though he had heard them every day of his life. The keening voices entered into him, became his voice, mourning for the dead Drummer.

His sister Kwaale, like a she-leopard caged, paced the room as she sang her mourning, arms clasped across her breast, sorrow distorting her handsome face, her strong face. She was the oldest child. She, not Nathaniel, should have been the son, for she was strong, strong, and the Kyerema had always known it.

> *'Father, do not leave me behind——*
> *Please do not leave me behind——'*

And her plea for gifts from the dead, that was a plea for love:

> *'Send us something when someone is coming this way——'*

The Drummer was also mourned by those of his own calling. The Drummer's drum was silent, and the drums mourned. The drummers, sons of the Crocodile who drums in the River, mourned their brother:

> *'The river fish comes out of the water,*
> *And asks the Crocodile,*
> *Can you drum your own names and praises?*
>
> *I am the drum of the Crocodile,*
> *I can drum my own names and praises——'*

The wake was a time of fasting. The drums were not still day or night. The dark air and the bright air, both were hot and wet, the air was sweat, the air was the sweet over-ripeness of palm-wine. And Nathaniel fasted and drank palm-wine and listened to the funeral songs for the dead Drummer, his father.

Somewhere there was another god, not Nyame, not Nyankopon, not Tano, not Asaase Yaa, Mother of the Dead. Somewhere there was another — God.

But He was far away. The Latin words were far away, and the altar and the wine-blood and the wafer that was a broken body. They were far away, and Nathaniel had come home.

Then one of the uncles spoke to him.

'They have not stolen your soul, Nathaniel, the white priests.'

— They have not stolen your soul.

In the compound, men were firing old Arab muzzle-loaders, a courtesy to the dead. Nathaniel could hear the now-wild voices of his sisters, wailing sorrow into the night. And the drums, the drums, the drums——

He knew then.

— I, the Lord thy God, am a jealous God——

Nathaniel had looked at his father's body. It was lying on its left side, dressed in the best cloth it had owned in life, a magnificent vari-coloured Kente. The 'kra sika', the soul money, was bound around its wrists, and the ears had been filled with gold dust. Beside it lay the food for the soul: eggs, mashed yam, roasted fowls, earthen pots of water. The Kyerema would not want on his journey.

Nathaniel's heart was gripped by a terrible love, a terrible fear.

'They have not stolen your soul,' the uncles repeated, satisfied.

And the boy had agreed, his aching body sweating and trembling lest the lie should strangle him and lest his father's gods should hear and slay him.

The noise of the drums was the howling of lunatics, and the palm-wine had the taste of death. Then he had drunk himself insensible.

On the third day, the Drummer's body was taken to the 'samanpow', the thicket of ghosts, for burial. Again, the drums, the guns, the heat, men reeling from hunger and exhaustion and palm-wine, the stench of the living and the stench of the dead. And the Drummer's only son, his voice more frenzied than the voice of the drums, shouted his confused despair into the ancient formula.

— Alas, father!

When he went back to the Mission, Nathaniel had gone alone to the chapel one night. He had stood before the statue of God's crucified Son. And he had spat full in the Thing's face, his heart raging to avenge his father. But it

31

did not work. For he believed in the man-God with the bleeding hands, and he could not spew that out of himself. For a moment, before an altar that was both alien and as familiar as himself, his fear became panic. He waited, waited, and the night chapel was a coffin. But God was sleeping. Or He had punishments more subtle than lightning. Nothing happened, and after a while Nathaniel's fear was only that one of the priests might discover him there and see the spittle on the plaster face.

It had occurred to him then that the Kyerema would only have laughed if he had seen. This was all his son could do — this secret slime at night. And there would have been bitterness in the Drummer's laughter.

Shame swamped Nathaniel. He had never been brave enough to burn either Nyame's Tree or the Nazarene's Cross.

Nine years ago. He had been a fool. He could see it now. Now he was different. Both gods had fought over him, and both had lost. Now he no longer feared.

Except sometimes.

* 3 *

'THE SAMPLE BOLTS have arrived from London,' Johnnie said. 'Cooper thought you might want to know.'

'Yes, indeed,' James Thayer said eagerly. 'I think I'll just nip down and have a look. Care to come along? You might find it interesting.'

Together they walked down the iron-banistered stairway. It was going to be a busy morning on the textile floor. The swarms of women traders were already pattering up and down the narrow aisles, their bare or sandalled feet slapping softly on the grey splintered wood. They would buy cloth wholesale and resell it in the markets. A twelve-yard bolt made two robes, and many African women who did not have the money for the whole piece were willing to pay more per yard to obtain half a length from the market mammies.

The huge room had a dim, cool, cave quality about it, away from the sun and shriek of the street. The walls were thick, the windows small and high. The building dated from the days when whitemen in the tropics never ventured forth without solar topee and flannel spinepad, and in their dwelling-places barricaded themselves against the marauding sun.

But dark and dank as it was, Johnnie could almost understand James' passion for the place. It was the Firm's

33

first building in the Gold Coast. Allkirk, Moore & Bright was an export-import firm which purchased cocoa and palm oil here, and sold soap, tradecloth, brass headpans, cheap enamelled pots and pans. There was a retail store in Accra and others in Kumasi and Koforidua. But the textile trade was the biggest branch of the business. Bolts of tradecloth had been piled on these low wooden platform-tables since the year of the last Ashanti War, more than half a century ago.

James and Johnnie crossed the textile floor and entered the stockroom. Pink-faced with exertion, Cooper and Freeman were helping the African counter-clerks to unload the new bolts. The Squire called them to one side.

'Gentlemen—' James' voice was quiet, but there was an unmistakable chill in it, 'you are meant to be supervising these clerks — had you forgotten?'

The two boys — they could not be more than eighteen or nineteen — blushed profoundly. They were apprentices. Ultimately, they might become branch managers, if they could stand Africa that long. But the training course was not an easy one. Johnnie felt almost sorry for them now, as they tried nervously to marshal their forces and to bark at the Africans in an authoritative manner, painfully conscious of the Squire's cold eyes on them. They looked pitifully similar, the two of them, both fair-haired and fresh scrubbed, both maidenly in their neatness and gaucherie, both miserable in their forced and feeble attempt to achieve the bellowvoice of the sahib.

The African clerks, understandably, were snickering, and James was annoyed.

'We're promoting young chaps far too fast these days,' he said in a low voice to Johnnie. 'Look at those two. It'll be ten years before they're any use, but I'll wager they'll be whipped away to more responsible posts within a year or two. When I began in this country, it was a different matter.'

He chuckled — a dry, thin, spun-glass sound.

'I worked with the Firm for fifteen years before I got my first promotion,' James said. 'Men were expected to prove themselves in those days.'

He went from pattern to pattern, examining, touching, clucking approval, like a master jeweller with a collection of rare stones. At last he raised his grey-fringed head and smiled.

'Seems odd to you, doesn't it? All this fuss about a few new bolts of tradecloth. Well, let me tell you something. The prestige and stability of the Firm depend to a very large extent on the right choice of patterns for tradecloth. If the Africans don't like a pattern, or if it offends them for any reason, they don't buy. And if you have more than one or two bad prints in a year, the word gets round that Allkirk, Moore & Bright are no good for mammy-cloth any more. You see?'

The two young men had gone back to the textile floor, and the African counter-clerks with them. James and Johnnie were alone now, with the gaudy bolts of new cloth.

The cold managerial stare was gone from James' eyes. Johnnie was startled at the expression on the Squire's face — an almost shy pride.

'I think I can honestly claim,' James said, 'to know as much about tradecloth as any man alive.'

Then he seemed embarrassed. He turned away with a cough.

'Well, all right, Johnnie, you'd better be getting back, I suppose. I want to look around here for a bit.'

Johnnie left him there, stooped in intense scrutiny over the bolts of cloth, his fingers stroking lightly the black giraffe, the orange palm, the sea-monster and the serpent, the red appalling eye, the green and blue entangled grasses.

Bedford was reading *The Illustrated London News* and eating an apple. He held out the paper bag to Johnnie.

'Have one. Six shillings a pound — "Saleh's" received a barrel of 'em this morning. Horrid little shrivelled things, actually, but it's refreshing to taste an apple that hasn't come out of a tin. Don't tell Helen. She worries incessantly. About the fruit, you know, not having been washed in pot. permang. When Helen breast-fed Kathie she used to scrub herself with potassium permanganate. Got blazing at me when I said her energy might be low but I hadn't known she was quite at the vegetable level.'

Bedford rumbled with laughter, then his handsome florid face grew morose once more.

'I asked the old blighter about the bungalow again this morning,' he said. 'Promised Helen I would. Not a bit of use, of course. Each time he simply says there isn't another bungalow available. He won't ask the London office for funds to build another one. Not he.'

'What's the matter with your bungalow?'

'What isn't the matter with it?' Bedford replied peevishly. 'It's the oldest on the compound. Built about the year One. Everything's falling to bits. Shutters blow off in every storm. Thousands of bats nesting in the roof. Helen can't bear bats — she nearly passes out when she sees one, which is roughly a dozen times each evening. I tell you, Johnnie, it's hell. I don't mind the house myself. Matter of fact, I'm rather fond of the place. But Helen gets in such a flap about it——'

'You should have had our bungalow. It's practically new.'

'Impossible. Too small. Your second bedroom wouldn't accommodate our young. Helen, of course, thinks we ought to have been given the Thayers' bungalow, as they haven't children. But really, one can't walk in to the Old Man's office and say "Look here, you must give me your bungalow", now can one? Women never appreciate the complexity of life. These things seem so simple to them.'

He sighed.

'Well, never mind all that. What can I do for you, Johnnie?'

'It's about the clerks,' Johnnie began, then hesitated.

Bedford Cunningham's position was a little vague, but he appeared to be responsible for office supplies and for the hiring of most of the African staff — clerks, drivers and messengers.

Johnnie, as the new Accountant for the Textile Branch, wanted to replace some of his clerks, and he wanted to hire the new boys himself. He explained it to Bedford as tactfully as he could. To his surprise, the older man did not demur at all.

'Go ahead,' Bedford said, waving one enormous paw. 'I wish you joy of them.'

'I expect you think I'm a bit of a new broom,' Johnnie said awkwardly. 'I'll try not to be——'

'No,' Bedford said. 'Don't try. It'll happen by itself, quite soon enough.'

'Somebody is waiting to see you, sir.'

Why was Attah smiling in that peculiar fashion? Johnnie looked sharply at his chief clerk, whose glance leapt away.

The African caller was sitting on one of the straight chairs just inside the door of the Accounts Office. He rose to his feet so slowly and languorously that there was something almost insulting about the action. He stretched his arms lazily above his head and gave an open-mouthed yawn. It crossed Johnnie's mind that the man might be after a job. But surely not even an African would try so deliberately to create a bad impression, nor present such a slovenly appearance. Crumpled khaki trousers, torn at one knee, sagged around the black man's hips. His yellow cotton jersey was splattered with food and grime. He wore canvas tennis shoes with no socks, and his heavy-jawed face bore a day's dark wiry growth.

'Ah, Mr. Kestoe,' the African said, 'I trust I have not intruded at an inopportune moment. Allow me to introduce myself. I am Victor Edusei, a journalist with the "Free Ghana Citizen". I promise you I will only take a few minutes of your valuable time.'

For an instant Johnnie could only look blank. He had expected pidgin English, or, at most, the heavily accented, stilted phraseology of the semi-educated African. But this man's speech had in it more of Oxford than Accra.

A clerk tittered, and Johnnie jerked himself into alertness.

'All right,' he said, 'in my office, then. But it'll have to be brief.'

When they were seated, Johnnie looked at the African curiously.

'Well, what is it?'

Edusei puffed thoughtfully on his cigarette for a moment.

'It has come to our ears, Mr. Kestoe, that your Firm is considering a programme of top-level Africanization.'

'Africanization?'

'Yes. You know — the process by which Africans are reluctantly permitted to take over certain administrative posts hitherto held by Europeans only.'

'Why ask me about it?' Johnnie said. 'Mr. Thayer is the Manager here, as I fancy you know quite well.'

'Oh yes, I know. But you have only recently come from London, you see. You might perhaps have heard things there — talk around the office——'

Johnnie stiffened.

'Mr. Edusei, do you seriously imagine I would tell you anything about the Firm's policies, even if I knew?'

'You Englishmen have such high principles.' Edusei's smile was a little more openly menacing than it had been. 'Never mind — relax, Mr. Kestoe — I knew you would not talk about Africanization.'

'What in hell are you doing here, then?'

The black man's languor dropped like a snake's sloughed-off skin. His powerfully built body seemed to coagulate, each loose limp muscle suddenly drawn together, tight and hard. He was on his feet, his face shoved close to Johnnie's.

'You visited the "Weekend In Wyoming" last Saturday, Mr. Kestoe. You remember the African girl you danced with?'

Johnnie drew back.

'What of it?'

'Nothing. Only — I watched you, and I didn't like what I saw. I just wanted to let you know — that happens to be my girl. You understand me?'

Unreasoning fear jangled along Johnnie's nerves; quieted; gave way to annoyance at the situation's burlesque quality.

'You're insane,' he said coldly. 'Why, I wouldn't even recognize her if I saw her again.'

The African's muscles went slack again. He laughed and sat down.

'Of course. I give you full marks, Mr. Kestoe. She was, naturally, only another black girl to you. And I am a bloody fool. How neat.'

'I don't know what you're talking about,' Johnnie

39

snapped. 'You don't need to worry, Mr. Edusei. I'm not interested in African women.'

As he said it, he could feel the wilful crimson staining his face. He turned away, as though to terminate the interview, but he knew the African had seen.

'Indeed?' Edusei drawled. 'I suppose it is against your principles.'

'It most certainly is. And now I'd like you to tell me why you gave me that line about Africanization.'

'I thought it would do no harm to let you know that a story could always be printed — if the need arose — as having come from you. You might deny having made such a statement, but would your Firm ever feel really sure about you again?'

Johnnie stared at him.

'Are you trying to threaten me?'

Edusei rose. Again he stretched, belly out, and yawned, flaunting coarseness.

'What a suggestion, Mr. Kestoe! I would never threaten a whiteman. No, no — I am much too timid for that. I know my place. Well, this has been a pleasure, but I must be going now.'

At the door he turned.

'Another reason — I really did hear the rumour about Africanization. I have many friends in London. It will be interesting to see if it is true, won't it?'

He bent in a spasm of soundless laughter.

'Goodbye, Mr. Accountant,' he said.

Nathaniel first met Miranda and Johnnie Kestoe at the British Council building, where an exhibition of landscapes by African artists was being shown. She was trying to persuade her husband to buy a picture.

'Johnnie — this one,' she said. 'I like it.'

'Sand and palm trees and a mouldy old fishing boat. Really, Manda——'

'It gets the atmosphere of the shore,' she insisted, and turning to Nathaniel as the nearest spectator, 'Don't you agree?'

Startled, Nathaniel stared at her.

'Pardon? Oh — the picture. Yes, yes, it is very fine.'

'You see — someone agrees with me,' she said to her husband.

'Who's going to disagree with you, Manda?' he said sulkily. 'You make people agree.'

Nathaniel felt awkward. He did not really like the picture. He had agreed only because he had been taken by surprise and could not think of anything else to say. He wondered now if the man thought he was one of those Africans who automatically agree with Europeans.

'Oh no, sir, not at all,' he said hastily. 'I assure you — I thought the picture was very good. I thought so before this lady asked me.'

'You would,' the European said rudely.

Of course, Nathaniel realized, the European thought he liked the picture only because it had been painted by an African. Nathaniel burned inwardly. He turned to go, wanting to get away as quickly as possible from the white-man's keen scornful eyes. But the woman caught at his sleeve.

'Please — don't go. We're Johnnie and Miranda Kestoe. Do you know the artist, by any chance?'

Nathaniel became agonizingly aware that his khaki slacks needed both washing and pressing, and that his blue shirt, although it had been clean that morning, was rumpled and transparent with sweat. He was conscious of his glasses, too. They were new, and had heavy horn rims. He had paid more for them than he could afford. He needed them — even with them, he wore the perpetual frown of myopia. But a lot of Africans wore spectacles only to give themselves dignity. Or, at least, that was what most white-men believed. Nathaniel wondered if Johnnie Kestoe would think the glasses were an affectation. Then he became angry at himself for caring, for even bothering to think about it.

'I am pleased to meet you,' he said stiffly. 'I am Mr. Amegbe. I am a schoolmaster. No, I do not know this artist personally.'

He realized too late that he had said 'Mr. Amegbe' and that the girl had said 'Johnnie and Miranda'. Nathaniel's hands tightened around his briefcase. In a moment he would say something rude, to even the score, and then he would despise himself and them.

The white woman was chattering on, in the determined way such women had. Her husband had moved on to the next picture, his jaws clamped hard together and his eyes narrow with disgust.

'I think these exhibitions are a good idea,' Miranda was saying. 'It must do something to encourage African artists. There aren't many yet, are there? Of course, it's no wonder. The early missions must have done a great deal to wipe out indigenous art here. By forbidding image-making, I mean.'

Nathaniel hesitated, and then plunged.

'No doubt,' he said. 'The missions tried to destroy our African culture——'

He stopped abruptly. He had overstated the case, over-stated it deliberately. Now a hundred details and qualifi-cations came to his mind, but he knew he could never tell them to her. There was too much to say. And so much that could never be said.

Nathaniel remembered the Drummer, and the boy who had trembled with the fear of many gods. What could be said? Not that.

And so his tongue would play him up, once again, and he would fail to make himself clear, getting deeper and deeper into illogicalities that he himself recognized. Nathaniel felt as though he were choking.

'Of course,' he said with a slight shrug, 'there is much more to it than that——'

He broke off again, wondering if he should tell them that he taught a course in African Civilizations of the Past. No doubt they thought he was completely uninformed. He ought to tell them.

'You're damn right there's something more to it,' Johnnie Kestoe said. 'This much-vaunted culture never existed — that's what. The missions tried to destroy it — nonsense! What was there to destroy?'

Miranda turned on him.

'That's not fair, Johnnie. You don't know.'

Nathaniel felt anger swelling in him like a seed about to burst its pod.

'I have made a considerable study of the subject,' his voice was harsh now, and he did not care, 'and I can assure you, Mr. Kestoe, that we in West Africa had civilizations in the past. Great civilizations. Ghana was a great civilization. I don't suppose you have heard of Ghana. Europeans do not know much about Africa. The school where I teach has begun a course in ancient African empires. As a matter of fact, I teach it.'

'How fascinating!' the white woman gabbled. 'I'd simply love to know more about——'

But the whiteman was looking at him suspiciously.

'What school is that?'

All at once Nathaniel felt defeated.

'One of the secondary schools,' he said.

'Oh?' the expression was insulting in its implications.

'I must be going now,' Nathaniel said hotly. 'As a matter of fact, I am already very late.'

'I — I'm so sorry we've kept you, Mr. Amegbe,' Miranda stumbled. 'It's been so interesting. I do hope we'll see you again——'

Her voice was young and bleak, and Nathaniel almost relented. She had meant well. Then his resentment gained command. She had tied him here, his hands damply clutching his briefcase.

'I think that's extremely unlikely,' he said.

Home, home, home, said the hum and whir of the bus. It stopped and Nathaniel climbed out. He was in his own territory now. He had been born far inland in the forests of Ashanti, but he had lived for six years in this decaying suburb of Accra and sometimes it seemed almost his own. It was good to get away from the centre of the city, with its white shops and faces.

But he carried the encounter with him.

He walked quickly into the maze of streets, towards his home. The air was thick with the pungent smoke from charcoal pots and the spiced smell of food being cooked in the open, outside every hovel, beside every roadside stall. Groundnut stew, bean stew, 'mme-kwan' — palmnut soup, with the rich sharp smell of the palm oil and the salt-and-woodfire smell of the smoked fish. The moist yeasty odour of 'kenkey', fermented corn dough, steaming in black round-bellied cooking pots. The sweet half-cloying smell of roasting plantains. And over all, the warm stench of the sea.

Beside the road, the petty traders' stalls sprouted, dozens

of little ramshackle tables made of old boxes and piled high with lengths of cloth, packets of sugar, mirrors, sandals, sweets, pink plastic combs, a thousand thousand oddments. Women minded the stalls, or children. One small boy slept, his charge forgotten, the goods arrayed for thieves. At another stall, a woman reached down to turn the half-done plantains on the charcoal burner at her feet, then glanced at the baby she held in one arm, her tired eyes growing momentarily rested as she watched him drink her milk.

The street was a tangle of people. Women in mammy-cloths of every colour, women straight as royal palms, balanced effortlessly the wide brass headpans. A girl breadseller carried on her head a screened box full of loaves and cakes. Coast men strolled in African cloth, the bright folds draped casually around them. Muslims from the north walked tall and haughty in the loose white trousers and embroidered robes of their kind. Hausa traders carried bundles tied up in white and black rough wool mats. A portly civil servant in khaki shorts wore with dignity an outdated pith helmet. And everywhere, there were children, goats and chickens. Vivid, noisy, chaotic, the life of the street flowed on.

Nathaniel was part of them, and yet apart. He did not any longer live as these slum-dwellers lived, and yet he lived among them. He was educated, but he was not so much educated that he had left them far behind. Sometimes they were his fear expressed, and he wanted to shun them lest they pull him back into their river. And sometimes, more rarely, they were his hope.

They lived in mud and thatch huts, but never mind. They sickened with damp and malaria and guinea worm and yaws and bilharzia, but never mind. They went to the ju-ju man to get charms for curing, but never mind. Most of them were illiterate, shrewd and naïve, suspicious and gullible.

Any political shyster could move them with luxuriant promises. But never mind. They were strong.

They would do something, do something——

The tailor's young son, leaping nimbly over the mangy goats that cropped dispiritedly at the weeds in the compound, ran up to greet Nathaniel. The tailor was one of the many inhabitants of the tenement. His sign was outside the main door.

'YIAMOO TAILOR — All For Mod, Dad & Kid'

Nathaniel sometimes wondered who had written the sign, but he never offered to correct it, for it was Yiamoo's greatest pride. All day long the tailor sat on the stoep, his bare feet working the treadle of his old sewing machine. Strung on a line above his head were the cheap cotton shirts he made, magenta and blue and orange, flapping like flags.

The compound was littered with the curious accumulations of many lives. The rusty shell of a car, stripped of tyres and engine, had been there for years. Under the mango tree stood a huge untidy pile of firewood and two smaller ones of sugarcane, belonging to a woman trader who lived in the house. An old upholstered rocking chair, its carved wooden swirls and roses white with mould and its springs protruding obscenely, rested beside a cage full of live pigeons and another of 'cutting-grass', the big bush rats. A weaver owned the cutting-grass and the birds. He claimed he bled them and used their blood in the making of dyes according to the ancient recipes. But Nathaniel always thought this was a story to impress European customers.

Weed-flecked and unkempt, the compound had never been touched by hoe or machete. But beside the open reeking drains a patch of portulaca flaunted a purple-red defiance to the barren earth.

Red, white and green, a Convention People's Party flag had been erected near the house. The flagpole was a crooked bamboo, striped in the same colours, with the party's red cockerel perched on top. Nearby, a dissenting tenant from Ashanti had put up a National Liberation Movement flag, green and yellow, with its cocoa-pod emblem.

The house itself was a massive two-storey pile made of sandcrete blocks, of the standard pattern built by Syrians for renting. Inside, it was a warren of tiny rooms. Nathaniel and Aya were fortunate. They had two small rooms on the ground-floor, a side entrance of their own, and a stoep where Aya set the charcoal pots to do the cooking.

As he had foreseen, Aya was cross at his lateness.

'Does Mensah pay you so much,' she demanded, 'that you have to give him his money's worth by staying until night?'

Aya was twenty-four, but she did not seem to have changed at all from the sixteen-year-old he had married. Despite the heartbreak of two previous miscarriages and the years of pining for a child, her face was still smooth and round, unlined except by an occasional exaggerated frown when she was angry. Nathaniel was glad she had not grown older in appearance. But she had not grown older in mind, either. There had been less difference between them eight years ago than there was now.

Nathaniel patted her shoulder. He found he did not want to mention his meeting with Miranda and Johnnie Kestoe.

'How are you feeling?' It was pleasant, after the daytime English, to speak again in Twi.

Aya touched her swollen abdomen proudly. She had kept this child, when everyone had given up hope of her holding one to full-term.

47

'Fine,' she said. 'Very well. He kicks all the time, now. I was thinking, Nathaniel——'

'Yes?' he looked at her suspiciously.

'Why pay?' Aya burst out. 'Why, why? I don't want to have the baby in hospital. All that money. And — I don't want to, Nathaniel. My mother said——'

'Your mother——' he shrugged. 'I know. She and her friends. They would do a fine job. It isn't right, Aya. My son isn't going to be delivered by old women with dirty hands. I know it isn't right. Why do we become educated, if we do the same things as before?'

'I was delivered that way,' she said, 'and so were you.'

'It wasn't any good,' he snapped. 'You must know that.'

'What was wrong with it?' she demanded. 'Children came, just the same. I don't understand you, Nathaniel. All this fuss.'

Nathaniel had waited eight years. It was as important to him as to Aya. And it had become a symbol. More than a safe delivery was the thought that if a child was started in the new way, it would be a favourable omen. The child would not go back, then. Its very birth would set the course of its life.

'You don't see anything wrong?' he cried. 'The child delivered in the hut where the dirty clothes are washed? We know more than that now, Aya. And if the birth was difficult, they would beat you, those old women, to force the child out — would you like that? I know these things — I used to hear my sisters whispering. And after it was born, for the eight days it would be nothing — a wandering spirit. No one knows if it plans to stay or go, so they ignore it, put it to sleep on a dirty rag, give it water from a filthy old banana skin. So unless it's very strong, it dies. Would you like that?'

She looked at him, her face shocked.

'You must not say it,' she murmured. 'You must not say those things.'

But he could not stop.

'And if it dies,' he said brutally, 'it is a disgrace. That small body, whipped because it died, and perhaps a finger cut off——'

'Nathaniel,' she whimpered, 'if I lose it now, it will be because you said — you said the things that should not be spoken.'

He stopped abruptly. He had upset her more than anyone had a right to do. For him, the mention of these things was a matter for anger. For her, it was terror.

'Aya——' he choked. 'Aya — I'm sorry. I have no sense. I'm sorry, sorry, sorry. It is just that those things must not happen — not to our child. They don't need to happen. Please — understand. Please try.'

She turned away.

'I will go to hospital if you want it,' she said resignedly.

'You shouldn't listen to your mother. How does she know? She's never been in a hospital.'

'My aunt has, and she says——'

'I don't want to hear,' Nathaniel said. 'It is settled.'

'But the money——'

'I have the money,' Nathaniel said firmly.

He would not send it to Kwaale. Not this money. Not this time.

'So foolish,' Aya said. 'Would my mother charge for delivering me?'

'Aya,' he said, 'you must learn.'

Aya sighed.

'The food has been ready for an hour,' she said. 'It will be ruined.'

As they were sitting down to eat, Victor Edusei arrived. Nathaniel was pleased to see him, but he remembered, too, that Aya always said Victor arrived just at meal times.

They had boiled yam and cocoyam leaves stew, the greens mixing fragrantly with the tomatoes, the smoked and salt fish, the rich yellow-red palm oil. Aya was a good cook. Her mother had taught her that, if nothing else. She heaped Victor's plate and urged him courteously to take more. But Nathaniel knew her eyes were cold with resentment.

Victor knew, too, and he did his best.

'So your friend is here,' he said pleasantly to her.

'Which friend? I have more than one.'

'Charity. Charity Donkor. From Koforidua.'

'Yes, she is here. I did not know you knew her, Victor.'

He grinned, his mouth open.

'I know her all right.'

Aya frowned.

'She is married,' she said primly.

Victor looked at her curiously.

'I wonder how well you know her, Aya?'

'All my life.'

'Well, that doesn't mean — never mind. You know why she is in Accra?'

'Yes,' Aya said. 'I know.'

They both glanced at Nathaniel, almost guiltily. Curiosity stirred in him.

'Why is she here?' he asked.

Victor laughed.

'You tell him, Aya,' he said. 'Sometime when he is in the right mood. He is shocked more easily than I.'

After chop, Aya obligingly left them. Nathaniel thought about the Kestoes and wondered if he should tell Victor.

Gloomily, he poured a beer for both of them. Victor would have known what to say to Johnnie Kestoe. He always had the right answers. Victor had a degree from the London School of Economics. He had, as well, studied both journalism and accountancy. He had spent six years in U.K. Nathaniel wondered if Victor knew how much he envied him. Probably. He was proud of Victor, as a brother would be, and grateful to him. He had learned more from Victor than he ever had at school. But yes, the evil thing was there, too.

And yet, why should he envy him? Victor had never made use of his advantages. He was a journalist on a hand-set newspaper. He could have been an assistant professor at the university here, or at least a journalist on a more important newspaper. Victor's paper was small, vituperative and — except for Victor's copy — largely ungrammatical. Even Victor described it as 'bush'. But he stayed. Nathaniel could never see why.

Nathaniel decided he could not tell Victor about the Kestoes. He told him instead about Jacob Abraham and the brass plaque. It was almost a reality now. Mensah had drafted a flowery letter to the parents.

'Fine,' Victor said. 'Up with the brass plaque, to show people how good we are. We all say it, so it must be true.'

'The roof will fall in one of these days,' Nathaniel said with a grin. 'The ceiling in my classroom has a crack that a python could hide in.'

'Who cares? As long as Mr. Mensah can sit on his fat ass behind his nice big "ofram" desk and see the nice big sign on the door that says "Headmaster".'

'I don't know,' Nathaniel said doubtfully. 'I think he really wants to be the headmaster of a good school, a proper school. Maybe he wants it so much he convinces himself he's got it.'

Victor's coarse face drew into a grimace and his eyes burned with a quick fury.

'The old dream,' he said. 'We're a race of dreamers. One of these days we'll wake up and find that the trains have stopped running — no one could fix them. We just hoped they'd keep going by themselves. The farmers will still be using machete and hoe, while the people starve. And we will say in astonishment — "But it's a rich country — where is the food?" The city will be piled six feet deep with the backwash from the sewers. The spitting cobra and the spider will be happily nesting in the Assembly buildings, and we will be sitting there gabbling about Ghana the Great——'

'You depress me,' Nathaniel said.

'I depress everyone,' Victor said cheerfully, 'even my own mother. She told me today if I couldn't talk about something pleasant, I'd better move out of her house.'

'So?'

'So I told her a very funny story. True. About a man at our paper, a typesetter who used to work for a European firm here. I had just pointed out about three hundred errors in a column. Do you know what he said? He said I was just as bad as his European boss, and he hadn't expected that kind of treatment from a fellow African.'

'Oh, fine,' Nathaniel said. 'And did your mother laugh?'

'No. She said she wished she'd had a daughter instead of me.'

Nathaniel's mind went back to Futura Academy.

'Victor — do you think I should leave? The school, I mean. Sometimes I'm scared that Mensah will give me the sack, and other times I think the school's no good, and I'm no good there, and I should look for something else. The term ends next week. I could give notice as soon as the exams are over.'

'He's got to have somebody to teach in his sweatbox. It's better that it should be someone like you, who actually does teach them something.'

'I wonder — if I do.'

Victor looked at him closely.

'What's happened now, to make you think that way?'

And so Nathaniel told him, after all, about the Kestoes. Victor nodded.

'Whatever you'd said, he would have twisted it to make you look like a fool. That is the trick such people use. But you shouldn't worry about it. He did the same thing with me — yes, that very man — I didn't tell you? But listen, Nathaniel, that whiteman is going to get a shock one of these days. You can say that for Ghana — these European firms won't be allowed to carry the whiteman's burden much longer. You'll see. As for Mrs. Kestoe——'

He shrugged.

'She wants to get to know Africa. She likes Africans, I've heard. Isn't that nice of her?'

'She seemed — sincere,' Nathaniel said grudgingly.

'Oh, she's sincere all right,' Victor said. 'These damn amateur anthropologists, they're all sincere. You couldn't insult them if you tried. Wait until one of them starts asking you about native customs, Nathaniel. You know, one of these ladies once asked me in what position Africans made love.'

Nathaniel laughed.

'What did you tell her?'

'I told her we generally did it suspended on a rope tied firmly around the neck,' Victor said. 'I suggested she try it that way sometime.'

After Nathaniel left the exhibition, Miranda turned on Johnnie.

'Did you have to be quite so rude to him?'

Johnnie laughed.

'Did you have to agree with every single thing he said? You wouldn't have, if he'd been white, would you?'

'Did I do that?' Miranda said in a low voice. 'I suppose one does tend to agree too much, to prove sympathy. To me that's the real meaning of whiteman's burden — the accumulated guilt, something we've inherited——'

Johnnie looked at her incredulously. Guilt — it was a word she used virginally, not really knowing its meaning. Miranda hated her inexperience, that was all. She had viewed almost all of life from the old-watercolour world of Branscombe Vicarage, but she burned to have been born dockside. Marrying him, he supposed, was the closest she had come to it so far. But now she had discovered another opportunity for vicarious strife.

'Listen, Manda,' he said patiently, 'I was damned lucky to get this job, and I don't want to risk it now. Do you want every European in the place to be talking about you?'

'I don't understand you,' she said. 'I would have thought that you, of all people, would want to do whatever you could, as far as Africans are concerned——'

'Why the hell should I?'

She hesitated.

'A few people helped you — to go ahead.'

'Did they? I don't think so.'

'What about that old man in the furniture store? Janowicz.'

'You're fascinated by him, aren't you? I wish I'd never told you.'

'You haven't told me very much,' Miranda said. 'Only that you went to work for Janowicz when you were fourteen, toward the end of the war, and that he taught you a lot —

gave you books, made you practise proper speech, started you off at night school——'

'I don't owe Jano anything — he'd be the first to admit it. Why, he was such an old soak, he was glad to find a kid willing to work for him. Anything he taught me, I'd have learned by myself, anyway.'

'You have to feel that, don't you?'

Johnnie tensed.

'That's right, Manda — get everything tidily analysed, and then you can read me like a report. I may turn out to be really weird — is that what you want?'

'I'm sorry,' Miranda said humbly. 'I didn't mean to hurt you.'

'Hurt me?' he cried. 'Don't talk bloody nonsense.'

It was true, what he had told her. He owed Janowicz nothing, unless you counted the cockeyed advice that flowed out of Jano's mouth as freely as the wine flowed in.

'Play it smart, Johnnie——' the Pole's asiatic face would twist into an imitation of a film gangster, 'play it smart, cockerel. I will tell you the secret of success — yes, I, Janowicz, seller of broken chairs, the man they say is as cracked as the china chamber-pots he sells. The greatest luxury in this life is not champagne or caviar, my friend, it is principles. Ideals. When you are really rich, you can afford them. Not before.'

More wine. Then Janowicz would fling himself into the heavy oak rocker at the back of the Anastasia Furniture Mart, and rock furiously to and fro, weeping and bellowing that he was the Devil's Advocate, and how could Johnnie stand there and listen to him without argument.

'For sweet Mary's sake,' Johnnie would say, laughing until he ached, 'do you want to ruin the only decent piece of furniture you've got for sale?'

Well, it had been the first good laughter he'd ever known, and they'd got drunk, the two of them, many a time, and cursed the world for its parsimony. But neither owed the other anything. For Johnnie, the shop had been a refuge from the grudging charity of Aunt Rose's child-infested house. As for Janowicz, only through constant talk could he maintain the sacred belief that his failure was on a grand scale. Two-fingered hand that hoisted the sour crock of cheap red wine; prophetbeard bristling with shed food snippets; stale shirt and rancid armpit; all verses in an epic poem, like the fall of Lucifer. Johnnie had been an obliging listener. It had been a fair exchange.

Johnnie and Miranda did not go out that night, and all evening there was a silence between them that neither tried to breach.

They went to bed early and lay side by side for a long time, still and quiet in the sweat-drawing night.

Johnnie's body was tight and hard, and deep inside him his need throbbed, like the tickling tic of an anarchical nerve, like a misplaced heartbeat. That was the worst — the absurdity of it.

'You asleep, Manda?'

'No. I can't sleep.'

'Cigarette?'

'All right.'

In the distance, the drums sounded. They would keep on all night. These were not the drums of highlife, slicked-up, sophisticated. These were the old drums, played out under some frayed casuarina tree, or beside shanties of mudbrick and tin, in any open space, where the sun and feet of centuries had packed the red earth hard as stone. There would be dancing — the pumpkin hips of women swaying, the muscles of men perfectly controlled even in frenzy.

'Blasted drums,' Johnnie said irritably. 'They never stop.'

He crushed out his cigarette.

'Turn over,' he said, 'with your back to me. Then at least you'll look like my wife.'

Almost meekly, she did so. But it was no use. He couldn't forget, even momentarily, how she looked from the other side, belly swollen nearly to her breasts. Like a cow's udder, blue-veined, heavy, drawn drum-tight with its contents.

'I know it's miserable for you,' she said. 'But — you could have kept on longer——'

'We've talked over all this before,' he said tiredly. 'I couldn't. I'm sorry. I can't explain, but there it is.'

'Johnnie — you do want this baby, don't you?'

'You were dead keen to have it,' he said, 'and you're having it. Isn't that enough?'

'Perhaps I was wrong.'

'Oh, for heaven's sake! Of course you weren't wrong. You needed it, I suppose. You can't help the way you are, any more than I can. Now let's get some sleep before it's morning.'

Johnnie lay limp as seaweed.

In the limbo between reality and sleep, thoughts merged and melted and changed. Magic symbols — a rune, a spell, a charm — the thing that made him different from any other man on earth. His name. John Kestoe. What proved identity more than a name? If you had a name, you must exist. I am identified; therefore, I am. If they say 'who are you?', you know what to reply. It makes for convenience. It might as well be a number, but numbers are harder to remember.

Kilburn, London N.W. The room was dark in day, cold as a corpse. The squeaking stairs wound up and up and up, tiring the legs off you, and the bits of untacked lino were traps to trip the unwary. He remembered how scared he always was of running into that nameless man-tenant who used to finger him, cursing sweetly into his ear all the while with breath that stank of sugared violets. The hallways smelled of boiled swedes and shop-fried fish and the harsh soap that was the women's last defence against chaos. The room was up so close to the top of the building that you knew the choking winter fog would still be with you after it had lifted from the street.

That was the room his mother died in, while he sat by and watched. Strange, how dim kids are about things. The red stain spread and spread on the quilt, and it was quite a while before he realized it was her blood doing it. His father watched, too, sitting empty-faced while she cursed and prayed by turns. The Irish had good lungs — you could say that for them, those who didn't have T.B. No feeble last gasps for them. People must have heard his mother dying all the way up Kilburn High Road.

Most of what she screamed you couldn't understand. The sacred and profane words tangled together in a raw hoarse cry. One phrase stood out stark — 'Jesus, Mary, Joseph, assist me in my last agony——'. In later years he realized that the words came from 'A Prayer For A Happy Death'.

His father, the halfman, gutless as always, kept repeating over and over to his son that they didn't have money for a doctor, and he was afraid to call the priest because 'she done it herself'. It was some weeks before Johnnie realized what it was that she had done, and why. His aunt Rose took pains to tell him his mother had been a sinful woman, and at first Johnnie had believed her sin to be suicide. It came as a surprise to him when he found out that she had not meant to kill herself but only the little blind humanworm in her.

For a while, after he discovered the truth, he had felt himself in some way tainted. The thought of himself issuing from that body — it had made him sick with disgust, as though he could never be anything more than a clot of blood on a dirty quilt.

At last, in desperation, Dennis Kestoe had shambled out to find the priest, leaving the boy to sit beside her in the evening-filled room, where the one weak ceiling bulb, far up and faint, only nibbled at the yellow-grey fog and the shadows.

He had watched and watched, terrified lest she realize he was there and cry out to him, to him who had nothing to give her in her need, not even his love.

So Mary Kestoe died, her black hair tumbling wild around her neck, her eyes open wide, as hard and bitter as they'd been in life, and staring her frantic fear of hell. And the high cold attic room grew silent at last.

'Heart of Jesus, once in agony, pity the dying!'

Father Duggan had hurried in, lisping, spraying spit through yellow teeth. The boy knew the prayer wasn't right, but he left the priest to discover that the dying was now the dead.

They questioned him, then, the priest and Aunt Rose, who, phone-summoned, had flurried in wielding a black umbrella as though Michael the holy standard-bearer had sent her in his stead.

Had Mary Kestoe made an Act of Contrition? Think carefully, Johnnie — did she say these exact words? Did she say 'O my God, I am sorry for having offended Thee, because I love Thee'? I don't know — I don't remember — she was yelling and yelling and then it was quiet. I don't know.

Think, now.

'I think she said it,' the boy whispered.

No flaming sword descended to cut him down for the lie.

He did not know if he had saved her from the deep pit and from the lion's mouth, that hell engulf her not. He did not know how they had finally settled the argument. She lay in consecrated ground and how she got there he did not care.

Because, chiefly, the words he remembered from the time alone with her were not words either of obscenity or prayer. From amid the shuddering sobs and the animal paingrunting had come suddenly the clear Irish girlvoice, surprised and frightened — 'Oh God, my guts won't stop bleeding — what am I going to do at all?'

When he was a little boy, there was a night prayer he used to say, a prayer to the Mother of God. He never said that particular one again. But he dreamed it sometimes.

'O Mary, my dear Mother, bless me, and guard me under thy mantle——'

★ 4 ★

THE SUN sucked everything into itself. The circle of gold, Nyankopon's image, which shot its arrows of life into man and leaf, now shrivelled the life it had made. The sun was everywhere, and men, dying miniature deaths before it, turned away and slept.

Only a few challenged the Lord of Creation, dimly aware in their liquid-feeling bones that they did so, fighting off His drug of sleep, angry at the melting of their minds in the golden fire of noon.

Nathaniel, sitting at his desk, fought to keep his eyes open and his attention from wandering. He looked at Jacob Abraham Mensah, scarcely seeing him. The big man, always slow-moving as a puff-adder, seemed unaffected by the noon lethargy. He stood huge in front of Nathaniel's desk, like a giant whose dignity is half ridiculous or a clown whose absurdity is sometimes transformed into nobility.

For the benefit of a wealthy but illiterate cocoa-farmer parent from Ashanti, Jacob Abraham was dressed today in an impressive Kente cloth. Normally he never wore African dress. But today he was all a man of the Ancient Land.

'We are Africans,' the headmaster was saying ponderously, as though he had just discovered the fact. 'We are Africans, Amegbe. We must remember the greatness of the past. As I was saying to Mr. Amponsah, we must remember our

61

responsibility to our past. The great kings — Osei Tutu, Opoku Ware, Mensah Bonsu, Prempeh the First——'

Nathaniel wondered uneasily if this apparently pointless recital were to have a political twist. It would be like Mensah to bait him about his politics. Nathaniel imagined fleetingly a life in which he did not have to worry all the time about Mensah. He gazed at the big man dully, hating him.

But Jacob Abraham was soaring above politics today.

'We have a responsibility to this country,' the clown-giant continued, 'to turn out men who can govern it. Statesmen and professional men. On every side, we need education and more education.'

Nathaniel nodded. Jacob Abraham was like Ananse, the Giant Spider, who, full of conceit and cunning, drew in the unsuspecting to his web. Nathaniel, who had harboured similar thoughts about responsibility, fought against agreement, trying to untangle the web and discover what the big man was really after.

'I don't see——'

'What I mean,' Jacob Abraham said, 'is that the time is approaching for Futura Academy to take the next step.'

Nathaniel looked at him blankly.

'I refer, of course,' the headmaster said, 'to the application for government inspection, which, if we pass it, will put us on the list of accepted Secondary Schools.'

Nathaniel gasped audibly.

The headmaster fixed him with an angry glance.

'Don't you think we could pass inspection, Amegbe?'

Nathaniel could not find the courage to reply. Did Mensah really believe that the school would pass muster? Mensah was capable of believing anything. To have government acceptance would mean financial aid. Mensah wanted that. But he did not seem to realize it would have to be earned and that it would not, in any event, be a personal gift to himself. Nathaniel waved his hands feebly, despising the weakness of the gesture.

'There are certain things——'

'What things?' Jacob Abraham demanded.

Nathaniel tried to judge how far he could go without giving offence. He wondered for a moment if Mensah had any real conception of how poor the school was.

'Well,' he said tentatively, 'the syllabus — perhaps a standard one should be drawn up — you know — more in accordance with government schools, instead of leaving it to each teacher to do as he wants——'

'Anything else?' Mensah said icily.

Nathaniel sweated.

'I do not mean any disrespect,' he stammered, 'but — the attendance——'

'It is up to you,' Mensah said, 'to hold their interest so that they attend your classes.'

Nathaniel felt sick. He lowered his head and did not speak.

'I thought you believed in Futura Academy,' Mensah sounded almost hurt.

'Oh, I do,' Nathaniel breathed.

He loathed himself, but he could not take back the words. He was afraid.

Then Mensah did a surprising thing. He put his hand on Nathaniel's shoulder, and when Nathaniel looked up, startled, he saw the other man's eyes were pleading with him.

'Maybe not next term, then,' Mensah said, 'but soon. Soon we will pass inspection. It will grow into a fine school, eh?'

Mensah would not spend money on more teachers or equipment. He would not have the buildings repaired. He believed that Futura Academy would, of itself, grow and improve. Nathaniel remembered a saying of his people —

'God is growing cocoa'. Not the people. God. One did not have to do anything except sit and wait for it to happen.

And yet — something was there, apart from the simple desire for wealth. Looking at Mensah now, Nathaniel saw a man whose eyes were aflame with dreams.

Nathaniel felt in himself, too, the terrible hunger to believe. Perhaps it would happen so. Perhaps the school would grow, slowly, into something fine.

Nathaniel thought of the boys who would be writing their examinations next week. Most of them would fail School Certificate, not because they were stupid but because they wrongly believed that Futura Academy had adequately prepared them to sit the government examination.

'I wonder,' he said slowly, 'what happens to the boys who fail?'

Jacob Abraham pulled his cloth tightly around him.

'How should I know?' he snapped. 'I am not running an employment agency. They take their place somewhere.'

Nathaniel wondered where that place could possibly be, the place for the semi-educated, the boys who failed and did not know why they failed, the hopeful applicants for engineering and medical scholarships who did not realize they must be able to do more than simple arithmetic, and could not write a business letter without making a dozen mistakes.

Because they had more education than the majority in this country, they wanted important and significant jobs, jobs for which they were not qualified. The past was dead for them, but the future could never be realized. Nathaniel felt a despairing kinship with them.

On his way home that afternoon, Nathaniel met Lamptey. The Highlife Boy wore a haggard face.

'What's the matter?' Nathaniel asked.

Lamptey jerked up his draped trousers with a defiant tug on the embossed leather belt.

'Everything go wrong, man,' he said. 'Can you lend me a quid, Nathaniel?'

'Sorry,' Nathaniel said coldly.

Lamptey grinned.

'Don't be sorry, boy, I never thought you could. Some life, eh?'

'Lamptey,' Nathaniel said on impulse, 'do you ever hear anything from any of the boys after they leave Futura?'

'Hear from them?' Lamptey shrilled. 'You crazy, man?'

'I mean——' Nathaniel regretted having spoken of it, 'what happens to them?'

'What do I care what happens to them?' Lamptey said irritably.

Then the sharp face softened. Leaning back on his heels, he gave Nathaniel a sad smile.

'I don't worry about those boys,' he said. 'They got their education. Let 'em go. The ones I worry about, Nathaniel, are the boys who leave before they finish. It's bad, man. It's very bad.'

Nathaniel was slightly taken aback at the other's concern. But he nodded his agreement.

'I was sorry when Cobblah had to go,' he said. 'He was a smart boy.'

Lamptey snapped the fingers of both hands, lightly and delicately.

'Oh, Cobblah——' he sniffed. 'He's not the one I'm worried about. You know Lartey?'

'I never thought he was much good.'

Lartey skipped most of Nathaniel's classes. He was a chunky, sullen boy of sixteen, utterly uninterested in education, and desperately homesick.

65

Lamptey hugged his green and gold spotted shirt tightly around him.

'No good,' he moaned, 'you said it, man. True as God. You remember about a week ago, that night I took some of the fellows out? Well, that Lartey was one. That bush boy finally made up his mind he wants to see Accra. Jesus, he was a real fancy man! Dressed real fine, buying drinks for us all. I had it fixed with this girl — Comfort, her name is. You should see her — fine girl. And clean, too. I could guarantee he wouldn't pick up a thing. Wha-at? Like a ripe paw-paw, she is, that's the truth. Man couldn't help biting her, she taste so sweet. Lartey say he'll see me next day. That's it. Finish.'

'So?'

'Next morning he was gone,' Lamptey said. 'He planned to leave all the time and I didn't know it. Hopped a mammy-lorry in the middle of the night. Went back to his village. Just like that. Twenty miles the other side of Koforidua.'

Lamptey flung out both arms and flapped them disconsolately.

'He just fly off like that, neat as a sparrow,'' he said, 'and never a penny I get from him, the fancy bugger.'

Nathaniel stared at the other schoolmaster, the Highlife Boy, the pimp. Then he threw back his head and laughed. And after an injured moment, Lamptey joined in. The two of them stood in the street howling with laughter, until they were weak, until they had almost forgotten why they laughed.

Aya was resting on the bed when Nathaniel came in. He still could not see the bed without a glow of ownership, for it had been the first piece of furniture they had bought in Accra and it was still the most splendid. It was a big brass bed, with a heavy frame above it for curtains or a mosquito-net. At the four corners, large brass knobs gleamed like gold, and the railings at foot and head were embellished with metal flowers and bows. Into the centre rail at the head was set a small mirror, and all four posts, enamelled black up to the knob, were painted with blue and pink flowers. Nathaniel had slept in it for six years, but it had never ceased to surprise him that he actually owned its magnificence.

Aya looked tired, and yet there was excitement in her eyes.

'My friend came today,' she said. 'You remember — Charity Donkor. Victor spoke of her. She is staying with her aunt at Teshie.'

Nathaniel began to wash, pouring the water carefully from the earthen vessel into the tin basin that stood on the dresser.

'You still haven't told me why she's in Accra.'

'She has been very unfortunate,' Aya said, giving him a quick appraising glance. 'She wants a child. She has been married five years.'

'Too bad,' Nathaniel said without enthusiasm.

'That is why she came here,' Aya went on. 'Her aunt was writing to her all the time about this new "suman"——'

Nathaniel swung around to face her.

'This new — what?'

'Fetish,' Aya repeated patiently. 'Its priests have brought it down here from the Northern Territories. Its home is near Tamale——'

'All right — go on.'

'Well, Charity said she tried her best with the "abosom" at Koforidua. And she prayed to her husband's "ntoro", and to Tano, Son of Nyame, who is the god of her people — as of ours. I mean — as it used to be. Also, Charity is a Baptist, and she said she prayed every day for a child. But nothing worked. So she is going to——'

'Aya!' Nathaniel cried. 'That's enough. She's a Baptist and a pagan, and she hasn't even the decency to stick to one pagan god. She's like a woman in the market — which piece of fish is the cheapest, the freshest? Which god shall I buy today?'

'She is my friend,' Aya said with dignity. 'It is not necessary for you to insult her. Victor was right, for once. I should not have told you.'

'Look——' Nathaniel said patiently, 'I've told you, Aya. We went into this long ago, when you miscarried. There are many reasons for a woman not having a child. I don't understand them all, but doctors do. Charity could pour libation every day for ten years, but it still wouldn't——'

'What harm does it do to try? You don't understand what it is, Nathaniel. You don't know how it feels to want a child, and not be able — but I know.'

Nathaniel's throat ached.

'And what "suman" did you try,' he said slowly, 'before, when you thought you couldn't hold a baby? What one did you go to, without telling me?'

She turned away.

'None,' she said in a low voice. 'I was afraid. You would not let me, and — oh, Nathaniel — I am ashamed of it now, but sometimes I hated you for it. For not letting me try.'

He believed her. But his desire to hurt could not be suddenly quenched.

'And when you were pregnant,' his voice ground out, 'I suppose you thought you wouldn't take any chances this time. I suppose you saw the "sumankwafo" to get charms so no one could harm the child by witchcraft——'

He laughed harshly.

'You couldn't have the cuts made on your forehead for the "boto" to be rubbed in,' he said. 'I would have seen it.'

Aya buried her face in the pillow.

'Why do you speak of it?' she cried. 'I would not go — where you said. We are Christians.'

'I am nothing!' he stormed. 'A man is better off to have no gods. They're all the same. They take, take, but they never give.'

She raised her head and looked at him, wide-eyed.

'You are a Christian,' she insisted. 'You went to Mission School. You go to church, sometimes anyway.'

'That makes me a Christian,' he said bitterly. 'Good.'

'It is Victor,' Aya said. 'He is a bad influence on you. How can anyone live without a god?'

'I knew you would say that. It isn't him. Sometimes I believe. Sometimes — I can't. But in the old gods — never. Not any more. That's gone. Don't you understand? It's gone.'

'For me, also,' she said. 'I would not go to the fetish priest.'

He looked at her, exasperated, and yet moved by her loyalty, which was loyalty to him.

'You lie like a child,' he said. 'Like a little girl.'

'I am not the right wife for you,' Aya cried. 'Why did you not marry someone who could read?'

He took her hands in his, and held them tightly, so she would not think the same question had ever occurred to him.

'You are beautiful,' he said.

She clung to him.

'You will not take a second wife, Nathaniel? I do not want that.'

'We are Christians,' he said with a grin. 'Don't you remember?'

She struck at his hands, half angrily, and he laughed.

*   *   *

The next day, when Nathaniel entered the gate, he knew Aya's mother was in the house. The hoarse throaty laughter was unmistakably Adua's. He could tell from the sweet-acrid smell that she was preparing palm-oil chop for him. He sighed. She did not do it for nothing. He wondered what she wanted this time.

The old woman sat unmoving beside the charcoal brazier, a gourd ladle in her hand. Her cloth was black and red, patterned in hands outspread. It billowed hugely around her, and the dozens of scarlet hands clutched at that massive body. She gave Nathaniel the customary greeting, but she did not smile or look up. Always the same — her laughter stopped when he appeared. He was glad to avoid her eyes. Once he had a dream about the old woman. All of her had melted in the sun, leaving only those wise-ignorant eyes, those eyes that searched him, running about on their own tiny legs in the puddle of oil on the ground.

Aya would never admit anything. And yet he knew that whatever understanding and knowledge of the new ways he patiently wove into her, the old woman busily unravelled it.

Aya looked pleased to see him, but something else as well. Frightened? Apprehensive? Her face was tired. The child was growing heavy, and the lines of strain showed in Aya's face. Nathaniel felt a sudden pity for her, who had to grow in her slow earth what he so quickly sowed.

'If Nyankopon gave me nothing else,' Adua said in her wheezy breathless voice, 'he gave me the hands to cook with.'

'You make the best palm-oil stew I have ever tasted, except my own mother's,' Nathaniel agreed politely.

'She has done it for you,' Aya said with a hesitant smile. 'She brought the fish and oil.'

Nathaniel nodded. He was getting a headache. He did not feel like dealing with another of those family arguments where everyone's heart gets sore and bruised and nobody wins. As Adua had promised, the stew was good, the palm oil just the right red-gold, the pieces of smoked fish succulent and plentiful. She had prepared 'kenkey' to go with it, balls of steamed fermented corn dough. No matter how much Nathaniel worried, it never made him lose his appetite. But he felt, with resentment, that each bite put him in her debt. When the women had eaten, after he had finished, Adua wrapped her cloth around her, belched, then sighed.

'Nathaniel,' she whined, 'Nathaniel, I am getting old. I have lived here too long.'

Nathaniel felt a rush of relief. She wanted to go back to her village. And then, despair. The fare for the mammy-lorry. He couldn't. He didn't have the money. He would gladly have borrowed it, at any interest, to get rid of Adua. But he had refused money to Kwaale, and if she heard of it she would never forgive him.

'If it is the money——'

She waved one hand, brushing his words away.

'No, no. My cousin owns a lorry. Had you forgotten? He will take me as far as Kumasi.'

'What is it, then?'

'Nathaniel,' she said eagerly, 'Aya should bear her child among her own people. And she is tired. Look at her. You can see how tired she is. She is alone here. I try to help her, but I have no man to work for me, no rich relatives. I must work. There, her cousins could help her. She would have help with the child, too, when it is young.'

She paused, and her heavy bosom shook a little. Her eyes searched Nathaniel's face. His own mother was dead, long ago. She was trying to make him believe it was his mother speaking. Her eyes held him, forcing her terrible terrible love.

'Nathaniel,' Adua said, 'come back, Nathaniel.'

Aya sighed, gently, as though she had been holding her breath until the thing was spoken.

Nathaniel felt stabbed, betrayed.

'Aya——'

Aya looked away so he could not see her face.

'You do not know,' she whispered. 'It is not easy for me——'

No, it was not easy for her. How could she hold to the future when the old woman kept on and on at her, touching her homesickness and her fears, using every trick?

He turned to Aya's mother.

'I do not want you to talk about it again,' he said. 'I am not going back. This is where I work and where I live.'

'You could work there,' Adua replied. 'This Accra, Nathaniel, it is no good.'

'What is wrong with it? Can you tell me?'

' "It is hard to meet a good man in a big city".'

He remembered the proverb from long ago. But he knew how to counter it.

' "Where you have had joy is better than where you were born",' he replied.

It was another proverb, and for a moment Adua did not know how to answer.

'You have grown to hate your own people,' she said finally.

It was an unwise remark. He could see that Aya knew.

'She did not mean——' Aya stumbled.

'I do not hate them,' Nathaniel said. 'You know I do not hate them. But I will not go back.'

'We send our sons to school, and they spit on us,' the old woman said bitterly.

Nathaniel peered at her. She really believed it. That was the impression his generation gave.

'No,' Nathaniel said. 'No. You do not know.'

— You do not know that I mourn everything I have lost. I mourn the gods strangled by my hand. You do not know how often I have wanted to go back.

'I live here,' he repeated stubbornly. 'I work here. I cannot go back.'

'For Aya's sake,' she pleaded, 'and the child's——'

'No!' Nathaniel shouted. 'It is for him that I stay! No! Do not talk of it any more. You hear? No more.'

Adua seemed to sag, as though the bones had crumbled within that hulk of flesh. Nathaniel saw that her eyes were no longer compelling. They were only the flat, unsurprised eyes of an old woman who plotted and plotted, scarcely expecting to win.

'Now I do not know whether to go or stay,' Adua said plaintively. 'I wanted to hear my grandchildren's voices.'

Nathaniel tried to remember all the superstitions and fears she had given Aya. He tried to be angry once more. But he could not. It is not the malice in a family that drowns us and not their greed. It is their love, stifling, inescapable.

Aya reached out and touched his arm.

'I think you have forgotten that a woman goes to her mother's people when she reaches the eighth month,' she said. 'But I will not do it, Nathaniel, even if Adua goes back. I will stay with you.'

It was a triumph for him, that Aya spoke the words in the old woman's presence. But Nathaniel did not feel triumphant.

'I am sorry,' he said helplessly, to both of them.

He felt he could not bear it. Anger was easier.

At last, well after midnight, Nathaniel slept.

— All night long my soul wrestled with the devil. Yes ——

— My soul wrestled with the devil in the night. The devil of the night. My soul wrestled with the Sasabonsam in the night. His fur was black and his fur was red and his face was a grinning mask of rage. His hands plucked at me, and his breath was evil. He jumped up and down like the great mad gorilla, and he drummed on his chest. Yes, he drummed on his chest like the mad gorilla. He drummed on his chest till the blood trembled in my heart. And he put on a sombrero like the happy boys wear, and he covered his fur with a pink nylon shirt. He pranced down the street in a pink nylon shirt, and everyone laughed as he danced a highlife. And he cried, 'I am the City. Oh yes, I'm the City, I am the City, boy, come and dance!'

— I knew he lied. I knew he lied. I'd seen him in the forest, old as the shadows. I knew he was the Forest. I knew he was the River. But I was afraid and I wanted to run. I wanted to run back and back and back.

— When I was a boy I used to swim in a green pool. The palms were green above it and around it, and the water was cool and green. The village goats came there to drink, stepping lightly, lightly, lightly, stepping lightly in the cool brown mud. And the old men sat in the shade chewing kola nut, and their voices, thin like spiderwebs, spun gossip while the young ones laughed. I laughed and I swam like a little lithe fish, until my mother called me home. She would be bending over the great wooden bowl, the wooden pestle in her hand, pounding yam or guinea corn. She would smile at me. She had four daughters but only one son. 'Is your belly empty, little fish?' Mammii-O! Mammii-O!

— I came to a forest and I stepped inside. And there in a clearing I saw a judgement. I saw the judgement, what it would be. The thief was there, with one hand severed, and the stump dripped blood as he howled with pain. The adulterer was there, and his face was gaunt with shame, and he bore a black gaping wound where the branch of life had been. And I was there, yes, I was there. I walked in the clearing with my head held like a dried gourd between these hands. And my neck shook itself at the self it could not see, and the eyes stared at the blind thing. And I fled, I fled, I fled. I ran away to hide myself in the streets.

— All night long my soul wrestled with the devil. You lie, Sasabonsam.

— Then the devil called down from his 'odum' tree— 'You will be cursed, Nathaniel. The blood in you, it is your mother's. Will it not turn sour, will it not clot with this damnation laid upon you who spit on your people? Have you not your father's "ntoro"? Will not your very spirit rise up against you?'

— When I was a little boy, in my mother's womb. When I was a little fish, in the place where my father poured out his life. When I was a little boy, in my father's tomb. I have drawn my blood from my mother, and I have drawn my life from my father's life. And they will curse me, for I have forsaken them. Alone, Nathaniel, alone.

— My soul wrestled with the devil, whispering doom in the night. And I was falling, I was drowning. Down, down, down.

— Onyame, the Shining One, Giver of Sun, help me. Nyankopon, Soul of Nyame, Shooter of Life's Arrows, help me. Tano, God of the River, Lord of the Planted Forest, help me. Asaase Yaa, Old Mother Earth, mother of the dead, help me.

— I called upon my gods. I called upon my gods. But I knew they would not answer.

— I knew my gods would not answer, for they were dead. My gods were dead in me. They died long ago. How can a god die? What a great death, when a god dies. The death of a king is only the death of a small boy, when a god dies.

— Onyame, the Shining One, is dead. In the compound where offerings were placed on the altar, only the chickens scratch in the dust. Nyame's Tree is bare. The altar is deserted.

— Nyankopon, the sun, has died in me and the sun still shines. Odamankoma, the Sculptor, He Who Hewed The Thing, he is dead. They say he created Death and Death killed him. It was not Death that killed him in me.

— My gods do not answer. Asaase Yaa, Mother of Earth, is dead with her dead. And Tano lies dead beside his River.

— Only, in the night, the Sasabonsam is not dead, and I fear, I fear, I fear.

— 'I am the City, boy, always and always. If you don't like me, you know where to go.'

— Hear him. Sh — listen.

— 'Sometimes I am known as Dr. Paludrine, sometimes Mr. Telephone, Q.C., or simply Sasabonsam Happy Boy. Charming names. I love them all, and have a silk tie for each. You see me every day. We often meet. I always smile.'

— You lie. I've seen you in the Forest, old as the shadows, mad gorilla with feet that point both ways. Mocker of men, doom-dark hunter, haunter of dreams — you lie. You lie. YOU LIE! (Oh — I cannot hear myself speaking. Am I speaking?)

— All night long my soul wrestled with the devil. Who will hear me?

— Jesus, my Redeemer, hear me (if You are there). Jesus, my Redeemer, be there. Hear me. For I am drowning. Save me. Jesus, I beg You (if You are there).

— King Jesus came riding on a milk-white horse. And He crossed the river of Jordan. Yes, He crossed the River. He crossed the River. He crossed the River, came up into the Land. King Jesus, reach out Your hand.

— King Jesus came riding, He Who Held The Beginning Of Time. King Jesus came riding and His armlets were gold. His bracelets were gold, His anklets were gold. King Jesus came riding, and His shoulder chains were gold, and the rings on His hands were gold. His robe was blue and gold, and the amulets on His headband were gold. King Jesus came riding, all in gold, and the brown skin of His body was afire with the dust of gold. Gold is the sun, gold is the King. He is my King, too. What do you think of that, you white-men? He is my King, too. King Jesus rides, all in gold; He rides across the River, and His hands stretch out to the drowning men. Oh hear me.

— All Angels Pray For Me. The song says, all angels pray for me. Pray, you angels, pray. Oh my Redeemer, reach out Your hand (if You are there).

— Sasabonsam, you lie. I will not be cursed. I am on the side of the King. See Him; He rides all in gold. And He crosses the River (Lord, take me with You!) and He comes up into the Land——

Nathaniel awoke, moaning. Beside him, Aya slept. His body was cold with sweat. He tried to remember. But it was gone. Then he remembered one thing.

Jesus, fantastically, had been arrayed like a King of Ashanti.

The insistent voice of the Forest did not cease. Like the menacing song of the wild bees, it hummed in Nathaniel's head. One evening, returning from work, he heard the chip-chip-chip of steel on hardwood, and a voice bawling a bawdy song in Twi.

The man was sitting cross-legged under a rough shelter of new palm leaves in the compound. Around him were woodcarver's tools, and already a little heap of shavings and splinters covered his feet. Yiamoo's youngest son squatted nearby, his eyes bright with curiosity and suspicion.

'I greet you,' the woodcarver said. 'You are the teacher? They told me you are from Asante, like myself.'

Nathaniel nodded, and they exchanged names and the names of their villages. The carver was Ankrah, and he had moved in that morning.

'You are at work quickly,' Nathaniel said.

'I am a poor man — I can't afford to do nothing, like some people.' The carver gave him a sly glance. 'Besides, my wife is fixing up our room. That's woman's work.'

Nathaniel felt a sudden mistrust of this man with his jutting pugnacious features and narrow eyes at once shrewd and stupid.

'What are you making?' he asked, without interest.

Ankrah held up his work. It was a mahogany block, still rough, but growing into the shape of an elephant.

'You know, my friend,' he confided, 'I have never seen an elephant, and yet I make my living carving them. Does that not seem wonderful to you? The whitemen like them. There is always a sale for elephants.'

He threw down the wood impatiently.

'I tell you,' he finished, 'all I want from the House of Nyankopon, when I die, is that there should be no elephants there.'

Nathaniel grinned.

'It must get boring,' he agreed. 'There are not many left who carve in the old way.'

Ankrah looked insulted.

'What is a man to do? If the whitemen will pay for elephants, I will make elephants until my own nose grows

78

into a trunk. But I remember, too, how my father taught me. My father was a woodcarver also. A real craftsman — learned his carving at Afwia in the old days, when they knew everything there. He knew all the royal stools, although he only made a few, of course. But ask him about any one of them — he knew them all, and could have done them. And everything else — the sword hilts, to be covered with gold leaf, the umbrella tops, the chief's "asipem" chair, the carved doors, the staves of the Akyeame — the Spokesmen, the "sankofa" birds and — oh, many others. He did them all. This is his "sekanmma" knife I've got here, and this chisel, a "bowere", the small one, see? He did masks, too, if a priest needed one for his fetish. He taught it all to me. I could do it, too. But how is a man to make a living from that, with everything so dear nowadays? The old chief and his ministers die, and the new ones need stools made for them, and maybe you make half a dozen stools in your lifetime. You won't drink palm-wine on that, my friend. It's not like the old days, when a chief helped you through the lean days. He's got no money for that now. The government's taken it all, these fancy boys from the coast, robbed him even of respect, coming in and putting up their flags all over the place, when anyone knows only a chief should have a flag——'

Nathaniel shrugged. He knew it all so well. It was partly true, but he did not want to listen to it.

'Don't you ever make anything but elephants?'

Ankrah nodded.

'Sometimes I make copies of stools. The Europeans like them, too. That's one, there.'

Nathaniel looked. It was a copy of a chief's stool, ancient symbol of kingship, badly done in poor wood. But Ankrah seemed proud of it. He reached out and patted it.

'Not so bad, eh? My father taught me everything he knew. He had three sons, all carvers, and he always said I was the best——'

'All the other things——' Nathaniel probed. 'If you haven't done them for a long time, how can you remember? It must be difficult, if you never use——'

Ankrah drew himself up.

'Does Nyankopon forget how He created man?'

It sounded brave. But Nathaniel, now regretting he had asked, knew it was not true. He turned to go.

'Well, I hope you like living here. It's not very quiet.'

'I don't care,' Ankrah said. 'I'm not a quiet man, myself. Of course, one could hardly like living here — in Accra, I mean. But the money's better. These coast people — you've got to watch them. They're slippery, like the fish they catch. They'd stab their mothers for tuppence in gold dust. And cheat! You've got to keep an eye on them. Here — I'll tell you what they're like. Just like those crabs you see on the sand here. Step this way to catch one, and it slips off that way. You move that way, it passes this way——'

He gestured vividly. Nathaniel wondered how he could get away from the woodcarver's clacking tongue without offending him.

'My wife will have the food ready——' he began.

'Wait!' Ankrah hissed. 'Who is that long-legged ape who sits on the stoep there, making shirts?'

'That's Yiamoo, the Tailor. He's a Togolander.'

'Why should he have all the stoep?' Ankrah demanded. 'I pay as much rent as he does. I tried to tell him so this morning, but he only laughed and said something in his own language. Well, I thought to myself, I've only come here today, so I'll wait and see. But I mean to have part of that stoep, I can tell you.'

'Yiamoo's been here a long time,' Nathaniel said quickly. 'I wouldn't argue with him if I were you.'

Ankrah spat noisily.

'Why not? Since when does an Akan take orders from a carrion-eater like that? I'm not afraid of him. I'm not going to take anything from him, I'll tell you that.'

'Have it your way,' Nathaniel said. 'But I warn you, Yiamoo's got a terrible temper. And when he's angry he's like a bush-cow — he charges everything in sight.'

Ankrah sucked his teeth and smiled scornfully.

'I thought you were from Asante.'

'Does that mean I have to pick fights with everybody I meet?'

'No-o. I suppose when you get to be a teacher, and wear a white shirt, you don't want to get it dirty.'

'Go ahead, then — fight with Yiamoo, if that's what you want. You'll find out quicker that way if there are elephants in Nyankopon's House.'

'Don't be angry,' the woodcarver said quickly. 'We are of one people. Here——'

He held out his hand, and Nathaniel, embarrassed, took it.

Nathaniel passed Yiamoo on his way into the house. The tailor was folding a pile of gaudy shirts, his big hands smoothing the material expertly.

'Morny,' Yiamoo said cheerfully, in pidgin. 'What you t'ink him?'

He yanked one thumb towards the carver. Nathaniel shrugged.

'He talks a lot.'

'I tell you true,' Yiamoo said, 'he say — go, you, I come here. I no agree. He say — chik, chik, chik, chik——'

He imitated the sound of a small lizard. Nathaniel could

not help laughing. Yiamoo's laughter boomed out, and the carver turned suspiciously and stared at them.

Nathaniel stopped laughing. He did not want to be involved in anything. He could fight, if he had to, but he resented this place imposing its problems on him. And there was Aya, here by herself all day——

He could see that Yiamoo was enjoying the situation. Once more there would develop the inevitable antagonisms, and some night everyone in the tenement would be wakened by the snarls and screams of two men who had come to hate each other.

Nathaniel felt tired of it all, the raucous squabbling life of this place. If only he and Aya could afford better rooms, a small house of their own—— Who did he think he was, a 'been-to' man, educated abroad, like Victor?

'Yiamoo——' he said suddenly, 'why African all time make palavah? We no got sense.'

The lanky tailor stretched himself luxuriously in the golden sunlight.

'Ahaa——' Yiamoo replied, 'we got sense. But we no got money. Man he be poor, what he do? Two t'ing he no cost. At all. He make pickin, he make palavah. God, He dash poor man dese two t'ing. No be so?'

Nathaniel smiled.

'Be so.'

He felt a surge of friendliness towards Yiamoo, almost a sense of comradeship. He knew he would never feel the same thing towards the sly woodcarver.

And yet he was not free to like whom he chose. Because the carver was from Asante, because their villages were not more than twenty miles apart, Nathaniel could not help feeling guilty that he did not sympathize with Ankrah.

*   *   *

Aya met Nathaniel at the door. She smiled in the half-anxious way she had when she hoped to placate him but feared it would be impossible.

Before she had time to speak, he heard the scuffle of feet in the back compound, and muffled laughter. Nathaniel groaned.

'Who now?' His voice was sharper than he had intended.

'Someone has come to visit,' Aya said apologetically.

'That is clear.'

'My aunt——' Aya went on, the words tumbling out, 'you know, Nathaniel, my aunt Akosua. She has two girls, you remember, one is five and the other eight. She is my mother's half-sister, but she isn't much older than I——'

'How long,' Nathaniel forced calm on himself, 'how long does she plan to stay?'

'I thought——'

Akosua Sackey came in from the compound at that moment. She was a tall, spare woman in her late thirties. Her face was handsome in a thin-boned hawkish way, and her wrists were slender and fine — they did not seem to own the wide, capable, hard-skinned hands.

'I greet you,' she said to Nathaniel. Then, looking from one to the other, 'You wonder why I have come, Nathaniel. Look at your wife's face. She looks tired. The child is heavy in her, and she needs help with her work now. I thought you would not mind.'

'You are welcome,' Nathaniel said stiffly. 'It is kind of you to come. If there is room——'

He looked helplessly around him. They had only the two rooms. Somehow, he did not want people sleeping all over, on the floor, as they did in the huts of his childhood. But it could not be avoided.

'It is all right,' Aya said hurriedly. 'They can sleep in here. My mother has loaned me the mats.'

She looked at him pleadingly, begging for his acceptance.

'All right,' he said. 'It will be good for you, Aya.'

He turned to Akosua, suddenly apprehensive.

'You know that Aya is having the baby in the hospital?'

She gave him, momentarily, a sour glance. Then her face was serene once more.

'I know,' she said. Then, as easily as though she believed it, 'She will be well cared for.'

Nathaniel nodded his satisfaction. At least she would not try to upset Aya about it: he could not hope for more.

'Well——' he said self-consciously, 'you are welcome, Akosua.'

Aya's quick childlike smile of gratitude made his heart contract.

After that day, life seemed to change at home. Aya became more relaxed, less liable to flare in anger. It was as though, having her aunt there, she felt she had come home. She let Akosua take over much of the work, and when the burden of the washing and the market shopping was taken from her, she was content to sit placidly in the sunshine, watching the two little girls as they played. Sometimes she seemed closer in age to the children than to anyone else.

When Nathaniel came home from work, he would find Akosua pounding cassava for fufu, while Aya and the children sat close by, listening to the stories she told. Aya's eyes would be soft and happy.

'Akosua——' she would cry, 'tell how Ananse stole food from the god Thunder — that is a good one——'

And Akosua would begin the tale of Ananse Kokuroko, Ananse the Giant Spider, the cunning one, the son of guile. And Aya would listen eagerly, her lips parted in a half

84

smile, her eyes tender with memory. Sometimes it seemed to Nathaniel that Aya was living, with a strange delight, in her childhood. Finally he spoke of it to her, ashamed of himself for placing the burden of his worry upon her.

'You are not a child,' he said. 'Why do you try to be one? Do you want so much to go back there?'

Aya looked away from him.

'You do not understand,' she said. 'After he is born, I will be different, different, different, all my life, until I die.'

It was her way of saying goodbye to herself. Perhaps she accepted not going back home more than he did, in the same way that she accepted the fact that once her child was born, her youth was over.

Nathaniel was frightened at the years that waited for them both.

★ 5 ★

SLOWLY THE CITY became familiar to Johnnie, and he no longer turned in the street to stare at the death-eyed beggars, or the trader mammies with trays on their heads and babies strapped to their backs. Any place was ordinary when one had lived in it for a while.

Then Africa began in various ways to taunt his knowing novice eye.

On a Sunday morning, the streets almost empty, Johnnie dropped into 'Saleh's' for cigarettes. The Syrian's shop resembled not so much a building as a form of plant life — some monstrous baobab with roots of cellars spreading deep and mould-encrusted underground, and branches in the form of innumerable wooden balconies, and latticed window shutters that fluttered leaflike in every tremor of hot salt wind from the sea.

The old man was the only one behind the counter this morning. Saleh was hugely fat, and his skin was yellow-brown. In the centre of that puffed pastryflesh, his blood and organs must have been quite lost, like the red dab of filling in a jelly doughnut.

'How you liking it here, Mr. Kestoe?'

'I expect it's as good as most places in Africa.'

The Syrian belched laughter.

'Sure,' he said, 'the best place in Africa. I been here — how long you think? Fifty-seven year. My parents bring me to this country when I was five year old. My father start a little shop — so small you couldn't hardly see it. We live at first in a hut, like Africans, and we eat kenkey and fishheads. But not for long. We are good businessmen. And now — my grandson Joseph, he buy a new Buick last month. He like American cars. He got three. He never remember when times was hard. His father — my son Edward — is dead. So unless I watch the boy, he spend like he was a king. Funny, eh?'

'Have you never been back to Syria?'

'Oh, sure. I been back four times. First time, I go back to get a wife. My wife never like Africa. I thought maybe I would send her back to Syria alone, she want so much to go. But she got sick first. So she die here. Let me tell something. If your wife want to go home, you send her. If you don't, you might be sorry. I was sorry. But what good was that?'

'I'll remember.'

The door to the back of the shop opened gently, and an African girl slithered in. She whispered to Saleh, and he replied with a hoarse grunt and a few words of pidgin. The girl giggled softly and shot a glance at Johnnie. She was tall and sleek, and her dark slanted eyes, half closed, seemed to convey her knowledge of men, a knowledge both amused and lustful. She smiled at him, and preened a little, her apple-breasts showing under the tight cloth. Then she was gone.

Saleh chuckled.

'You like?'

'Mm,' Johnnie said carefully. 'Not bad.'

This amused Saleh vastly.

'Not bad — yes. I am glad you think so. She is my daughter.'

Johnnie stared at him.

'But she's——'

'Oh — did you not know? After my wife die, I take an African wife. I have three children by her. That one, and two younger boys. Good children. Joseph don't like them, naturally, but he never dare to say anything. She is his half-aunt. This he don't like to be told. The two young boys will be educated in England. I have it in my will.'

A trace of malice appeared in his fatly smiling face.

'We Syrians are not like you English, Mr. Kestoe. My woman is old now, and she is not beautiful any more. But I keep her. She always been a good wife to me. But you English — you want to try a black girl, see what she's like. But all very quiet and secret. Then, if a baby come, you say — "Who, me? Impossible! That girl, she's crazy — I never seen her before in my life. I bet you it was some Italian or Frenchman did it!" Eh?'

Johnnie laughed awkwardly.

'Please to understand,' the Syrian went on, 'I don't care what a man does, just so he don't pick on Saleh's daughter to do it with. A man should go to the proper place — don't you think so? If you should be interested sometime, I can give you a name. Clean — so I heard.'

'No, thanks,' Johnnie said, too quickly.

Saleh laughed.

'Whatsamatter?'

'I'm not interested,' Johnnie said curtly. 'That's all.'

'Oh——' Saleh said, 'you're not interested. From the way you look at my daughter, I thought maybe you was wondering — well, never mind. You know, a young English-man come in here the other day — nice boy, I know him well — he don't mind an old man who talk too much — well, he says to me, "Saleh," he says, "tell me what it's like to sleep with an African woman." You know what I tell him? "When you're my age," I says to him, "you'll know all women are the same. There's no difference." Well, he don't believe me, see? "C'mon, Saleh," he says, "you can do better than that." So I tell him — "If there's a difference, it's that an African woman knows when to move and when to keep still."'

The Syrian's belly shook with laughter.

'A lie, of course,' he finished. 'Some do and some don't. What a woman is like — it depend on the man who taught her. But I tell him what he want to hear. And he stand there, breathing a little — you know — hard——'

Saleh leaned across the counter, his warlock's eyes narrowing.

'Like you are now,' he said softly.

The mid-morning sun gave a metallic lustre to the hibiscus leaves and flowers, making their green and scarlet appear as hard and gaudy as the enamels on a brass bowl. In the niim branches the ravens cawed disdain, painted birds, birds with brazen throats.

The cook's wife, pounding cassava out in the compound, sang to the rhythm of her work. Her voice rose shrill and mournful, and the wooden pestle thudded again and again, like a slow metronome.

Johnnie put the car in the garage and walked into the bungalow. Miranda's voice came from the kitchen, talking to the cook.

'Surely you must save something, Whiskey. There's just yourself and your wife.'

'No be so, madam,' Whiskey cried. 'You no savvy African family. My bruddah, my sistah, all time dey say— "Whiskey, why you no give we more money?" Trouble me too much, madam. Now my bruddah — he got some small case. Poor man no be fit for mek case, madam.'

'What's the case about?' Miranda asked.

'My family got land near Teshie. Mek farm long time. Den family come small-small. No got plenty man. No look-a de farm propra. Nuddah family, he go for my land, plant corn, plant cassava. My bruddah say "Go, you". Nuddah man, he say "You no mek we go". Too much palavah. Go for court. Madam — I beg you. You help me.'

'What do you want?'

'I no ask dash,' Whiskey said. 'I beg you, madam. You give me five pound advance on my pay.'

'I guess that would be all right,' Miranda said slowly.

'I t'ank madam! You be fine too much!'

'What will you do,' she asked, 'if you lose the case?'

'If we no win,' Whiskey said, with a croak of apologetic laughter, 'I tell my bruddah we go for ju-ju man.'

'Whatever for?'

'Mek some small ju-ju for mek nuddah family go somewhere.'

'If it's poison,' Miranda said, 'that's murder. And if it isn't — well — you don't believe in that sort of thing, do you, Whiskey?'

'I no fear ju-ju!' Whiskey cried. 'But nuddah family, he fear. I fear on'y small-small. Madam, I be Methodist!'

Johnnie burst out laughing, and in the kitchen there was an offended silence.

A quiet, sweltering, ordinary Monday, the clerks drowsing and the Europeans irritable and dyspeptic after the weekend. Nothing in the day's beginning to indicate that it would be **different** from any other.

But in the middle of the morning, Johnnie was summoned to the Manager's office, and there James told him. Word had just been received from Head Office in London that the Firm's Gold Coast branch was to adopt a speed-up policy of Africanization, in line with current social and political changes. In essence, the policy meant that as many Europeans as possible were to be replaced by Africans. Department managers were to begin training suitable African senior clerks at once, so they could take over the junior administrative jobs by the time of Independence, now only a few months away.

Absurdly, Johnnie's first thought was of Victor Edusei's ugly smile. A caged and helpless rage speeded his heartbeat. How the African would laugh.

'James — why?'

'The Firm wants to keep on the right side of the Africans,' James said wearily. 'Don't forget that ninety percent of our business is in selling to Africans. Oh — as a publicity gesture, it's understandable.'

His fingers drummed on the desk.

'The only trouble with it,' he went on, 'is that it won't work. I know Africans, Johnnie. Trustworthy, efficient men who can handle an administrative type of job — they just don't exist.'

All at once the Squire's face became suffused with a dull red anger; his neckveins stood out like crimson-black ropes as though his fury were about to hang him.

'Even if they did exist——' the thin voice shook, 'even if they did exist, by God, I wouldn't have them! I've been here for over thirty years and I never thought I'd see the day when common bush Africans——'

Johnnie gazed in reluctant fascination. The Squire was on his feet now, his pawhands gesticulating, capering in the air a weird ballet of rage, like something from a Punch-and-Judy show. His simian face wrinkled more and more until it seemed that one extra crease in the soft skin would accomplish the sad betrayal into tears.

'Ruin it in a month — corruption — laziness — sheer ignorance. People don't know how long it takes to build up a system that works. In London, they don't know — they don't understand——'

He stopped abruptly and sat down.

'I'm sorry, Johnnie. I shouldn't have burst out like that. It's just that this whole business has — upset me. I practically made this department, you know. You'd hardly believe how small it was when I came here. A few bolts of cloth — most of it striped, I recall. All but one, yellow and brown, patterned like leopardskin. D'you know, we still sell that pattern? We had only one clerk, and he could hardly write his own name. We used to administer a smart kick to his backside when he made mistakes — he learned pretty quickly, I can tell you. There was no nonsense in those days. An African did what he was told. And now — they want to run my department. Well, I won't have it. I promise you that.'

'You're not going to start looking for an African accountant, then?' Johnnie tried to make his voice sound casual.

'I most assuredly am not,' James said. 'Nor for Africans to replace any of my officers.'

Johnnie looked at him in surprise.

'If it's policy, how can you——?'

James' expression was oddly conspiratorial.

'We simply won't be able to find any suitable Africans, that's all. We must just stick together in this business.'

James had been here a long time, and he knew. There was no cause for alarm. But Johnnie could not entirely put from his mind the gesture of James' hands when he burst into the tirade. In recollection, it seemed that not only anger but fear had been the puppetmaster.

The clerks had all heard the news, of course, and they could scarcely conceal their jubilation. Nothing was openly spoken. But a snatch of highlife tune was whistled, and an answering snicker, soft as rain, pattered through the room.

Johnnie sat at his desk, sweating heavily. He wondered if the Firm would ever see fit to instal ceiling fans. Probably he wouldn't be here by that time. Someone like Attah would be sitting at his desk, smirking at the sign 'Accountant.'

Johnnie threw down his pen. No one could concentrate on work this morning. He gave it up and went in to see Bedford.

'Come in and shut the blasted door,' the massive knight growled.

The small pink object, carefully shielded as a rare butterfly in the huge hand, turned out to be a paper cup such as children use for orange squash at birthday parties. Bedford fished another out of a drawer and poured it half full of scotch.

'Here——' he handed it to Johnnie, 'we must toast the great event. You've heard, of course?'

'Yes. Thanks, but I'm not sure I want this, Bedford — a bit early in the day.'

'Nonsense! Never too early, when our black brethren are making history. Drink up. To Africanization, to the black keys and the white, old boy, to Ghana, to the star that is rising over Africa——'

He set his glass down gently on the desk.

'Isn't it an absolute bugger?' Bedford said.

It was close to midday when Johnnie's office door opened and Helen Cunningham walked in.

93

She had been shopping, but she wore the same tired cotton skirt and blouse as she wore around home. But despite dust and perspiration, there was still a magnificence about her sunflower hair and her eyes. She looked straight ahead, utterly ignoring the clerks' curious stares.

The poise lasted only until she had closed the door of Johnnie's inner office. She sat down on the edge of a chair and groped in her handbag for a cigarette. Johnnie offered her one of his, and she took it. She was shivering, like someone who has just awakened from a nightmare and still believes it real.

'Helen — for God's sake, what's the trouble?'

'Sorry. I'll be all right in a moment. Shock, I guess.'

'Oh — Bedford told you, then?'

Her eyes opened wide in fresh alarm.

'Told me what? What is it, Johnnie? What's happened?'

'Don't panic,' he said. 'It's nothing. It's not important. Everything's all right. But if he didn't say anything, what——?'

'Bedford's in no condition to tell anybody anything,' Helen said, 'for the simple reason that he's out cold.'

'Oh Christ, what next? Wait, though, you don't mean he's sick?'

She gave him a withering glance.

'Don't be a fool. Sick, yes, with an empty Johnnie Walker bottle beside him on the floor, and another in his desk.'

She began to cry, gulpingly, and the sight of her wet distorted face sickened Johnnie. Then she stopped, blew her nose, and sat up, her face tight and hard.

'James mustn't see him,' she said. 'He simply mustn't. He warned him the last time——'

'It's happened before?'

94

'When I said — shock — did you think this was the first time? You don't know us very well yet, do you?'

'I'm beginning to think not.'

'The last time was when the Thayers moved into the new bungalow. I — I guess that was partly my fault. Damn it, I did resent it — why not? They have no children, and here we are, with Kathie and Brian in that ghastly old wreck, and the scorpions underneath the stoep. Whenever he can't cope, Bedford simply——'

She broke off.

'He never used to be this way, you know, Johnnie. He's had rotten luck, poor dear. It was fine in the war, but ever since — well, you can't really blame him, I suppose.'

She put her palms to her eyes.

'But why does he do it at the office?' she cried. 'We've got to get him out of there.'

'Helen,' Johnnie said patiently, 'we can't get him out, and you know it. What do you want me to do — conceal him in my briefcase? He only weighs about fifteen stone. I'll do my best to keep James out of there. That's all I can do, I'm afraid.'

'I — I'm going back to his office, to be there. When you go home for lunch, will you ask Miranda if she'll go over and put the children down for their rest? And tell Kwaku he's not to leave the bungalow until I get back.'

He nodded. At the door, she turned.

'I'm sorry to bother you with all this, Johnnie.'

He shrugged in embarrassment.

'It doesn't matter.'

'Oh — I know. But — you liked him, before.'

'Don't be daft. I still do. It doesn't make any difference.'

'You——' she hesitated, 'you respected him. He was pleased about that.'

'I don't expect anything of people,' Johnnie said curtly. 'It never comes as a surprise. So it makes no difference.'

But it did, of course. He had thought Bedford would be a strong and useful ally. And now it seemed that the massive knight was only a leaden soldier, weirdly dissolving in this fire.

That afternoon, the African reporter phoned. Johnnie had known that he would.

'Ah, Mr. Kestoe,' Victor Edusei's voice flowed with oily ease out of the receiver, 'we have just received an interesting press-release from your Firm. I suppose you know the one I mean?'

Johnnie grunted.

'I have excellent informants in London, don't you agree?'

'I don't want to discuss the matter with you,' Johnnie said.

'Wait, wait,' Edusei said, 'don't hang up yet. Am I to understand, then, that you are not in favour of an Africanization policy?'

'Go to hell,' Johnnie said.

As he replaced the receiver, he heard what he had expected — the peal of hoarse exultant laughter from the black throat.

⋆ 6 ⋆

THE PRESENCE of Aya's aunt Akosua seemed to pacify Aya's mother, for she said no more about a return to the village. Aya did not mention the hospital; Nathaniel's sister Kwaale did not send another letter, and for a while Nathaniel almost convinced himself that his family had begun at last to accept his life here and the birth of his child in the city of strangers. But the lull meant only that another wave was accumulating its strength to pour upon him.

The mammy-wagons jounced and rattled from Ashanti down to the coast, bearing cocoa and bananas and people. And the day came when Nathaniel answered the knock at his door and saw his uncle Adjei. Nathaniel had not seen his uncle for six years, but the old man greeted him calmly, as though they had met yesterday, and stepped inside the house.

Adjei's face was hard and deeply seamed like a cocoa pod. He was a small man, and his arms stuck out like crooked sticks from the folds of his cloth. But he bore himself well, sitting with stiff dignity on the edge of the chair, scorning to lean back. His cloth was dark purple and green, patterned with long-legged cranes as lean of shank as himself. His sandals were shabby and the toe thongs were nearly worn through, but once they had been embossed with gold.

He looked around the room, his eyes dwelling on each object as though he were mentally listing everything. The

97

dining table, the thin blue cotton curtains, the old wireless, the striped green and orange coco-matting on the floor, the pictorial calendar whose message 'Happy New Year From Mandiram's The Quality Shop' was mysterious to him.

Then the old man looked at Nathaniel thoughtfully.

'You have a fine house.'

'I do my best,' Nathaniel said awkwardly. 'I do not have much money.'

The old man clicked his tongue unbelievingly.

'You must be a wealthy man. All these things——'

'I am not wealthy,' Nathaniel said hopelessly.

'Nathaniel——'

'Uncle?'

The old man's voice had a high silvery quality, like an ancient tinkling bell that has not quite lost its throat.

'You are my sister's son, and my heir,' Adjei Boateng said. 'I wish for your sake I were a wealthy man.'

Nathaniel involuntarily clenched his hands. Let it be only money that he asks. I cannot afford it, but let it be only money. Please, I beg you, not the other.

'I know.' Nathaniel tried not to sound impatient. 'It is of no importance.'

'We are not wealthy, our families,' the old man continued slowly, 'not like some men I could tell you about, who started with two pennyworth of gold. And now — ahhaa! House like the Asantehene's palace — fine clothes — everything. And how they made it, it is best not to enquire, for shame. You remember Mintah?'

'Yes.' Nathaniel felt his nerves cracking, but it was no use — like the seasons, Adjei took his own time.

'He is a contractor now, a big man. A loyal member of the party of apes and strangers. That is how he gets his contracts. Some men would sell their own mothers into slavery.'

Nathaniel sighed. To his uncle, anyone not born in Ashanti was, now and forever, a stranger. No doubt he was right about Mintah. But politics was not a clean game.

'I am not a boy,' Nathaniel said, a trace of sharpness in his voice. 'I know all this. What has it to do with me?'

'Our two families are not like such men,' Adjei went on solemnly. 'We are poor people, but loyal to our own. That is the way you were brought up, Nathaniel.'

'Uncle——' he could stand it no longer, 'I beg you — come to the point!'

'The young——' sighed the old man, with exaggerated sorrow, 'have no respect. That is what happens.'

Nathaniel wanted to shout — I am not young; I am twenty-seven and I have a wife and an unborn son and very little money. Will I never be rid of the gentle plucking fingers, the soft whine of the old? Then he felt ashamed. You spit on your people, Nathaniel. He is an old man, and he loves you. You are his blood. When you are old, Nathaniel, your sisters' sons will spit on you.

'I am sorry,' Nathaniel said humbly.

Adjei snorted suspiciously. But he decided to state his business.

'Nathaniel, you remember Nana Kweku Afrisi?'

'Of course.'

'He needs a clerk,' Adjei said. 'He remembers you.'

Nathaniel stared at him.

'You will come?' Adjei said smoothly. 'It is a big town, and near your village. He is a fine man. It is a wonderful chance, to be clerk to a chief.'

For a moment Nathaniel could not reply. The old man's eyes looked confident, certain. Nathaniel reached up automatically to adjust his glasses, and his fingers slid along the brown plastic frames as though drawing strength.

'I can't go,' he said finally.

Adjei Boateng looked at him without surprise, as though he had expected an initial struggle. Nathaniel squirmed in his chair.

— The drowning man would struggle for a little while and then he would be quiet, and the River would lap him around with its softness, the brown murky stillness of its womb.

'I can't go!' Nathaniel repeated desperately.

— How many times have I cut the cord that fed me? How many times have I fought with the Mother to give me birth? How many times has the fish, feeling his gills aflutter with the stars, dragged himself from the womb of water, painfully to breathe?

'You will come, I think,' Adjei said. 'It is your duty. I try to look after your sisters, my nieces. They live under my roof, and I do what I can for them. But I am an old man, and I have no sons. Your sisters need you. You are their children's uncle, the man of the "abusua", the blood-clan. They need the uncle's guidance. It is your duty. The burden of the family has fallen on Kwaale. She is a fine woman, but her husband is dead and she has many troubles.'

'I know,' Nathaniel said heavily. 'I know.'

'How much do they pay you at the school?'

Ashamed, Nathaniel told him.

'Is that all?' Adjei said, not believing him. 'Nana Kweku will pay you more than that.'

'You do not understand.'

'Then tell me.'

Nathaniel looked away.

'I do not think I can explain.'

The old man nodded his head, and his eyes showed a flicker of amusement.

'The young always think the old cannot understand them. Try. Perhaps my feeble mind can follow you.'

'It is not that,' Nathaniel said. 'It is just — well, I have changed. I do not want to be a chief's clerk.'

For the first time the old man looked confused.

'It is an honour to work for a chief. Surely you see that it is an honour?'

'Not to me,' Nathaniel said clearly. 'How can I tell you? You will not understand. The chiefs are dying out, uncle. I do not want to work for the dead. I mean no disrespect. Nana Kweku is a fine man, a good man. But I do not want to work for him.'

'He is chief only over one town and a handful of villages,' Adjei said bitterly, 'is that it? Who are you, Nathaniel? Who do you want to work for — the Asantehene himself?'

'It is not that at all. I knew you would not see it.'

The old man sighed gustily.

'Are you well, Nathaniel?'

Nathaniel threw out his hands in despair.

'Yes,' he grated through his teeth, 'quite well.'

The old man's eyes gleamed cruelly.

'I thought you must either be mad or very wise,' he said. 'Try me again, Nathaniel. You say Nana Kweku is a good man, and yet you refuse to work for him. Why? I am perhaps a little deaf these past years. That part was not quite clear to me——'

'Because I would end by hating him, if I worked for him,' Nathaniel snapped. 'Oh — many clerks of chiefs despise their masters, make no mistake about it! I'd have to watch him, every day, every day, not able to read or even write his own name, not knowing anything outside his little province, but still able to command, to move people this way and that. I don't want to see it.'

The old man looked at him in astonishment.

'Now I know you are mad. Your sisters will grieve. Certainly, they will grieve.'

Nathaniel looked at him helplessly, as though from a great distance.

'Listen to me, uncle. Just once. I mean no disrespect. Can't you believe me?'

Adjei's eyelids lifted a little.

'Wonderful,' he murmured, 'wonderful. You would strangle your brother, I suppose, telling him all the while that you meant no disrespect?'

'I know,' Nathaniel said, 'I know it sounds like that. But it is not. I do not say anything against the chiefs. Only that their time is past.'

'You think,' the old man's voice was a soft hiss, 'that because we have fallen low, and are ruled by foreigners and apes from the coast, that it will always be so? I tell you, Nathaniel, there is a wind rising in Asante more scorching than the Harmattan. It speaks of fire and it speaks of blood. Asante will be again what it once was.'

His words rang out clearly, the thin-voiced silver bell gathering itself to toll.

'I know — you believe that,' Nathaniel said. 'The nationalists are trying to break Asante away from the union, to get a separate independence, to establish the old kingdom again. But I do not want my people to be what they once were. I want them to be something more.'

'And what is wrong with what we once were?' Adjei demanded angrily. 'Our people are not the apes and dogs of the coast, eating their filth and living godless in caves.

We have borne kings, and their strength gave us strength and their life gave us life. And they are with us, and the strength of their spirits will be as the fire of the sun in our veins——'

The old man's eyes burned, and Nathaniel felt himself being drawn into that fire, fire of the sun, fire of gold.

'No—' he said, then, bringing his hand down hard on the table, 'no! Old tales, all of it. Our souls are sick with the names of our ancestors. Osei Tutu, he who made the nation, and Okomfo Anoye the priest, he who gave the nation its soul, and Nana Prempeh exiled by the English — I know, I know them all. I respect them, although you do not believe it. I honour them. But they will not save us. They are dead, dead, dead, and we are alive. Our future does not lie with them, or with the living chiefs, or with Asante alone. Africa is a big place, uncle.'

'That is like a young man,' Adjei said. 'You would throw it all away. You would let the souls of your ancestors die for want of tending, not seeing that you die with them.'

'I do not want to throw it all away,' Nathaniel said painfully, then his voice rose to a cry, 'but how can you keep part without keeping all? Keep the chiefs, the linguists, the soulbearers, the drummers, and you will keep the "sumankwafo", dealers in fetish, and the "bayi komfo", the witch-doctors. You will keep the minds that made "atopere", the dance of death, a man hacked slowly to pieces and made to dance until too much was butchered for him to move. That is what you will keep.'

'"Atopere" has been forbidden for many years,' Adjei said sternly, 'and it is not fitting for you to speak of things you do not understand.'

'All right,' Nathaniel said. 'So I do not understand it. I am a city man. I do not know about these things. I do not want to know about them. They do not interest me. Things are changing, uncle, changing more than you see. The wind that is rising is rising all over Africa, and it speaks of something new that has never been before.'

The old man's expression told Nathaniel he had gone too far, had wounded more than could ever be excusable.

'Adjei — I'm sorry,' he said. 'I cannot help it. But I'm sorry.'

Adjei scuffed one sandal on the floor and stared down at it, avoiding Nathaniel's eyes.

'No,' he said, and his voice was not quite steady, 'I do not think you are sorry. Because you have forgotten your own land. That is a strange thing to do, Nathaniel.'

Nathaniel could not speak. The old man's voice seemed to repeat the words over and over, buzzing in his head like the shrill voices of a thousand cicadas.

— You have forgotten your own land. You live in the city of strangers, and your god is the god of strangers, and strange speech is in your mouth, and you have no home.

— Oh, Nathaniel, how can a man forget? A man cannot forget. Deep, deep, there lies the image of what the eye has lost and the brain has lost to ready command.

— The forest grows in me, now, this year and the next, until I die. The forest grows in me. See, there are the high trees, the tall hardwoods, mahogany and ofram, and the iron-grey cottonwoods buttressed from their roots like great forts, the cottonwoods with their high green umbrellas of leaves. From the half-rotted trunks of the oil palms the parasite ferns grow, clothing the old bodies of the trees with obscene frivolity, tickling them with their fronds, their green green plumes. The forest spills over with life and death. The trees are hairy with strangler vines, beautiful green-haired death. The jungle lilies and the flowers of the poinsettia are red as the fresh blood of a sacrificed cockerel. The small blue commelina clutches the soil, the flower we call 'God will die before I do'. The forest floor is carpeted with ferns, and beneath the live green lies the rotting flesh of the plants' last growth, and their death gives new life to the soil. The forest is rank and hot and swelling with its semen. Death and life meet and mate.

— The forest grows in me, rank, hot, terrible. The fern fronds spread like veins through my body.

'I have not forgotten,' Nathaniel said in a low voice.

His uncle glanced at him, the old eyes unblinking as a lizard's.

'You want to forget, then,' Adjei said, 'and that is just as bad.'

Did he? Did he want to forget? Nathaniel looked away.

— When I was a boy, on my father's farm, the forest was peopled with a million ghosts, a million gods. Stone and tree and root, a million eyes. I was not brave. I was slight and small for my age, and my mother had protected me too much. I was not brave. Was anyone? I thought the other boys were, then, but now I am not so sure. Perhaps they were afraid, too. The forest was enclosed, shadowy, like a room filled with green shadows. It was my home. The voice of the forest was shrill all day — a million million bees, a million million cicadas, a million million screaming birds. And at night the silence of the snake.

— The farms were hewed and hacked out of the bush. The matted brush closed in like a solid wall, and the bush paths were hacked out with machetes, until you had a tunnel through the undergrowth, a green tunnel where the ant-men scurried to and fro from their farms. The cocoa trees grew richly, with their pale brown-stained trunks and yellowing pods. The cassava grew, and the guinea corn, and the yams with leaves like elephants' ears.

— It was not so bad, when I was young. I did not know I would ever leave, then. I did not know that soon the mission school would give me a new name and a new soul. It wasn't so bad. At dusk we used to go back home, running through the green tunnels. We used to come out onto the road the whitemen had forced through the forest, the great road. And there was excitement! It seemed then that the world walked on that road. The women trudged along with the baskets of bananas, plantains, cassava on their heads, the bundles of firewood on their heads. But we boys stopped to stare at the lorries that passed, or we loitered beside the palm shelters where palm-wine was sold in old beer bottles. Sometimes we saw strangers, men with shifty eyes, thieves or God knows what, or just travellers who couldn't afford to ride a mammy-wagon. And sometimes we saw bands of northern desert men, dressed in their coarse blue and white tunics, driving their herds of long-horned cattle to the coast. It seemed the world must be passing by on that road.

— It wasn't so bad, it wasn't so bad. But I always wanted to know where that great road went, and what was at the other end.

Adjei Boateng was looking at him curiously. Nathaniel turned away. He did not want to see the pain in the old man's eyes.

'Do not forsake your own people,' Adjei said gently, 'or life will be a bitter leaf in your mouth.'

'It will not happen so.'

'You are young,' his uncle said. 'Some day you will know where you belong.'

Nathaniel grinned, and bitterness welled up in him.

'I belong between yesterday and today.'

Adjei Boateng smiled also.

'But that is nowhere.'

'I know,' Nathaniel replied. 'Yes, I know.'

Adjei had friends whom he wanted to visit, so he refused Nathaniel's invitation to stay. Nathaniel felt ashamed at his own sense of relief.

Aya and Akosua had stayed in the other room while Nathaniel talked to his uncle. Aya emerged now, but she did not ask him what the old man had said; she would certainly have listened and heard it all. Instead, she held up a length of new cloth for him to see.

'My church,' Aya said, 'is going to have a parade.'

She always referred to it as 'my church'. Nathaniel did not belong. He still attended the traditional church in which, as a boy at the mission school, he had been brought up. Sometimes the old anger stirred and he would not set foot in the church for months. Then, out of need or habit, he would return, never entirely believing, never entirely disbelieving, doubting heaven but fearing hell.

Aya went with him on Sunday mornings, but her real enthusiasm was for the evangelical church she attended with her women friends. She would arrive home from the sessions strangely exalted, and she did not seem to mind when Nathaniel made fun of her. Maddeningly, whenever he asked her about it, she could never tell him, only that the singing had done her good. Nathaniel sometimes wondered how much of the teaching touched her at all. Jesus did. But Aya did not see Him as The Redeemer.

'That Jesus,' she would say, clucking her tongue in soft sympathy, 'that poor boy.'

'He grew up to be a man,' Nathaniel would remind her.

But to Aya He remained a child-god. Men had brought Him gifts of gold, honouring his godhead, and then, envying his powers, they had slain Him. On Good Friday, she mourned Him like a mother.

'It was a hard command God laid on Him,' she said once.

And she was astounded when Nathaniel laughed. But Aya had said 'hyebea' for command, and for God, 'Nyame'. Nathaniel had seen it, for a moment, through her eyes and had known by what beliefs she interpreted it. She thought of it in terms of the faith of her people. The 'kra', the soul, of some royal sinner, probably David the King, to whose house Jesus belonged, was reborn in that poor boy, that miraculous child, and told to come to earth and perfect itself. And the solemn command of Nyame to the 'kra' could not be evaded.

But when Nathaniel questioned her, Aya grew bored and restless, and denied thinking anything at all.

'I suppose you think that Sunday was Jesus' name-day,' he teased her once, 'and that He used to take part in the soul-washing ceremony then.'

And Aya had looked confused, knowing he was making fun of her, but not quite understanding how.

Now she draped the material around herself. It was deep blue, with a pattern of drift-tailed fishes and unnamed sea-creatures in swirling lines of yellow and orange.

'We have all bought new cloth for the parade. How do you like it? No — do not say it is too expensive. It is my own money. Remember when I sewed for Mrs. Ansah?'

'You should not go,' he said. 'Not — like that.'

Aya laughed.

'How can it harm the baby? He does not have to do the walking.'

She would never change. Never. The country might go on, leaping century after century overnight. But Aya would remain the same.

'Why do you want to go?' he asked peevishly. 'A bunch of women dancing highlife to the hymns — showing their foolishness from Christiansborg to High Street. It's almost as stupid as the fetish priestess dancing with ashes on her breasts——'

She stood quite still for a moment, and her oil-dark eyes shone with anger.

'What do you want me to do?' she cried. 'I must have nothing to do with the "abosom" and now I must not go to my church, either. What do you want me to do?'

What did he want her to do? Nathaniel knew. He wanted her to go to church on Sunday mornings only, unobtrusively, to his staid and respectable church.

'I'm sorry,' Nathaniel mumbled. 'You will go with your friends. It is all right. And the cloth is a fine one.'

'Why did you change?' she asked bluntly. 'What made you change like that?'

Nathaniel shrugged.

'Truly, I do not want to tell you everything you must do,' he said helplessly. 'If you want to go, then go. If you think I am always telling you what to do, it is only because——'

Already she had grown tired of the talk, and was folding the cloth with practised hands.

He did not want to tell her what to do. It was not right. He knew it.

But why did she not learn?

It was that night that Ankrah the carver stabbed Yiamoo. Nathaniel and Aya were wakened shortly after midnight. The compound had become a cage where anger roared and struck. They could hear Yiamoo's deep thundering voice, cursing hotly in his own tongue. Then the carver's voice, a snake-hiss of hatred, a high-pitched squeal as Yiamoo hit him.

The wooden shutters of the house banged open, and anonymous voices cackled in the night. From the street, the noise of cars blurred the pattern of sounds in the compound.

'Ankrah tried again today to get the stoep for his work,' Aya whispered, 'and Yiamoo spat in his face.'

They heard the scuffling of feet, then the strangled grunt of a wounded thing. A second's terrifying silence, then the sound of feet, running, running, stumbling. Strangely, the wooden shutters of the house began to creak closed, one after another, quietly, as though upon an agreed signal. The next morning, if the police came, no one would have seen or heard anything.

'Which one?' Aya whispered, frightened.

'I don't know.'

But he did know. Nathaniel was not surprised when, a few minutes later, they heard the soft desperate voice of Yiamoo's wife at their window.

'Come——' she said. 'I beg you. Come quick.'

Nathaniel pulled on his trousers and went out. She was standing beside the window, shivering, her eyes wide with panic. He helped her drag Yiamoo into the house.

It was a shoulder wound, and the knife had pierced from behind. It had not been meant for the shoulder. If Yiamoo had not been crouching, his wife said, already half-turned to find his slippery opponent, the knife would have slid up under the ribs and into the lungs.

Yiamoo's wife moaned in a low voice as she washed and bound the wound. She produced, from among an untidy pile of earthen pots, a small bottle of cheap gin, and handed it to Nathaniel questioningly.

Nathaniel did not know what to do. He could not remember if it was a good or a bad thing to give spirits. Finally he poured a little of it into the tailor's mouth.

Yiamoo was not unconscious, but he seemed to be dazed. His breath came in short gasps. He almost choked on the gin, then he drew a deeper breath and opened his eyes. When he saw Nathaniel, he put out one hand towards him.

'Mek I go die?'

'No,' Nathaniel said. 'You no go die. You rest. I go for doctor.'

Yiamoo made a violent gesture, then grimaced in pain.

'No,' he said. 'No go for doctah. I no 'gree.'

Nathaniel shrugged. Yiamoo was a strong man. Maybe the wound would be all right without treatment. Maybe not. But he knew he could not persuade the tailor.

Yiamoo's wife had thrown herself down at her husband's feet. She was sobbing noisily, thankfully, as though she could hardly believe he was still alive. It was true that Yiamoo beat her, shouted at her, tried to take her market-earned money from her. But she had no life apart from him.

'What he do?' Nathaniel asked. 'Why he cut you?'

He pieced together the story from Yiamoo's halting pidgin phrases. After the day's argument, Ankrah had gone off and Yiamoo — so he said — had forgotten about it. Tonight, as he was walking out to the latrine, someone tripped him. In a rage, he had made for the man, not knowing who it was. When he saw it was the carver, Yiamoo's temper had given way completely and he had fought in a blind anger. He had hit Ankrah once, then the carver had twisted away and come up behind him with a knife.

Nathaniel asked him if he would go to the police. Yiamoo shook his head.

'Police palavah, he no be good,' he replied. 'I no got money. Ankrah, he no got pickin. He got money, I t'ink, small-small. He go dash plenty man, den dey say Yiamoo he mek trouble.'

It was true. But Nathaniel, if he chose, could give evidence for Yiamoo. He felt, angrily, that he would like to do it.

But they said no more about it. When Nathaniel left, Yiamoo's wife pressed into his hand the only present she had to give, a bead necklace for Aya. Nathaniel took it, feeling once again that strange companionship that needed no blood allegiance as its base.

He was determined to go to the police on Yiamoo's behalf.

At his own doorway, Nathaniel felt a hand on his arm. He swung around to see Ankrah standing there, his sharp face contorted with fear.

'Is he dead?'

Nathaniel shook off the hand.

'No,' he said brusquely. 'No thanks to you.'

The other began to whine.

'I swear to you, I did not mean to hurt him. I tell you, it was an accident. Look — here's what happened. I speak the truth, may Tano bear me witness. I tripped him, sure, as a joke — can't a man take a thing like that without going mad? That's what he did — he went mad. You should have seen him, like the big ape he is, his arms going this way and that, trying to grab me. He would have broken my neck. It's true. Well, I slipped under his arm, and I had to stop him, so I thought I'd just touch him with the knife, just to scare him, you know. But he lunged right against it. I couldn't help it, I swear to you——'

'I don't want to hear,' Nathaniel said.

'Listen, Nathaniel,' Ankrah pleaded, 'you won't tell the police?'

'Why shouldn't I?'

A semblance of dignity came over the carver. He looked straight into Nathaniel's eyes.

'Because we are of one people,' he said. 'Does a man

betray his brother? Do you think the spirits of your ancestors would give you any rest, ever again, if you did a thing like that?'

'There are more things——'

Nathaniel stopped. He had been going to say there were more things and more important things than being of one people. But he knew he could not explain.

'You will not tell?' Ankrah insisted.

Nathaniel looked at him, feeling sick.

— Oh, Nathaniel, would you spit on your people and have in turn your sons spit upon you?

—Nathaniel, Nathaniel, life is a bitter leaf in your mouth.

'Speak,' Ankrah said in agony. 'What is the matter with you?'

— The 'asamanfo', the spirits of the dead, speak in every whisper of breeze through the niim branches. The voice of the Drummer. My son, my son. I was betrayed in your heart — must I now be betrayed again and again?

— Jesus said, love thy neighbour as thyself. Nathaniel, love thy neighbour Yiamoo as thyself. And Jesus said, one of you will betray Me.

— Choose. Must a man always betray one god or the other? Both gods have fought over me, and sometimes it seems that both have lost, sometimes that both have won and I am the unwilling bondsman of two masters.

— Does a man betray his brother?

'Nathaniel,' Ankrah was saying, 'does a man betray his brother?'

Nathaniel turned away, his heart pounding.

'I will not tell,' he said in a low voice.

The carver's eyes shone with triumph, and he sucked in a relieved breath.

'I bless your name, my brother. I promise you——'

'Go,' Nathaniel said fiercely. 'Go now before I hit you.'

With Adjei, with Kwaale, with Aya and Aya's mother, even with Ankrah the carver, Nathaniel expected to have to fight the Forest and the part of himself that wanted to listen to the voice of the mother-pleading River. But not with Victor. He and Victor had always stood together, like brothers. Nathaniel was unprepared for the day when he and Victor seemed to stand opposed.

Victor clenched his powerful hands together, cracking the knuckles unpleasantly. He had not shaved all day, and the black hair stood like burnt spikes of spear-grass on his heavy jowl. A soiled green shirt was glued with sweat to his chest, and half his stomach swelled in a thick roll of fat over the top of low-slung shapeless corduroy trousers. He yawned and half-closed his eyes.

'Where's Aya?' he demanded, 'and the relatives?'

'In there,' Nathaniel said. 'When I saw you downtown you said you wanted to talk to me alone.'

'So I did,' Victor said absentmindedly.

They were silent for a while.

'Did Aya tell you?' Victor asked finally.

'No.' Nathaniel tried not to sound annoyed. 'About what?'

'About Charity.'

'Who — Charity Donkor? You still seeing her?'

Victor laughed.

'Seeing her——' he said. 'Yes, I've been seeing her. The great fetish from the north has worked.'

Nathaniel looked at him sharply.

'You mean she's——'

Victor nodded.

'Wonderful what the right fetish can do, isn't it?'

'Is it yours,' Nathaniel demanded, 'the child?'

'Naturally,' Victor said. 'She's been living with me for — oh, I don't know how long.'

'Are you sure it's yours, though?' Nathaniel insisted. 'I mean——'

Victor grinned.

'I know what you mean,' he said. 'Don't be shy about saying it. Charity is a whore by nature. But I'm pretty sure it's mine, as it happens. Not her principles, you understand. It was only that she liked what I had to offer. My offering to the fetish was to her taste.'

Nathaniel gazed into his glass of warm beer, smelling its sour yeastiness. He was willing to say anything, but he was not sure what Victor wanted to hear. The folds of flesh around Victor's eyes were creased into jeering laughter. Nathaniel felt that Victor must think of him as stolid and humourless.

'Make no mistake about it,' Victor continued. 'I was honoured, man. Why, she never even asked me for money. That's not her usual habit, you know.'

Grotesquely waving one hand to the rhythm, he sang a verse from the 'Club Girl' calypso:

> '*But when you want to rest,*
> *You lose a lotta dough,*
> *That's how the business go——*
> *So please forget about marrying.*'

'My beloved,' Victor said. 'That's how she used to be with men. She is a fine woman, my beloved. Don't you agree?'

'Aya will be furious,' Nathaniel said abruptly. 'At you, I mean.'

'Oh, come now. Aya knows what Charity's like. She's too loyal to admit it, that's all. Besides, who said I was going to forget about marrying?'

'I don't understand——'

Victor looked suddenly tired and the heavy features of his face went slack.

'Charity wants to leave her husband,' he said quietly, 'and come to me. You see, she's grateful. She really wants that baby.'

Nathaniel looked at him, unable to speak. Charity was grateful. She was so grateful she wanted to ruin Victor's life. Of course, it didn't appear that way to her. She would cook for him, sleep with him, bear his child, and be — what she was.

'You won't——' Nathaniel stammered.

'Why not?'

'Don't be crazy, man. It's impossible.'

'I need a wife,' Victor said. 'Isn't Aya always telling me?'

'Look——' Nathaniel said desperately, 'don't misunderstand me. I don't mind what she's done in the past, or how many men she's slept with and got paid for it. But she went to the fetish priest, Victor, and she can't read or write — she doesn't know — she doesn't know anything——'

'So?' Victor's eyebrows went up.

'So you couldn't stand it,' Nathaniel said firmly. 'You're an educated man. You need some woman who——'

'I know — one of the "been-to" girls,' Victor snarled. 'One of the girls who straighten their hair and forget how to speak Twi and tell you they can't possibly eat African chop, thank you, it doesn't agree with their stomachs. Is that what you mean?'

'They're not all like that,' Nathaniel said hopelessly. 'Why do you exaggerate every time? What's the matter with you, man? You hate all the old ways, and now you go and hate all the new ones as well. You've got to stand by something.'

'All right,' Victor said. 'I'll stand by Charity, then.'

'Listen, Victor, you're educated. Maybe you don't like it, but that makes you different. You hear? Why hide from it?'

'Is that what you think?' Victor said slowly. 'Is that what you think of me, that I hide from it?'

'I don't mean it bad,' Nathaniel said quickly. 'You know that. But why don't you do something, Victor? Look at you — you could get a better job — easily. Marry a nice girl who would help you. What's the matter? You want to hold onto the mud with both hands, just because everything above that isn't perfect?'

'Go on,' Victor said, between his teeth. 'Is there much more to the lecture?'

'There's no more,' Nathaniel said, surprised at his own calm. 'Only — I remember a proverb from a long time ago — "I face upwards and can't see Nyankopon, but what of you sprawling downwards?"'

'Fine,' Victor said sullenly. 'That is the difference between us, then? Good. I'm glad to know it.'

'If I can't say something to you, who can?'

Victor's eyes flickered amber. He meant to hurt now.

'You can't see the sun, but you think there's something there, don't you? You put your faith in Ghana, don't you? The new life. Well, that's fine, boy. That's fine for you. But as far as I'm concerned, it's a dead body lying unburied. You wait until after Independence. You'll see such oppression as you never believed possible. Only of course it'll be all right then — it'll be black men oppressing black men, and who could object to that? There'll be your Free-Dom for you — the right to be enslaved by your own kind. You can see it happening already. We've been ruled too long by strangers, Nathaniel. We've got the slave mentality. I don't mean we're humble. Slaves aren't humble; they're ruthless. They don't want freedom for everybody — all they want is to be the man who holds the whip. Maybe we'll learn differently, in a hundred years or so. Maybe we'll have civil war, and maybe we'll need it. Who knows? But I'm afraid I haven't got your optimism. You can keep Ghana. I'll take Charity.'

The cruelty in Victor's ugly-handsome face all at once dissolved, and there was in his eyes an anguish that made Nathaniel turn away, not wanting to see it.

Then Victor heaved his shoulders in a vast shrug, and his laughter rumbled.

'You see?' he cried. 'You see? Charity and I will go fine together. It's like my mother says — it's a pity to spoil two families.'

Nathaniel looked at him squarely.

'You really mean it? You'll let her — you'll have her——'

'Oh yes,' Victor said cheerfully, 'I'm serious, all right.'

He reached out and laid his hand on Nathaniel's shoulder.

'You won't understand, boy,' he said quietly, 'but I'm fond of that woman. You see, whatever I do, she'll think it's great.'

Nathaniel's throat hurt, as a woman's might, with unshed tears.

★ 7 ★

No MOON, no touch of wind, and the night was soft and smothering, like black velvet against the face. Johnnie walked up the wooden steps to the Cunninghams'. Even in the dull glow of the stoep-light the bungalow's creaking age was all too apparent. Slatted shutters hung crazily at prison-narrow windows. The square yellow stoep-pillars were weather-gnawed. Shrubs, planted long ago, had grown beyond control, until now they formed a miniature jungle. A tangle of bougainvillaea all but obscured one wall, and the blossom clusters hung down like bunches of crimson grapes. The veranda was enmeshed in a net of morning-glory vines, and the moonflower delicately stretched its strong green tentacles around the door.

Johnnie knocked.

'Who is it?' Helen's voice was tense. 'Oh — it's you, Johnnie. Come in. I'm nervous as a cat when Bedford's not here.'

'I thought you might be,' Johnnie said. 'I just came over to make sure you were all right.'

'Oh, quite all right, thanks. I've got the children off to bed, and I was having a quiet drink by myself. Will you join me?'

Helen's long hair was drawn back and coiled haphazardly at the nape of her neck. She wore a white housecoat, its collar splotched with facepowder. On her feet were the cheap toe-thong sandals which the Africans made out of old car tyres and scraps of leather. Almost any other woman would have been painfully embarrassed to greet a visitor. Not Helen. She wore the soiled housecoat as though it were a court gown, and the car-tyre sandals like glass slippers.

'I know it's stupid to mind being alone,' she said, 'and after all, Bedford will be back from Takoradi tomorrow. I wouldn't mind, if only we had a decent bungalow with screens. I know I talk about it too much. Bedford says it's courting disaster, to worry so much — about the children, I mean. Perhaps it is. But so many things can happen to a child here. Tetteh killed a puff-adder in the front garden last week. It was coiled up under a hibiscus bush. Kathie had brought me a flower from that bush, not ten minutes before. If she'd gone a little closer——'

She broke off and began to shiver, the way she had that day in Johnnie's office.

'It's not only the wild-life,' she went on, 'it's — oh — malaria, dysentery, the sudden high fevers. Two years ago there was an outbreak of unidentified fever. The Evans' little girl had it. I went over one morning to see if I could do anything, and I — I was with her when she died. I was pregnant with Kathie at the time — perhaps that's partly why the whole thing unnerved me so much. The child had convulsions and then — I guess her heart just stopped. When Bedford came home that night, he found me holding Brian in my arms — too tightly: the child was terrified — and I couldn't stop crying. At least, Bedford says it was that way. I didn't remember, the next day. I guess I went off my head, a little. I remember, afterwards, though, thinking I had to go back to England. But of course I couldn't. It still happens — that sense of desperation, the feeling that something will happen to them, and it'll be my fault for not taking them home——'

Her handsome face was haggard.

'It's awful to feel afraid all the time,' she said in a low voice. 'I feel so — ashamed. But I can't seem to stop it.'

'Why don't you take them back to England, then? I know you wouldn't want to be separated from Bedford for such a long time, but——'

'If I left Bedford alone out here,' Helen said, 'he'd drink himself to death in six months. I thought you realized. Everyone else does.'

She suddenly jumped to her feet.

'Hear it? That shushing sound — the wind's coming towards us. It's going to rain. I just know it.'

'Does that bother you?'

'The storms are so fierce here, not like rain at home. I wonder if I should close the children's windows now?'

'Can't you do it when it starts raining?'

'You don't know our windows,' Helen said. 'Those horrible old wooden shutters. They bang and crash so. The wind turns violent all at once. It doesn't give one time to shut everything.'

As she was speaking, the wind came, bringing with it the smell of rain, a moist earth smell. The wooden shutters began clattering. Helen ran into the children's room while Johnnie shut the windows in the main room.

He could hear Brian's excited chattering and Helen telling him to hush or he'd waken Kathie. Then Kathie's sleepy confused crying. Finally Helen quieted them and came back.

Then the rain. It was as though the clouds had formed a solid bowl across the sky, and the bowl had now tipped, spilling its entire contents in a sudden deluge. The water drove into the ground, hammered and thudded at trees and bungalow.

A ravenous wind tore at the bougainvillaea and casuarina branches.

Sometimes white, sometimes blinding blue, the lightning switched on and off, each flash close enough to light the room. The thunder that followed was an explosion so deafening that the steady roar of the rain seemed subdued by comparison.

'I hope Miranda won't mind it,' Johnnie said.

'Oh dear. I do hope not. But you can't possibly go out in this, can you?'

'No,' he reassured her, 'I can't.'

She was sitting on the edge of her chair.

'I wonder if I ought to go in to the children again——'

'They're all right,' Johnnie said. 'You're more frightened than they are.'

'It's true,' Helen said, as though she resented it. 'They're never very bothered. Brian loves storms. I can't understand it.'

'They've lived here all their lives. They don't know anything else.'

'Why is it that the lightning always comes so close here, Johnnie? I never remember it like that at home. It seems evil and malicious, doesn't it? That's what all of Africa is like to me — vicious. It's all in the same pattern. The sea, the sun, the storms, that snake the other day, even the people. Cruel and hard and menacing.'

'If you hate it so much here,' Johnnie said, 'why doesn't Bedford get a job in England?'

She hesitated.

'Well, it's the money, really,' she replied. 'We wouldn't do half as well in England. We've got to think about Brian's schooling. Bedford wants him to go to Walhampton — that's Bedford's old school, you know.'

So that was it. Brian would go to Bedford's old school, and they would make a gentleman of him there. He would be charming, well-mannered and without any real qualifications. He would be one of the relics of a dead age, the men who insert advertisements in the Situations Wanted: 'Public school man, go anywhere, do anything'. For this, the Cunninghams were chained to Africa as long as Africa would have them.

'That makes it difficult,' Johnnie said.

Helen gave him an odd glance.

'I hope you never discover how difficult.'

She picked up her glass and rose unsteadily to her feet.

'Another?'

'No, thanks,' Johnnie said, 'and — I don't honestly think you should, either.'

'No,' she said. 'One in the family is quite enough, isn't it?'

She turned to Johnnie with a sudden vehemence.

'Shall I tell you the chief reason why we can't go back to England?' she cried. 'It's because Bedford can't get a job there. He can do a little of everything and not enough of anything. And even if he could get a job, he couldn't hold it. Do you know the last job he had in England? He was office manager for a tuppenny-ha'penny firm that manufactured glass eyes for teddy bears. I expect that sounds riotously funny to you. And he was sacked — yes, even from that. It was the only job he'd been able to find at home, the only job of any kind. Now do you see?'

Johnnie nodded wordlessly.

'Sometimes I worry myself sick that he'll lose this job,' Helen said. 'And he mustn't. He mustn't! It isn't all his fault. He did awfully well in the war, you know. He was very well thought of. We hoped those contacts might help, but they didn't seem to, much. If he'd ever been able to get a really decent post after the war, I think he might have been quite different. But — it hasn't worked out that way.'

And Johnnie, listening to her, knew that it could scarcely have worked out any other way. Bedford's world was dead, and he did not know the language or currency of the new. Nobody wanted gentlemen nowadays. They were like the beautifully carved monstrosities Johnnie used to see when he went to furniture auctions with Janowicz — cheap enough to get, but what could you do with them, who had room for them any more?

Helen's mouth twisted.

'It's all very well to say it mustn't happen,' she said, 'but he will lose this job, Johnnie. He might just have managed to hang onto it, if Africanization hadn't come along. What's the point in everyone wondering who'll be the first to go? They all know perfectly well it'll be the Cunninghams.'

She put her hands to her forehead and pressed her fingers against the bone.

'It's true that I'm afraid of Africa,' she whispered, 'but — if we're sent home, what shall we do? What will become of us?'

There was nothing he could say to her. If he had known any reassurance, he would have used it on himself.

The rain had stopped, as suddenly as it began. For the moment, the storm was over. He could go home.

When Johnnie walked into Mandiram's it was mid-afternoon. Cora should be finished her shopping by now.

She was looking at brocades. She smiled at Johnnie and made small winglike gestures with her hands. He explained that James needed the car and driver, and would she mind his driving her home instead.

'Oh — thank you,' Cora said, as though he had made the

request purely out of a desire for her company. 'I shan't be long. You won't mind waiting a moment?'

She turned again to the clerk, a Hindu youth with a long mournful face and pimply skin. He drew out several bolts of cloth, handling them tenderly, flicking the brocade over his arm to display the material's radiance, touching here and there. Cora's hands lingered on one.

'How much?'

Johnnie was surprised at the intensity of longing in her voice.

'Thirty-eight and six a yard,' the clerk said nasally. 'Feel it, madam. Best Indian brocade. All hand-woven.'

The brocade was scarlet, with small perfectly woven peacocks in turquoise and thread of silver. With her dark hair, Miranda could have worn such a material. But on Cora it would be even worse than the insipid colours she normally wore. She would look like a poorly stuffed antique chair with frail wooden arms and legs.

She turned to Johnnie.

'Do you like it? I know it's an extravagance, rather——'

Johnnie struggled to be tactful.

'It'd make a nice cocktail outfit——'

Cora seemed to stiffen and draw away.

'Oh no——' she stammered, 'I wouldn't wear it——'

She stroked the material.

'I know it wouldn't be — becoming — on me. I collect these brocades. Sometimes I get remnants and they're much cheaper. I keep them in a little mahogany box. James had it made for me, just for the purpose. My bits and pieces — that's what I call them. I just — well — I look at them, you know.'

She turned once more to the clerk.

'Half a yard, please,' she said defiantly.

At the Thayers' bungalow, Johnnie helped Cora to carry in her parcels.

'I wonder——' she hesitated, then rushed on breathlessly, 'I know you must be in a hurry to get home, but — would you stay for a cup of tea — or a beer?'

'I won't have tea, thanks — Miranda will be expecting me. But I'd like a beer.'

She went to summon the steward, and Johnnie looked around. Big faded English roses were profusely printed on the chintz curtains, and the walls were faded rose, hung with innumerable little watercolours of Windsor Castle, the Lake Country, a Kentish oasthouse. The sideboard was crowded with pewter and copper objects — candleholders, mustard pots, beer mugs, snuff jars. A leather band bearing a dozen horse-brasses was tacked on the wall beside the door, and on the other side there hung an enormous copper bed-warmer with a long walnut handle. In one corner stood a grandfather clock, its brass pendulum backed with a panel depicting nymphs and shepherds.

Cora returned and sat down primly.

'I always like this room,' Johnnie lied obligingly. 'It's so un-African.'

She began to unfold, like some pale graveyard peony in the charitable sun.

'In the old bungalow, we had such a lot of African things about — ebony heads, fetish figures, goldweights — stuff that James had picked up. I simply put it all away when we moved in here. I sent to Harrods for the curtain material. James wanted mammy-cloth, but I said no, Africa shan't enter here at all. Just this one small place — I felt I'd earned the right. Of course, James likes Africa.'

'And you don't.'

'No—' even her voice was pastel, 'no, I don't.'

She poured a cup of tea from a china teapot shaped like Ann Hathaway's cottage.

'Getting this bungalow meant a great deal to me,' she said. 'It's the first one I've wanted to fix properly, like a — a real home. The others were far too dilapidated. We've lived in so many old bungalows.'

'I can imagine.'

'No — you really can't imagine——' it seemed unfair that anguish should be condemned to chirp and tweet in that birdvoice, 'you really can't, Johnnie. No one can, who hasn't lived here as long as we have.'

'Oh — well, I suppose that's right.'

'The first five years I was here,' Cora said, 'we lived in a bush station in Ashanti. It was really the jungle, you know, but one never called it that. The whole place seemed to be shut in, enclosed, so hot and dank, as though it were under glass. The first year, I had malaria three times, and James nearly died of typhoid. The nearest doctor was in Kumasi, fifty miles away. That may not sound far, but the roads were only bush tracks. I had to take James by myself, in the truck. We were the only Europeans in the place, you see. None of the African drivers would help me — they were too frightened of catching typhoid, and they were certain he'd die on the way. I suppose they thought his spirit would curse them or something. My steward-boy came along — I told him I'd take James' whip to him if he didn't. I would have, too. He was useless, though — quite terrified. He was only a child, really, just thirteen. It took me a day and a night to reach Kumasi. The night was the worst. Of course, I had James' revolver.'

Johnnie looked at her in astonishment.

'You drove a truck through that kind of country — by yourself?'

'Well, I had to, you see,' Cora sounded almost apologetic. 'There was no one else to do it.'

All the adjectives of mediocrity applied to Cora. She was faded, pallid, lukewarm. Had it actually happened? He could see from her face that it had. He knew nothing of that Africa, and now it was gone.

'Can you see — a little — why I wanted this bungalow, Johnnie? I waited a long time for it. And for James' position here, as manager. A very long time.'

The social position and the big new bungalow — these were her harvest, after a lifetime.

'Do you know,' Cora said, 'the Cunninghams actually thought they ought to have this bungalow, when it was built. Can you believe it?'

'Well—' Johnnie said awkwardly, 'I suppose they didn't realize — and they were thinking of the children——'

Cora laughed, and Johnnie felt apprehensive.

'Yes, the children. Helen ranted and raved and finally told me I hated children and was doing it out of spite. I didn't tell her, of course. Why should I?'

'Tell her?'

'Not many people here know,' Cora said, almost proudly, as though the secret were to her some kind of power. 'It was two years after I came to this country. I had a bout of malaria, and the baby was born two months premature. It was a perfect little girl. I saw her. She was all formed, very tiny and thin, of course. But she was dead.'

She saw his expression.

'You don't need to worry,' she said quickly. 'I won't tell Miranda — I wouldn't upset her.'

But Johnnie was not thinking of Miranda. He was wondering how many heat-sodden afternoons Cora spent here, her fingers stroking the silken eternal skin of the brocade.

'It never occurs to Helen——' Cora said. 'She just doesn't see — well, never mind. At least, they'll be the first to go.'

It was the first time she had mentioned Africanization. Johnnie looked at her questioningly.

'You know what I mean,' she went on. 'I haven't much faith in the Africans' ability, but really and truly, almost anyone could do Bedford's job, couldn't they?'

'What do you think will happen to — to the rest of us?'

Cora sat perfectly still. Even her hands were quiet, but he saw they were knotted tightly together.

'Oh, Johnnie—' she whispered, 'I'm frightened.'

'But you've no cause to be——'

'Yes — more than anyone. You're young enough to start again.'

'But James won't — there's no chance — the Firm would never——'

'Once it begins,' Cora said, 'where does it stop? They'll be everywhere, the Africans, everywhere.'

'Is James——?'

He could not say it, but she understood.

'He says not. He keeps telling me not to worry. Men always say that, don't they? I suppose it's their way of fighting a situation they can't alter. They keep on saying don't worry, don't worry, it's nothing serious, and all the time there's a sort of brittle irritation in their voices that betrays them. He hardly eats a thing these days, and at night I hear him getting up and trudging all around the bungalow, until I think I'll go out of my mind. I know I oughtn't to be talking like this. You won't say anything, will you? I can't talk about it to James, of course. He has to keep up the pretence that everything's all right. But he's afraid, too. I know he is. What'll happen to us? Where will we go?'

'You'd have a pension——'

'Do you know what it amounts to? We'd be able to live, but only just. We had hoped to save enough, by the time he retired, to buy a house in Cornwall and have at least — oh, you know, a country girl or someone, to cook and that sort of thing——'

Her yellow parchment face crumpled.

'I can see myself in some hateful poky little flat,' she said. 'Do you know, Johnnie, I haven't cooked meals in twenty years? It's funny, isn't it? The whole thing is really almost funny. What will I do? What will I be able to do?'

The fall of a dynasty. All at once, he could see her in the hateful flat, too. It would be small, of necessity, and James would clutter it with the ebony heads and the brass figurines she loathed. James, obsessed with Africa's rejection of him, would prophesy doom: Africans had been fine when they were bushmen but they were ruined now; Africans would never make a go of governing themselves; the Firm's West African branch would be bankrupt within a decade — mark his words. James would have no one else to talk to, and she would hear it all, day after day, until he or she died.

She would be tired all the time, for physical work was now completely alien to her. The flat would get drabber as she slowly stopped trying. The tines of the forks would be clotted with egg-yolk she somehow hadn't been able to wash off. Forgotten dabs of milk pudding would sour in little bowls on shelves. The sinks would be brown as tea. She would wear shapeless cardigans and heavy shoes, and would cry because she could not get the coal fire lighted.

Cora had waited patiently to reap the harvest of her exile. And now even that meagre fruit seemed likely to be destroyed by a storm she had never foreseen and would never comprehend.

★ 8 ★

TRADITIONALLY, Sunday was the time for curry lunch parties. The genuine Coasters' curry was an imposing meal consisting of curried lamb or veal so peppery that even the most hardened gullet required a frequent antidote of chilled beer, and a conglomeration of side-dishes, each ingredient chopped or grated very finely — groundnuts, coconut, green peppers, bananas, paw-paw, tomatoes, onions, okra, oranges, pineapple, and any other tid-bits that the cook's imagination might discover. The Cunninghams' cook was particularly adept at preparing curry, and Helen made full use of his one great talent. On this Sunday, as on so many others, the cars began arriving at the Cunninghams' about eleven.

Johnnie stood at the window and watched the nearby bungalow.

'She's got quite a throng there this morning. Isn't that Nelson's car? He's manager of Coast Chemists. And there's old Cruikshank — contractor's agent — got a new Humber, I see.'

'You should have gone,' Miranda said. 'Why didn't you?'

Johnnie turned from the window.

'I didn't especially want to go without you.'

'I'm sorry,' Miranda said, 'but I simply couldn't. The last time I thought I'd pass out with hunger before they finally served lunch at three-thirty. And then the curry gave me the most awful indigestion. I wish you'd gone, though. You enjoy curry, and Helen's always so pleased when people do. She hasn't got another good word to say for Kwaku, but she maintains he makes the best curry in the country. He's never been known to serve less than fifteen side-dishes, she says.'

'He cheats,' Johnnie said. 'He serves everything twice — raw banana and fried banana, and counts it as two.'

'I sometimes wonder how the Cunninghams can afford these curry lunches. Not so much the food, but the drink. It adds up.'

'They can't afford it,' Johnnie replied, 'but their credit's good. For how much longer, I wouldn't like to say.'

Miranda glanced at him sharply.

'You've heard more, then? About Africanization?'

'We've heard nothing else all week. Bulletins from Head Office nearly every day, telling us what to do and how to do it. The Firm's very much in earnest. Black men in, white men out — for all the junior posts, anyway. That's as far as they've gone at the moment. But once they get their African sales-managers and confidential secretaries and pattern-researchers, what will they look for next? An African personnel man to replace Bedford, then an African accountant to replace me.'

'What does James say?'

'James isn't budging an inch. He's simply ignored instructions. Sooner or later, though, the London office is going to realize that nothing's been done, and then what?'

'I've told you what I think will happen,' Miranda said promptly, 'but of course you haven't paid a blind bit of notice.'

'And what do you think will happen, then?'

'The Firm can't afford to let everyone go. They need some

continuity. But the only Europeans who do stay will be those who show they can work with Africans.'

'Well, that's just too bad. You don't know what it's like, Manda. I've tried out four new clerks in the past fortnight, and not one is any damn good. And that's simple work. What would it be like in more responsible jobs? Besides, I'm not exactly enthralled by the idea of having African colleagues.'

'That's what really decides your opinion about Africanization,' she said angrily.

After lunch, while Miranda lay down for a rest, Johnnie went out to the garage to tinker with the car. It was not a type of work he enjoyed, but Bedford had emphatically told him that one could not trust African mechanics.

Whiskey was shutting up the kitchen for the afternoon, and as Johnnie walked past, the old man gave him a hostile glance. He and Whiskey had been on bad terms ever since the loan business.

As Johnnie had predicted, Whiskey had not used the money for his brother's court case at all. He had turned up the following week with a girl he called a 'small wife'. Whiskey and his old wife had no children — a state that was, apparently, considered a disgrace. The old man had finally succumbed and taken another wife, hopefully. African Christians, of course, weren't meant to practise polygamy, but many still did. Perhaps if they termed the second one 'small wife' they felt it scarcely counted. This girl was fourteen, but she was as ripe and developed as necessary.

Johnnie worked on the car for nearly an hour. The garage door was open, but it was hot and airless inside. Bad as it was, though, it was better than taking the car out onto the drive, where he would have had the sun on his neck the whole time.

He straightened and reached for a cigarette. It was then that he became aware of the watcher.

The girl had slipped into the garage so silently he had not heard her. Whiskey and the old woman must be having their afternoon nap, or they would never have allowed her out of their sight. She stood in the doorway, her large dark eyes fixed on him. She wore a length of mammy cloth casually wrapped around her waist, and on top nothing but a shift cut in a deep half-moon at the neck and leaving her round brown breasts partly exposed. She seemed to hover as though prepared every instant to turn and disappear.

The afternoon was quiet, all the morning noise of the house hushed in the time of intense heat. No stewardboys sang mournful lovesongs as they worked; no brown women pounded fu-fu with the resounding mortar and pestle. Even the raucous blackbirds and the white egrets were still, wings folded in baobab or niim tree.

Everyone seemed asleep except himself and this girl.

Moved by some inner compulsion he dared not consciously consider, Johnnie stepped closer to her. She stiffened but did not move. Watchful as a jewel-eyed lizard, she held herself quiet.

Johnnie reached out one of his hands, and touched her breast.

There was a sense of unreality about it, as though it did not matter what happened because it was happening only in a lone mind and no one could look there or know at all. He knew the unreality was unreal, the girl actual, but he did not believe it.

She averted her eyes from his. She was tense, but he was certain that she had been awakened by someone, sometime, before she came here to be the wife of a man old enough to be her grandfather.

He knew the whole thing was impossible. But his body would not obey his mind's frantic command to turn and go.

Then she looked at him.

Johnnie disentangled himself abruptly and jerked away. The girl's eyes were filled with a quivering rabbitfear, the flutter of the frail furred thing caught, the bird that dances witless before the snake.

Comprehension filtered slowly into his mind. She was a bush-girl, and he, a whiteman, was of a species so strange to her that she could not see him as a man at all.

But the concept that had made her afraid to stay, also made her afraid to go. Doubtless she had been warned against displeasing him.

He had not intended his half-instinctive action to lead anywhere. He had not really intended anything. But he had wanted her. He had wanted a bush-girl. And she had rejected him.

Swiftly and without thought, Johnnie hit her hard across the face. He felt a quick flare of pleasure, then nothing. She crouched on the ground and her breath came jaggedly, soundlessly. He turned and walked back into the bungalow.

A few minutes later he heard her screams. The blow must have made a betraying welt. Whiskey was beating her. Johnnie grasped the chair-arm and closed his eyes. But he did not go out to stop the beating. It was none of his business.

He felt afraid, yet even in his fear he knew it would be passably all right. Whiskey would never speak of this day — not to Miranda, or anyone, for it gave the old man too good a trump card. Whiskey would be quick to realize that however poorly he worked from now on the master would never dare to sack him. Johnnie was quite safe.

Monday mornings, always difficult for Bedford, seemed to be growing a little more grim each week. This morning he had passed Johnnie's office without his usual greeting, and for several hours had maintained absolute silence. At mid-morning, however, Johnnie heard him shouting in the corridor.

At first Johnnie paid no attention, but when his clerks began to giggle softly, he left his office and went out to see.

Bedford's face was suffused with a purple rage. Before him stood Kojo, the Stores Clerk. Kojo was young, but he was one of the better clerks. He was bright; he knew his job; and lately he had carried a heavier work-load than usual, since Bedford had taken to drifting around to Johnnie's office so much, ostensibly to give reassurance but actually to receive it.

'You damn idiot!' Bedford's bull-voice must have reached all the way out to the street. 'What do you mean he didn't have any in stock? How could he run out of typewriter ribbons? Probably had some in the back of the shop. Couldn't be bothered to look, that's all.'

'He looked, sir.'

'Well, you should've told Chebib he's got to keep things in stock, if he wants our trade. Why didn't you get 'em somewhere else?'

'The chit was made out for Chebib, sir, and so I had to come back, first, and get it changed.'

'Why didn't you make him go and get them at another place, then?'

'I did that with the carbon paper, the last time, sir, and you said I was not to do it.'

'The hell I told you that!' Bedford bellowed. 'Never said any such thing! That's the trouble with you people. You're all alike. Never know what to do unless somebody tells you. Don't think, that's your trouble. You're all the same. Not one of you uses his head.'

Johnnie stopped listening. He had heard it all many times before. He looked at the African boy. Always, before, under such circumstances, the faces of African clerks had been defiant or filled with a sullen hatred. But this time it was different.

Kojo looked patient, indifferent, almost bored.

Johnnie knew, with sudden sick certainty, that Kojo could handle Bedford's job quite easily, if he were given the chance.

The old order was changing already. The African clerk did not any longer need to look defiant or sullen. Kojo knew he could afford to wait.

For the first time, in the eyes of an African clerk, Johnnie saw that Africanization, like Independence, would go ahead whatever he or anyone else thought of it.

Perhaps a similar concept had penetrated Bedford's fury, for he broke off in mid-sentence, as though he had forgotten what he was going to say. He frowned, trying to recall, then he waved the boy away, wordlessly. His face was drawn and grey. He looked up and saw Johnnie.

'Oh — you heard, then,' Bedford mumbled. 'Stupid — to lose one's temper.'

Miranda sat under the niim tree, half asleep in the bright air that at midday was becoming steamy once more. The season had kindled a flame tree into flower. Its blaze of red blossoms covered the top branches, spilling embers down onto the ground. A gold and ebony salamander lay sleek and still in its hunting blind, the bed of marigolds. A pair of mudwasps, trailing hair-thin legs like vines, came out of their dwelling, a tube of clay they had painstakingly built on the stoep wall. Their dance was slow and perfectly measured, the dance of hunting, their delicate poisonous bodies absorbed in the dream-like gyrations of their flight. A battalion of warrior ants threaded its persistent way across the garden. They left a path in the dust, and all the larger creatures, even the dragon-lizards, moved out of the way. On the bungalow walls the big spiders had come out to weave the gossamer of death.

Johnnie told Miranda about Bedford. She was silent for a moment.

'It's a terrible shame,' she said finally.

'He's a rank imperialist, you know,' Johnnie said with a wry smile.

'Don't make fun of me,' she said. 'I guess it's not so simple when you know the person.'

'No. It's never so simple then.'

'Where does it leave you, Johnnie?'

'I don't know. Perhaps it means that your idea is the only practical one, after all. That would be a laugh, wouldn't it?'

'Johnnie — if you could discover a few really promising clerks, why couldn't you begin giving them extra training?'

'Surreptitiously, you mean? Without James' knowledge? My own Africanization project?'

'What's wrong with that?'

'Just whose jobs do you think these model blacks would take over, Manda?'

'There are those four bachelors,' she said without hesitation. 'What are their names? Cooper's one, I think. I scarcely know them.'

'It's all right to boot a man out, then, as long as you don't know him personally?'

'They're awfully young,' she protested. 'It might be a disappointment to them, but I can't think it would ruin their careers.'

'Perhaps not. But don't you see that any training scheme would entail the co-operation of all concerned? And James still believes he can defeat Africanization ostrich-fashion, by ignoring it.'

'You think James won't change — ever? Even if the London office——?'

'It isn't that he won't change. He can't. He's too old and he feels too strongly on the subject.'

'Well, even so, if you had some boys who seemed to be administrative material,' Miranda said determinedly, 'you could find some way of letting the Firm know——'

Johnnie looked at her steadily. There was an inexorable logic in her idea. But it seemed strange, coming from Miranda. Then he saw that she had no idea of the implications in the scheme she presented so blithely.

'Yes,' he said. 'I suppose I could do that.'

It was true. All he needed was a handful of promising candidates, boys of Kojo's calibre. They need not be trained in any specialized way. They need only exist — gold-ore ready to be mined. He might contrive then to let Head-office know that, despite James' inertia, Africanization could be achieved promptly if the right man handled it. Inquiries would be made, and with any luck, he would be allowed to go ahead. James would be replaced. The new manager would be more in tune with the times, and Johnnie would act as his lieutenant. Johnnie's advice would be asked, and he would have to reveal the fact that Kojo could step into Bedford's shoes. The old guard would all go.

Johnnie felt a sudden disgust — at Miranda, for not seeing, and at himself, for being able to see, the whole treacherous scheme.

The Club was the last sanctuary of whitemen, yet even here the present climate of change was apparent.

Johnnie walked slowly back to the table beside the dancefloor. He dreaded the dreariness that awaited him. He'd had a fair amount to drink, but he was cold sober. The Club had that effect on him.

It might have been all right in the old days, when everyone knew everyone else and the Club was a gathering place of the clan. The exiles of three generations had met here to drink and to mourn the lost island home for which they longed but to which they did not want to return until they were old. One could almost see them, those mythical men, sitting here on the stoep where hibiscus flowers drooped half-asleep and the niim branches shushed throughout the hot quiet night. One could almost hear their voices, talking of the Masai, Somali, Watusi, Matabele, Bantu, Ashanti, Hausa, Yoruba, as though they had been discussing the Jenkins of Paddington. The long-dead tamers of a continent seemed more real to-night than the living, who drifted spectre-like up the steps and along the corridors.

From the tables came shreds of conversation.

— if they let the blacks in, I'll resign my membership —

— every bush cocoa-farmer will be able to come in and raise hell —

— they say the government's got plans for a road through this exact spot, if we don't allow Africans —

— I've no objection to educated Africans, but —

— they're all the same, they're all bush —

— you should have seen it before the war —

— everything's different — everything's changed —

The band's music seemed to swell the dirge. On their own ground, the local nightclubs, the African musicians played highlife lustily, but here they merely performed with listless stoicism the required cycle — waltz, slow foxtrot, quickstep.

Primly, the dancers pirouetted, the long pastel skirts of pale girls swishing sedately over the parquet floors. On the stoep, where vined moonflowers burned their last faint incense, the drinkers' glasses clashed cymbal-like and their laughter boomed loud and hollow as drums. And in the Gentlemen's Bar, a few old Coasters communed with ghosts.

'My round,' James said. 'What'll yours be, Johnnie?'

'Oh — gin and tonic, thanks.'

Only James and Cora and himself were here, and they were all bored stiff, but no one would admit it, no one would give up and go home. Once a month James dutifully spent an evening at the Club in company with selected members of his staff. The Cunninghams had been unable to attend this evening, and Miranda had begged off. But this was the appointed staff night, so the gathering took place despite the depleted ranks. James never altered a long-standing custom under any circumstances.

The Squire was giving the usual patter.

'The province of Ashanti contains almost all the country's wealth,' he intoned. 'Cocoa, gold, timber. No wonder they don't want to be governed by a political party dominated by coast men. And of course the C.P.P.'s death on the chiefs and the old traditions, and that's got the Ashantis raging, too. The N.L.M.'s getting stronger all the time. The two groups will never agree on a constitution. I think, myself, that there'll be civil war — or tribal war, one should really call it. You mark my words, Johnnie, March sixth will come and go, and Independence will still be just a word. If we weren't here to maintain order, they'd be at each others' throats in five minutes.'

A month ago, Johnnie would have believed him. He would have been impressed. Now he only nodded wearily.

'Please, James——' Cora said it like a prayer to a deity one knows to be deaf, 'please let's not talk about it.'

James ignored her, as she had known he would. She beckoned to a passing steward-boy, and her drink was renewed, and James did not notice.

The Squire hunched his leprechaun body halfway across the table.

'The parallel between government and business is exact,' he said. 'Africanization will no more work in business than it will in government. Of course, you realize one thing, Johnnie. If Independence is delayed, the Firm won't worry about Africanization. The whole thing will be conveniently dropped. That's what I anticipate.'

'That would be convenient,' Johnnie said dryly.

'We simply have to wait it out. I will say this, Johnnie — I think I know the African mentality pretty well. I wouldn't be surprised to see Ashanti secede, and of course if it does, there'll be no Independence.'

'Yes. I see.'

James chuckled.

'The Ashantis are great fighters when they really get started,' he said. 'We were at one of the gold mines in Ashanti for a time, you know. I opened a branch there. The shop was just outside the mine gates. The mine settlement was behind a high wall, and the European mine staff lived inside. The African miners lived outside, in the village, and of course they had to be carefully searched each evening before they were allowed out. They used to try to hide bits of high-grade gold-ore around themselves, in the most unlikely places sometimes.'

James looked up expectantly, and Johnnie dutifully smiled.

'I remember one time,' James continued, 'when an African, working inside, had been caught tossing a dead rat over the wall and the creature was found to have been stuffed full of ore. Well, of course, there was the devil of a row about it. The African swore he thought it was just an ordinary rat. He accused another man, a Northern Territories chap. No one believed him, naturally, and he was sacked. That night in the village there was a proper riot. The two men began fighting, and all the Africans joined in on one side or the other, the N.T.'s against the Ashantis. Cora and I lived above the shop, and we could see the whole thing from our balcony. Remember, Cora? It was a real sight. Machetes, knives, rocks, and everyone shouting like lunatics. The police couldn't cope. I phoned the Mine Superintendent, and he wired to Kumasi for troops. Well, well, the Ashantis are certainly fighters, I can tell you——'

Johnnie felt a gratifying anger. Who gave a curse how the Ashantis fought in a village brawl twenty years ago?

Cora rose.

'Johnnie — dance with me?'

As they walked around the edge of the dancefloor, Cora turned to him.

'James didn't tell you one thing about that night of the riot. He finally sent me in through the mine gates, to a friend's house. James wouldn't leave the shop. In case they tried to burn it, you know. He — stood out on the balcony, all night, in plain view. He had his .303, but some of the Africans had spears. Towards morning, the mob shifted in the other direction.'

She hesitated.

143

'He really was quite brave, you know,' she said.

When they arrived back at the table, James did not even glance up or appear to notice them at all. After a moment, however, he roused himself and leaned towards Johnnie.

'Did I mention Cameron Sheppard to you?'

Johnnie shook his head.

'The name rings a bell, but I can't think where I've heard it.'

'London,' James said. 'Sheppard's one of the junior partners in the Firm. He's coming out here in a week or so.'

'What for?'

'In connection with the Africanization programme. Quite ridiculous. He'll be here for several days.'

James' voice took on a note of petulance.

'I shall have to put him up, I suppose. I expect he'll be asking all sorts of stupid questions — probably want to hold sessions far into the night. I tell you quite frankly, Johnnie, I'm not looking forward to it. Seeing him at the office is one thing. One's — prepared, you know. But to have the wretched fellow in one's own home——'

Johnnie drew a deep breath. It might just possibly be worth a try.

'I'll put him up, if you like,' he said casually.

James' eyes lit up hopefully.

'Oh — would you? Well, I must say that's very decent of you. If you're sure Miranda wouldn't mind. It wouldn't be too much trouble?'

'No trouble at all,' Johnnie said.

★ 9 ★

NATHANIEL HAD NOT expected to meet Miranda Kestoe again, but he did. This time, of all unlikely places, it was at a party, a European cocktail party, the first that Nathaniel had ever attended. He was there almost by accident.

Victor had introduced him to Eric Banning, an American who was studying the drum language. Nathaniel had forgotten most of the things the Kyerema his father had taught him as a boy, but some he remembered, and Banning was grateful. It never occurred to the American to doubt that Nathaniel would be at ease at one of his parties. Nathaniel felt flattered but in a vague way resentful as well.

He and Aya stood by themselves. No one spoke to them. Nathaniel could feel his muscles tightening, like the leather thongs on a 'dono' drum.

The Drummer would have done better. He would not have been ill at ease. He would have worn a Kente cloth and sauntered among these people, his eyes cold and amused. And they would have flocked to speak with him. But he, Nathaniel, wore a badly fitting suit and spectacles, and he was a schoolteacher. So he was not interesting to them, because they could see no further than to think he was trying to be like them and not succeeding.

The glasses clinked, and the laughter of tipsy women shrilled up to the whirring fans. Outside the bungalow, the thorny bougainvillaea boughs, purple-black in the night, scratched and tapped at the windows.

Out of the crowd Nathaniel saw Miranda Kestoe walking serenely towards him, smiling, her straight black hair braided across her head, her yellow smock clinging to the swollen lines of her body.

Pregnant European women looked all belly. Their legs were so thin and their breasts so small in contrast. Nathaniel looked with pleasure at Aya. She was big-breasted, and the folds of her green and orange cloth took away her body's clumsiness.

He smiled. False Nathaniel. He wanted only to scowl, as Victor would have done. There was honesty in that. But he smiled.

'Well, hello — how are you?' Miranda cried. 'I'm so glad to see you again.'

Reluctantly, he introduced her to Aya. Miranda spoke to her in a great flood of cheerful words, mainly about the baby. It transpired that their children were due about the same time. Miranda made much of this fact.

Aya looked confused, answering Miranda's questions in one or two abrupt words. Nathaniel felt ashamed, and angry at his shame.

'My wife understands quite a lot of English,' he said, 'but she does not speak much.'

'Oh——' Miranda's face fell, 'of course. I'm so sorry.'

'It is nothing,' Nathaniel replied uncomfortably, fingering his spectacles.

He could feel the sweat gathering on his thighs. He thought it must be soaking through the thin grey stuff of his trousers. Horrified, he glanced down at himself. But of course it was not so.

'I was so interested to learn that you're teaching a course in African civilizations of the past,' Miranda was saying gravely. 'I'd very much like to find out something about that subject. How could I?'

Nathaniel mentioned several books, and fidgeted with embarrassment as she produced a pencil and wrote down the names on the back of a cigarette packet.

'Your school——' she went on, 'it's a private school, is it?'

'That is correct.'

'Can anyone start a school here?' she asked innocently.

'Yes——' his voice was cautious, 'anyone can start a school.'

'I mean — I'd always wondered. There seem so many private schools here. Isn't there any check on standards?'

'Not unless you want to get your school on the government-aided list. Then you must have it inspected by government. Otherwise — no. Some schools are good. Some only take the villagers' money.'

He wondered dimly why he had said so much.

'And yours?' she asked.

'I am an employee, Mrs. Kestoe. Naturally I think it is a good school.'

'Oh yes,' she breathed, 'of course. I'm sorry. I didn't mean——'

'Do not worry,' he said, suddenly magnanimous, 'it is a natural question.'

'Your students — what do they do after they leave school?'

He looked at her suspiciously.

'I do not know,' he said at last.

'You don't help them to find posts, I suppose?'

'No.'

He wished she would go away. He could not see what she wanted. But the fact that she had hit upon this particular problem seemed uncanny and rather frightening to him.

'I don't know if this would be in their line at all, but my husband's been looking for some intelligent boys to train as clerks. They might be groomed for administrative posts later on. I just wondered — do you think any of your boys would be interested?'

'They would be interested,' Nathaniel said politely, without enthusiasm.

'Why don't you go and see him about it?'

'I do not think your husband would be very pleased to see me, Mrs. Kestoe.'

Miranda flushed.

'I'm sorry he was rude. He doesn't realize how people will take what he says. Please — I wish you'd go to see him.'

'Perhaps,' Nathaniel lied. 'Perhaps I will go.'

Miranda seemed satisfied. She veered away from the subject now, as though she felt it might become unresolved once more if they touched it.

'Tell me — those wonderful names on the mammy-lorries — I suppose they have some significance? Flee Oh Ye Powers Of Darkness, Lead And We Follow — there must be hundreds. Political significance, I mean, as well as religious?'

'Oh yes,' Nathaniel said agreeably, 'they have significance.'

He wondered what he could possibly tell her if she enquired further.

'I always liked the one called Baby Moon,' Miranda said.

Then she was gone. Around Nathaniel, the glasses clinked and the laughter shrilled. He stood quietly, wondering how soon it would be polite to leave.

'What troubles you, Nathaniel!' Aya asked.

'Nothing. I — I do not like these people.'

148

She shrugged.

'You talk to them well.'

'Do you think I do?'

'Yes,' she said. 'You have something to say.'

He looked at her, unaccountably moved by her determination. He did not want to receive this kindness from her, but he could not stop himself.

'Do you really think so?' he said.

Aya nodded and turned away, but not before he saw the tears in her eyes.

Nathaniel knew he was not the sort of man who was fated to meet friends on the street. It was always his luck to run into someone he didn't want to see. He was not surprised one afternoon, therefore, to see the Kestoes.

They did not see him. He wondered momentarily if they had purposely not seen him. He was about to turn and walk in the other direction. Then he saw what the trouble was. They were sitting in their car and Johnnie was stabbing angrily and futilely at the starter.

Glancing up, Johnnie saw him.

'Hi!' Johnnie shouted. Then, in a low voice to Miranda, 'There's your pal, Manda. Maybe he'll give us a push.'

Miranda waved cheerily to him, and Johnnie leaned out the window.

'Hey, Amegbe, I'm stuck. My battery's low. Give us a push, will you?'

Nathaniel was paralysed. He did not know what to do or which way to move. His white shirt had been clean that morning. He would get it all smeared with grease, or dust anyway, and Aya would complain.

From the corners of his eyes he could see two crippled beggars squatting beside the gutters, grinning up at him.

Several khaki-clad drivers in peaked caps were waiting for their European masters' wives to finish shopping. A few mammies had pitched their vegetable and fruit stalls on the street. Over the tomatoes and the heaps of green oranges, their eyes stared up at him, beady and avid. A gaunt, sharp-featured Hausa trader in a white Muslim robe stopped spreading out his wares.

They were all looking at him, waiting for the joke. Waiting to see the teacher, the man of business, with his briefcase and glasses, push a car like a bush-boy.

Nathaniel's sweating hands shifted the briefcase from one side to the other.

To Johnnie Kestoe, he was just another African, to summon like a servant.

And what if, having buckled to this humiliation, he put his shoulder to the car and it would not move?

All those drivers were standing around, and the street was full of men who were obviously labourers. Why did not Johnnie Kestoe ask one of them? Because he would have had to dash them? Or because any African was the same as any other to him?

'Well, come on!' Johnnie Kestoe shouted.

Nathaniel half staggered a step or two. He stretched out his hands in a kind of mute appeal, and then, despising the gesture, clamped them to his sides.

'Really, Mr. Kestoe,' he said, 'it is not easy for me — I suffer from rheumatism — always, this season, with the dampness——'

'Oh God!' Johnnie exploded, his dark hair dancing angrily over his forehead.

Miranda's face was strained. She touched her husband's arm.

'Please, Johnnie — if he's got rheumatism——'

But Johnnie was out of the car. He did not even glance towards Nathaniel.

'Rheumatism, my foot. Bloody Africans are all the same. You'll have to take the wheel, Miranda.'

He put his hands and right shoulder to the back of the car.

Miranda leaned out of the driver's window, towards Nathaniel.

'I'm sorry——' she said. 'He doesn't mean——'

'O.K. Now!' Johnnie yelled.

Miranda released the hand-brake and put the car into gear. The street sloped down, and although Johnnie had to push hard, he did not have much trouble in getting the car rolling.

He jumped in, still shouting directions to Miranda, and they drove off. Neither looked back.

The beggars began their steady whine again — 'Mastah, I beg you——'. The drivers returned to their gossip. The Hausa trader stacked the rest of his wares and began advertising them in a deep monotone. The mammies plucked at dresses of passing European women — 'Madam, I got fine fine tamantas. Fine too much. You like?'

Nathaniel stood there woodenly. He felt ill. Where was the triumph of showing them he was not a servant, not a slave to be summoned? Gone. Only a sour taste.

Then it occurred to him that Johnnie Kestoe had not pushed the car himself before, because Miranda, being pregnant, had not wanted to take the wheel.

He realized suddenly that if Johnnie had seen a European acquaintance, he would have asked the European to give the car a push.

And the European would have done it. Unquestioningly, as an equal, with no thought of insult.

Why had he not thought of that before?

Rheumatism. Rheumatism. The first thing that came to mind. Of course they knew he lied.

His muscles ached with shame.

Nathaniel sometimes went to the British Council reading room to look at the periodicals. The chairs were upholstered and comfortable, and in the late afternoon there was rarely anyone to bother him.

But he had forgotten that today was the class in African drumming. Miranda was standing beside the pair of Fontomfrom drums in the corridor. With her belly carried round and rigid before her, she and the Fontomfrom looked like a trio of drums. Nathaniel could not help grinning, and she, trustingly, took the grin to be one of greeting.

'I'm a little early for my class,' she said, breathlessly conversational. 'I usually am. I don't want to risk missing anything. It's so tremendously interesting.'

'Have you been taking the drumming class for long?' he asked politely.

'Only a month. I'm not much good yet, of course.'

Shyly, she reached out to the Fontomfrom and her hands beat a few clumsy rhythms. Nathaniel, who could not look at her for embarrassment, shifted his briefcase from one hand to the other. In a moment, if she did not stop, he would be forced to sneeze or blow his nose.

She did stop. She turned to him, smiling.

'It's fascinating, isn't it?'

'Yes,' Nathaniel agreed obligingly, 'fascinating.'

Why not? Make her happy. He waved one hand extravagantly.

'Our people are wonderful drummers,' he cried.

'Oh yes,' she said reverently, 'I know. It's very compli-cated, isn't it, the drum language and the symbolic meanings? I wonder if I shall ever be able to understand any of the messages? I do want to find out a great deal more about it.'

The English were incomprehensible. Either they despised Africans or they seemed to want to turn themselves into Africans. Nathaniel remembered Victor telling him of a certain European woman who married an African doctor. That woman used to wear 'cloth' and carry her baby on her back, thus disappointing her African in-laws who had hoped she would bring back from England a fine pram with a fringed top. Her husband, Victor said, always dressed in expensive English suits and spoke of 'going home on leave' to London.

Miranda was even more extreme. She wasn't satisfied with learning the 'dono', the thonged drums African women used. Oh no. Not at all. She had to be the Kyerema himself.

'You will learn, Mrs. Kestoe!' Nathaniel cried. 'It is only the language of a simple people. You will learn easily. Why not?'

She looked at him doubtfully.

'Do you know anything about drumming?' she asked.

'No,' he said. 'I know nothing.'

'The man in the moon is a Drummer,' his father had said once, hawk eyes glinting with a cruel humour. 'You must be very careful. If you watch him for a long time you may see him lay his drumsticks on his drums, and then you will die.' And the child Nathaniel had peeked up at the sky between his fingers and then snapped his eyes shut and run back to the hut in blindness, tripping over tree roots as he ran.

Miranda Kestoe would be enchanted. Folklore. The mythology of the drums. Poor little black boy, afraid to look at the moon. How quaint.

'I know nothing about it,' Nathaniel repeated angrily, 'nothing.'

She dropped the subject with that obvious tact that English people had.

'By the way,' she turned from the drums and faced him, forcing him to look at her, 'you haven't been to see my husband yet about those boys.'

'I have been busy,' Nathaniel said.

'Is it——' she hesitated, 'is it because of what happened the other day? The car, I mean? It must have looked awful to you. I'm terribly sorry. Johnnie's not like that, really. Only, he doesn't think I ought to drive now——'

'It was not that,' Nathaniel interrupted desperately. 'I prepare my next term's lectures in the vacation. I have much reading to do.'

'Oh, well——' she said, appearing to believe him, 'in that case — you'll go when you can?'

Nathaniel almost told her bluntly that the meagre cream of the crop did not interest him, that it was only the failures he worried about. But something stopped him from saying it.

Some of the boys who would fail School Certificate this year would be bright and ambitious. If they could get in with a business firm——

He must be crazy.

'I will think about it,' he promised casually.

'There's something else I wanted to ask you,' she said. 'I've been looking for someone who could explain the things in the market to me. It seems a bit of an imposition to ask you, but — do you suppose you could come with me one day? Just for a quick whip round.'

'There's nothing much to see. It's just — an ordinary market——'

'To you, perhaps. It's all new to me. I've been around

once or twice by myself, but there's so much I'd like to ask about, and I——'

'I'm very busy,' he evaded. 'I work in the Public Library every afternoon these days——'

'After work, then? The market doesn't close early.'

Nathaniel fingered his glasses. The memory of his lie about the rheumatism made him unable to think of an excuse now. Why did he not tell her the truth? But she stood there, waiting confidently, certain he would be delighted to go with her. He did not know what to say.

'All right,' he said finally, and it was almost a sigh, 'I'll go.'

So Nathaniel did show her the market, one afternoon the following week.

Miranda's car was waiting for him when he left the Library. The driver gave Nathaniel a long amused stare. Nathaniel was thankful when they reached the market and got out.

They were sucked into the whirlpool of humanity that swirled unceasingly around in the small square. There were rough shelters for the sellers, but these had long since been outgrown and the stalls spilled out onto all the paths and crazily winding by-ways.

'Come on,' Miranda said, 'let's go to the vegetable stalls first.'

It was his own doing, this. He would see it through. He would be calm, perhaps a little amused. The way Victor would have been.

He tried not to look at her, pressing ahead, huge in her billowing smock. The mammies at their stalls grinned at him. Nathaniel did not speak good Ga, but he had no trouble in following the gist of their comments.

A rag-clad labourer, carrying a headload of empty kerosene tins, passed close in front of them. His eye caught Nathaniel's.

'Is it yours?' he shouted gaily in Ga.

'Be quiet, you!' Nathaniel snapped.

It would have been easy to reply in kind. He could have had the whole market shaking with laughter. But he could not.

'Oho!' the man said rudely, jostling him, 'it's easy enough to put it in, but when it comes out, it's a different colour. Watch out, brother!'

The big-breasted market women showed their teeth in wide bawdy grins, and their laughter, warming as liquor, entered into Nathaniel. They could not read, but they could read him or anyone. No one was private, but what did it matter?

Nathaniel threw back his head and laughed, and the deep warmth of his voice made Miranda turn around.

'You watch yours,' he called to the labourer, whose headload rattled and banged with his mirth, 'and I'll watch mine.'

'Mastah, you got sense,' one of the women cried in pidgin.

Miranda was smiling.

'They're very friendly,' she said.

'Yes,' he cried, in a voice like Victor's, 'very friendly, Mrs. Kestoe! We Africans are very friendly!'

She gave him an odd glance.

'I can guess what they're saying,' she said dryly.

Startled, Nathaniel saw from her face that she knew. He had underestimated her. Victor would not have made that kind of mistake.

All around them, African women walked tall with their laden brass headpans shining. In the mud, a child crawled, crying, its mother lost, its nose pouring mucus onto its lips.

Almost under the host of padding, pushing feet, a man sprawled sleeping, nearly naked, his head on his hands, his genitals lying flaccid across one leg.

At the vegetable stalls, Miranda asked innumerable questions. The big round wooden platters that held the neatly piled tomatoes — where did they come from and could she buy one? Nathaniel did not know. And the red and green peppers, where were they grown, how were they used?

She fingered the green okra, the yellow garden-eggs, the groundnuts, the yams, the calabashes full of corn and dried cassava, the trays of coarse salt and onions. She asked him about African cooking.

'I don't know much about that sort of thing,' Nathaniel said. 'My wife knows.'

'I'd love to ask her about it someday.'

'Someday,' Nathaniel said uneasily, to pacify her.

They passed the stalls that sold mammy-cloth, the stalls where women were cranking out shirts on hand-run sewing machines, the stalls where clay cooking-pots were stacked.

But Miranda was forging her way determinedly towards those other stalls. Nathaniel knew all this was only a prelude. He tried to distract her. But it was impossible. Quite clearly she had been here many times before, and she knew exactly where she wanted to go.

Here they were, then. The medicine stalls.

Miranda was only mildly interested in the bundles of roots, herbs, leaves, twigs, the raw materials of brews that could cure or kill, depending on which of the two you required.

'Look——' she insisted, 'over there.'

The place was a blind alley, and there were only three or four stalls. It seemed dark and airless as though it were out of the sunshine of the general market.

Miranda's fingers, eager, alert, touched, touched, touched.

What was it that made some Europeans behave this way when they came in contact with these piles of rotten bones? What was it made them want to touch, touch, touch, and stare — as though to remember a past that was for them so comfortingly long ago?

'What's this?' she cried. 'How do they work? How do they make ju-ju out of them?'

'You don't want to see this rubbish,' Nathaniel said gruffly.

'Yes, I do,' she said. 'It's tremendously interesting.'

She could draw back any time she chose, into the safety of the thousand years that parted them.

Nathaniel stood beside her, staring stupidly. He had a headache, and his briefcase felt heavy in his hands.

— What can I say? That this is my heritage? The heritage of Africa, the glorious past.

— The crocodile head was put out in the sun, and the sun rotted its flesh, and the ants picked it clean. And here it is, the bones grating against the husk of brittle skin. Here it is, in its power. And the monkey head, dried and hairy, eyes closed, dead nostrils puckered with the stench of death, here it is in its power. And the clenched hands of dead monkeys, they are here. And the putrid bird heads, blood dried on the mouldering feathers, they are here, their beaks sharp in their power. And the skulls of small animals that died running, they are here. And the patches of crocodile skin, leopard skin, snake skin, half scraped, stinking in the sun. And the dead chameleons, tails curled as they curled in life, bones rattling inside grey decayed almost-transparent skin. They are here in their glorious power.

— Oh my people. Oh my children.

— Soul is abroad in the world. Soul is stronger than flesh. We believe it. And believing it has led us to this. The taste of death is in our mouths. The stench of death is in our nostrils, and we pray to old bones. Our crops are blighted and our children die. The husband is cut down by his enemy, and the wife bleeds to death in birth. What can we do? The taste of fear is in our mouths, and we pray to old bones.

— My heritage was the heritage of gold, the heritage of kings, of women splendid as silver, and the brave message of the drums. And my heritage was reeking bones, dried leaves, stones, sea-shells curiously curved, small jingling bells, medicine yam like dead brown phalli, rock sulphur, blue-stone, gourds that rattle when you shake them. Death beats his drum in the quiet night. Oh my people. Play with your toys. Pray with your toys.

— The fetish priest danced, and his eyes were topaz, his eyes were flame, his eyes were the sun. Writhe, writhe, and work the work you were paid to do. The priestess danced, and her breasts were painted white, white as the moon. Writhe and work the work you were paid to do.

— My sister was ill. It was a long time ago. She was two years old. She vomited again and again, and her skin burned to the touch. My mother had some money saved. She kept it buried in a clay pot deep in the earth beneath her sleeping-mat. She dug it up. She went to the fetish priest. They are very skilled in medicinal herbs. Oh, quite true. But some are more skilled than others. This one said the child had been polluted by an evil touch. She was two years old. I crouched in a corner while the rites went on. I was frightened, and there was so much noise. The child cried, but only a little, and then she died. My mother did not cry. She did not cry or wail or move. She was stone and her eyes were dead.

'This little clay vessel,' Miranda was saying, 'it looks as though it were meant to mix medicine in. Is it?

Nathaniel almost struck it from her hands.

'Why are you interested?' he cried. 'What does it matter to you? Let it be!'

'I don't understand——'

'I know,' he said. 'I know. I know.'

Slowly, she put the vessel back on the heap.

'You don't want to think about it, do you?' she asked.

He did not reply.

'I'm sorry,' Miranda said. 'I didn't know——'

'Come,' Nathaniel said roughly. 'Let us go.'

Meekly, she followed him.

'Have I offended you?'

'Please,' he said. 'It is nothing. I am sorry.'

She looked at him, wanting to understand. Her eyes pleaded with him to explain.

'It is nothing,' Nathaniel repeated. 'I — I have a headache. It is very hot and noisy here. Yes, that is all. I just have a headache. I must leave.'

Jacob Abraham stuck his massive head inside the door of the classroom where Nathaniel was sorting out last term's essays. He beckoned urgently, and Nathaniel, surprised, followed him out.

'You have a visitor — a lady,' Jacob Abraham leered. 'A European lady.'

Nathaniel stared at him, appalled. It could be only one person. Why did she keep troubling him?

'I have told her she could see you in my office,' Jacob Abraham hissed, his fish eyes agape with curiosity.

Nathaniel blinked and wiped the sweat from his chin. Now she had seen Futura Academy. In all its glory.

'Well,' Jacob Abraham said, with a trace of impatience, 'don't keep her waiting, Amegbe.'

Stiffly, as though he were performing in front of an audience, Nathaniel stepped into Mensah's office.

Miranda was leaning back comfortably in one of the armchairs. She was regarding with interest the lace doilies and gilt-framed photographs on the small tables.

Her face, well-carved in the angular way the English admired, looked young, and incongruous above the unwieldy body. The severity of her hair, plaited across her head, made her face look even less like a woman's. It was something Nathaniel had noticed before in whitewomen. Their faces grew yellow and tired here, but retained a strange look of boyishness. They could bear children, even, without seeming aware of their own womanhood, as though it were unimportant to them. He wondered if these boy-women could change, suddenly, at nightfall, become soft and hungry and supple. It was ridiculous. He could not imagine it.

'Good morning,' Miranda said humbly. 'I hope you don't mind my coming here, Mr. Amegbe.'

And then he was conscious again of the building outside this carpeted office — the cracked plaster, the corridors strewn with refuse, the empty classrooms with their unswept mud floors.

'I know you must be busy,' she hurried on, 'but I wanted to tell you — look here, though, before we go further, you're not still annoyed about the other day, are you? The market, I mean——'

'No, no, it was nothing,' he mumbled. 'I have told you. I had a headache.'

At her quizzical look, fury rose in him.

'A simple headache. Why do you trouble me about it?'

Miranda Kestoe flushed, a bright dye along her cheek-bones.

'I — I'm sorry,' she said hesitantly. 'I never seem to——'

Either they never apologized for anything or they apologized all the time for everything. Nathaniel's face went blank.

'Please,' he said, 'I beg you — forget about it.'

He realized too late that he had said 'I beg you'. It was a pidgin phrase. Every beggar, every market urchin used it. She would think he could not speak proper English.

— Mastah, I beg you. You go dash me one penny.

Nathaniel could not look at her. But she did not seem to have noticed.

'Very well,' she was saying, 'let's forget it, then. The thing is — my husband tells me he's got to find boys for those posts within the next week, if possible. It would be a shame for you to miss the opportunity——'

Nathaniel did not know what to say. Because now he wanted to go and wring those jobs from Johnnie Kestoe, a niche for the dispossessed, an awakening for the dream-addicts who had chewed the sweet bitter kola nut of unreality.

That was the terrible thing — he wanted to go. She had talked and talked, and he had begun thinking about it, and now the wish was there.

And yet he held back. He did not want to accept anything from her. She was so eager to offer help. She urged and pleaded. She thrust her goodwill down his throat. And Nathaniel gagged on it.

'I don't know,' he said, 'I don't know——'

He wondered if Miranda would tell her husband what the school looked like, its every crack and stain, the bedraggled goats lying in the courtyard, the stench of the open latrine.

Then he knew, and even in his relief he despised her for it, that she would not tell.

'Why are you so anxious for me to do this, Mrs. Kestoe?'

'Well, it would help Johnnie tremendously in his job, you see, and also, it might show him — it might convince him——'

She stopped, as though realizing the implications of what she had said.

'I don't mean that you're just a means——' her words faltered and fell into silence.

Nathaniel looked at her gravely, hardly able to contain his elation. He owed her nothing. If he arranged for the jobs, he would not owe her any thanks. She wanted him to go for her own reasons.

'A fine opportunity!' Nathaniel cried. 'A fine opportunity to show what Africans can do! To show what good fellows we are! Eh, Mrs. Kestoe?'

> — *Black man, black man, come down from the trees,*
> *Show how you pound those typewriter keys!*

'I will go!' Nathaniel's mouth twisted with soundless mirth. 'Yes, yes, I will go!'

Miranda looked mildly surprised.

'I'm so glad,' she said simply. 'I'm sure you'll find it worth while.'

He walked with Miranda to her car. She talked about the most recent in the series of bribery trials. Corruption in high places, she said, was a social phenomenon that appeared in every culture. There was more excuse for it here, she said, because the first loyalty of an African was to his tribe and family. The nation, as a social unit, was new here, she said, and could not hope to command the same loyalty for at least another generation. Nathaniel, sipping the sweet poison of his soul, agreed loudly and profusely with everything she said.

When he went back to the school, Jacob Abraham was hovering in the corridor like a jovial vulture.

'Well,' he said, 'what did she want?'

Nathaniel saw curiosity bulging from the eyeballs, protruding like rolls of fat under the skin.

'An invitation,' he said, 'she wanted to give me an invitation.'

As the vulture stared at him, he howled with laughter. His cruel laughter boomed and howled around his head like the voices of the unresting dead.

Even to his own ears, there was desolation in the sound.

Wriggling his shoulders so that his orange shirt shimmered like fire, the Highlife Boy capered up to Nathaniel on the street. He pulled a grimacing face.

'Hey, boy!' Lamptey cried. 'Seen 'em?'

Nathaniel felt a tremor of excitement.

'You don't say the results finally got here?'

'They are here. Sure, man. I got a belly-ache, I laughed so much.'

'Did anybody get through?'

'Oh, sure,' Lamptey said. 'Two. We got two bright boys, Nathaniel. Fine, eh? Last year, four bright boys. This year, two. Next year, none. Best thing Mensah can do is turn old Futura into a nightclub. Wha-at?'

'Who got through?' Nathaniel asked dully.

'Ofei and Ampadu. When I saw old Jacob Abraham's face, man, I thought sure I'd throw a fit, I want to laugh so bad. Old man's face, it looks like — well, I swear to you I can't say what it looks like, he's so insulted. Goddamn boys, he says to me, goddamn bastahds, are they trying to ruin me or what? But when some of the boys come in, he says — my dear chaps, I'm deeply grieved, deeply, but don't you worry your good selves too much, I pray you consider all the members of the Legislative Assembly who never in their life got their School Cert.'

Lamptey was still wheezing with mirth when Nathaniel walked away. At least he would have plenty of candidates to choose from now.

Nathaniel entered the old whitewashed building that housed Allkirk, Moore & Bright. He had felt reasonably confident when he started out. But at the door of Johnnie Kestoe's office, he had to pause and remind himself that he was a professional man, a teacher of History.

Johnnie looked up from his desk. His dark hair was tousled over his forehead, and beads of sweat glistened around his mouth.

'Oh. It's you,' he said. 'Well, what do you want?'

Under the scrutiny of those eyes, Nathaniel found himself growing angry before he had said a word. He must not. It would be stupid to have come here only for that.

'I came to see about some students of mine,' Nathaniel said loudly. 'Mrs. Kestoe said——'

Johnnie Kestoe's pencil tapped impatiently on the desk.

'My wife,' he said, 'has nothing to do with this office.'

'Didn't she tell you——?'

'She told me nothing,' Johnnie Kestoe snapped.

'I thought——' Nathaniel stammered. 'I mean, she told me you were looking for reliable clerks — boys you could train for higher posts——'

Surprisingly, Johnnie rose and closed the door to the outer office.

'Perhaps I am,' he said, a little more civilly. 'But I certainly hadn't thought of you as a possible source. These boys of yours — they have some semblance of education?'

'They have Secondary School education,' Nathaniel said quickly. 'They have knowledge of typing, which we teach as an extra. They are keen and ambitious.'

Johnnie Kestoe looked thoughtful.

'Well,' he said at last, almost as though he were talking to himself, 'it's as good a chance as any, I suppose. There's no one else in sight.'

Suddenly brisk, he turned to Nathaniel.

'All right. When can you send them?'

Nathaniel hid his surprise and his glee. He was business-like, competent.

'One day next week?'

'Can't you make it sooner? If they're any good, I'd like to have them within a few days.'

'I don't know,' Nathaniel said doubtfully. 'I have to find out who is interested and pick the most suitable. Perhaps by next Wednesday——'

Johnnie Kestoe grinned sourly.

'Typical of this place. Nothing ever happens when one wants it to. Well, I suppose it can't be helped. Wednesday, then, about this time. Send two, to begin with, will you? And make sure you pick them carefully. I want boys who are capable of learning something. That's the main require-ment.'

'You will be pleased with them,' Nathaniel said earnestly. 'I can assure you of that.'

'I suppose,' Johnnie said, 'that if I employ one of them you will expect some kind of fee, Mr. Amegbe?'

Nathaniel's brief elation was gone.

'No, no,' he muttered, 'nothing like that——'

The European lifted one eyebrow.

'I see. It works the other way round, then?'

It was a moment before Nathaniel understood.

'I take no fees from anyone, Mr. Kestoe,' he said roughly. 'These boys are my students. If I can help them——'

Johnnie Kestoe laughed.

'Well, it sounds good, anyway, doesn't it?'

Nathaniel said good morning, smiling pleasantly. He walked out, closing the door quietly behind him. The building was silent, but as he walked down the stairs it seemed to him he could hear the whiteman's laughter echoing in his ears.

— If I had stayed a boy on my father's land. If I had stayed a boy in my father's village, clearing in the forest, huts of mud and grass. If I had stayed, where would I be now? Beating back the forest, from now until I die.

— I would be happier and not happier. No fumbling, no doubt, no shame. No 'Mastah, I beg you'. No. None of that. Only sweat and the forest, and at night songs and love. That was Eden, a long time ago.

> — *Nathaniel, plant the koko yam,*
> *Nathaniel, plant the water yam,*
> *Nathaniel, plant the koko yam,*
> *And never wonder why.*

— But something said — GO. Something said — vomit it out, the forest, the stinking hut, hoe and machete, dead men's bones. Something said — don't stay here, boy, sure as God don't stay here. Something said — a man got to live until he dies, and that's a long time, Nathaniel, a long time to wonder what he might have done if he'd tried.

— So now you're finding out. The city of strangers is your city, and the God of conquerors is your God, and strange speech is in your mouth, and you have no home.

This Side Jordan

'Where shall I go, where shall I go,
Seeking a refuge for my soul?'

It was a song he had heard in this city that was now his city. But he could not remember the answer, or even if there were an answer.

★ 10 ★

JOHNNIE poured two more drinks, a little whiskey and a good deal of soda. They had been drinking cautiously, making one drink last a long time. Neither wanted to say more than he intended. But for all that, they had talked like old friends.

Cameron Sheppard had none of the qualities Johnnie had once admired in James and Bedford. He had to be admired for another reason: he knew exactly what he wanted and he was going after it, methodically, scientifically, and without the slightest scruple. He didn't ask whether a thing was right or wrong. He only asked if it could be made to work. Perhaps that was why Miranda didn't like him.

Cameron hadn't left them in any doubt about his African policy. And yet he hadn't held forth on the subject, as James did. His grey-framed glasses gave the necessary executive touch to a face that was, at forty, still the face of a young man. Behind the glasses his eyes crinkled often into a smile as he expounded his theories in a casual and conversational way.

'Personally, I neither like nor dislike the Africans,' Cameron had said. 'There's been entirely too much emotion in our dealings with them in the past, and it's done no one any good. It's essential for our own self-preservation that we should understand them, though, but it must be an objective study, without the personal involvements of hate or love. We can't afford the luxury of such irrationalities in these lean times. Britannia's no longer a buxom wench who can give or withhold her favours. She's a matriarch, and an emaciated one at that, and she'll have to be very sharp-witted if she's to hang onto her family and keep them from straying. Don't you agree, Johnnie?'

Johnnie had nodded, and Cameron continued smoothly.

'Take Independence, for example. It's an inevitable development here, and there would be no point in our burying our heads in the sand about it. The question is — what can we salvage from the whole thing? The British government's taken the only possible course in agreeing to grant Independence to this colony. Certainly, we all know the Africans aren't ready. But what was the alternative? To do as the French have done in North Africa, and have an interminable rebellion on our hands? Or as the descendants of the Boers have done in South Africa — segregate black and white, and create such hatred and tension that civil war is almost bound to result one day? Admittedly, we were forced to suppress the Africans in Kenya, chiefly, I think, because Mau Mau wasn't a genuine movement towards independence. It wasn't a forward-going thing, you understand, but rather a return to the past, to the old secret societies and horrifying rites of their ancestors. And, of course, there was the ghastly complication of the white settlers. But this country — well, independence was bound to happen first here. All the conditions were right. No white settlers have ever been allowed. The country is rich in resources — cocoa, timber, gold, palm-oil. And there exists a certain minimum of educated Africans who can take over. We did the only sensible thing. We gave in gracefully. And the new Ghana will probably stay in the Commonwealth because of it. Maybe they'll make a mess of things at first, but it can't be helped. We've made them a partner in the Commonwealth, and let's hope it keeps 'em happy for a while. We've cut our losses. We've salvaged what we could from the maelstrom.'

He had smiled at Johnnie then, and given him a meaningful glance. Johnnie knew he was being flattered, but he could not help feeling pleased all the same.

'What is true in the macrocosm, so to speak, of Empire,' Cameron had finished, 'is equally true in the microcosm of a business firm. There you have the whole thing in a nutshell.'

'Expediency,' Miranda had said. 'There you have the whole thing in a word.'

Miranda had gone to bed soon after dinner. From then on, the atmosphere had been entirely agreeable.

Now it was midnight. The ceiling fan still churned the sour air. Outside, the only sounds were the trilling of the tree toads, and the bougainvillaea vines scratching at the thief-netting on the windows.

Cameron leaned back in his chair and stretched his arms.

'It's getting late. Well, we've had quite a discussion, Johnnie. Do you realize, though, an amusing feature of it?'

'You mean we've talked about everything under the sun except the one specific thing that concerns both of us most at the moment?'

Cameron laughed.

'Just what do you think of Africanization, Johnnie? I'm asking you in a competely unofficial way. I simply want to know, for my own information. Quite frankly, we've hit a number of snags in the Textile Department, and I want to know why. We have our own views in London, but I want to get a reasonably unbiased view from someone here. And that's not easy to find. I think you can give it to me.'

'Exactly what do you want to know?'

'Do you think we can make Africanization work, especially in the Textile Branch? If so, how, and how soon?' Cameron's staccato questions seemed to be typed in the air.

Johnnie drew a long breath.

'Yes, I think it can work quite well,' he replied. 'As to how soon — that depends.'

'On what?'

Here it was. The course had to be set now.

'You'll never have Africanization in this department,' Johnnie said slowly, 'unless someone sets the wheels in motion.'

He glanced up uncertainly. But Cameron was nodding encouragingly.

'You don't have to be afraid of saying it, Johnnie. That's why I'm here, you know. To find out why nothing's been done.'

Faint and far away, Johnnie heard the womenvoices — what will become of us? where will we go?

He remembered Cora's eyes as she looked at the brocade. And James' hands that had danced a ballet of anxiety, the anxiety of an old man who had created only one thing with his life and now stood to lose it. And the massive knight, clutching in his hands not a sword to go with armour, but a child's paper cup full of his consolation and his grief. And Helen, obsessed with a double fear — the fear of staying and the fear of being forced to leave.

These were all the reasons why nothing had been done.

'It's not easy to say it——' Johnnie stammered.

'I know,' Cameron replied soothingly, 'and I respect your reticence. You mustn't think I'm trying to pump you. If you'd rather not go into details, that's fine. But — you're the only man here who can tell me what I want to know. I suppose you realize that?'

If he remained silent, he would not save those others. He would only make certain his own destruction as well.

'Well, never mind,' Cameron was saying. 'It's getting late, now, and perhaps we'd better——'

Johnnie made a quick movement with his hands.

'No — wait a moment, Cameron. It has to be said sooner or later. I think I can — tell you everything you want to know.'

And everything was what it turned out to be. Not one thing, or several, or a selection. Once he began, it all poured out, everything he knew about the other Europeans in the Textile Department, everything he knew about their wives.

It took two hours, and when it was over, Johnnie's shirt was drenched with sweat and his hands were shaking.

Cameron was looking at him curiously.

'It wasn't easy to say all that, Johnnie. I know. But I'm grateful. It makes a lot of things clearer in my mind. It's not easy for me, either, you know, coming out here for a few days and having to grasp the whole complex situation and remedy it. You've helped. I won't forget.'

A look passed between them. Two men who understood each other. Two realists. Johnnie felt strength and assurance flow into him. He told Cameron, then, about the boys.

'I'd hoped to have a few definitely lined up by the time you got here,' he finished, 'but it couldn't be managed by then. I'm seeing these chaps next week. It would save us a good deal of time and grief, it seems to me, if we could go straight to the schools and have them do a preliminary screening of applicants. This particular schoolmaster — he's a pedestrian sort of chap, really, not too imaginative, but very earnest and serious. If he can find me some promising boys, I can begin grooming them, if you like, to take over from men like Cooper and Freeman.'

'Yes, I see. Look here, Johnnie, you haven't mentioned the scheme to James?'

'No. I could scarcely — I mean, he's so dead-set against——'

'Quite right. We don't want anything underhanded, of course, but I don't think you need go into details with James just yet. I'll assume responsibility. It's merely — what shall we call it? — a pilot scheme. I can't give you any definite authority, you understand. But you go ahead with it. It's the first promising sign I've seen here.'

'That's very decent of you,' Johnnie said. 'Thanks.'

Cameron was leafing through his wallet.

'Here —' he held out a card to Johnnie, 'my home address. If you care to make the odd progress report——'

Johnnie took the card. The dead voices were still. Now there was only his own voice, shouting inside him, shouting his identity.

When Johnnie went into the bedroom, he found a dead gekko on the floor, belly uppermost. It was already covered with black ants. They swarmed around it in a loosely organized army, and their combined strength was shifting it. Swaying from side to side, in jerky halting movements, the lizard corpse was being carried away to have its bones picked clean. The ants had not been obvious in this room before, but they must have been here, unobtrusively waiting. In its strength of life, the lizard had preyed upon them. Johnnie looked at the gekko coldly. Then he kicked it away, out of sight, and the ants with it.

'I'll tell you something,' Bedford said, closing the door behind him, 'it's eleven a.m. and I'm tight as a tick, and I fully intend to stay that way.'

Johnnie looked up from his desk.

'Well, keep out of James' way, then, for God's sake.'

'James!' Bedford snorted, lowering himself onto a chair. 'It's not James we have to worry about any longer, Johnnie. It's that pipsqueak Sheppard.'

'Has he been talking to you, then?'

'With a vengeance,' Bedford said heavily. 'I tell you, Johnnie, the man has simply no manners whatsoever. Barged into my office without so much as a by-your-leave, and demanded to see all the staff records and God knows what else. Well, I mean to say, one can't always produce that sort of thing on the spur of the moment, can one?'

Bedford certainly couldn't. Johnnie knew something of the chaotic state of the big man's office.

'And that chummy manner of his,' Bedford went on, pulling at his grey moustache, '"Now tell me, Bedford, old chap, what do you think of Africanization?" So I bloody well did tell him.'

Johnnie groaned.

'Why on earth did you do that? You knew he——'

Bedford drew himself up, and for a moment Johnnie saw him as the massive knight once more.

'Oh, certainly, I know he's flat out for Africanization,' he said, 'but, as it happens, I'm not.'

Johnnie felt a grudging admiration for Bedford's staunchness, his immovability. But such qualities weren't worth tuppence any more.

Bedford leaned forward and spoke in a confidential and rumbling whisper.

'Sheppard's angling for a senior partnership, of course. Old Mr. Bright plans to retire soon.'

'Oh,' Johnnie said with interest. 'I hadn't known.'

'Yes. I suppose he thinks this is the way to impress the Board. Howling success in West Africa — lots of publicity —

that sort of thing. So he flits merrily in here, bursting with all sorts of sociological theories, and we're expected to lap it up gratefully. Well, I'm blowed if I will. James says the same.'

Bedford laughed without amusement.

'You know, Johnnie,' he finished, 'I'd never have thought it possible, but I find myself of late becoming quite fond of old James. At least he understands the situation here. And he's in the same boat — you and I and James, we're all in the same boat. We're on our way out. No use beating around the bush. There it is, plain as paint.'

Johnnie flushed and looked away.

'It may not be as bad as you think——'

'No,' Bedford said steadily, 'I'm afraid it's finished, old chap. Well, there you are. No use moaning about it. I wouldn't so much mind if it weren't for Helen——'

'What does she——?'

'Oh, you know Helen. She storms and rants, but she knows it's all quite pointless, really. She'll calm down after a bit. She always does. It's not been easy for her, bringing up two youngsters — this way. I haven't exactly helped the situation, ever. She thinks I don't realize. But actually, I very rarely think of anything else.'

He glanced at Johnnie in embarrassment, as though he had not intended to reveal this much. Then he rose to his feet, straightened his cumbersome body and assumed once more, with effort, his military bearing.

'Stupid to talk this way,' Bedford said. 'Of course we'll make out all right. Something will turn up, although it's hard to see what possibly could. But as far as Sheppard is concerned, and all this nonsense about Africanization — well, I mean to say, a man's got to draw the line somewhere, hasn't he? We'll be a pack of nobodies quite soon enough, I expect. At least we needn't let it happen to us here.'

He lumbered out of the office. His pace was careful and measured, and the expression on his face, for the benefit of the African clerks, was strong and self-contained. Whether he had been accepting the enemy's flag, or handing over his own, his expression would have been the same.

Watching him go, Johnnie would almost have traded his own cleverness and an assured future to be that stiff-spined and unbending figure.

When Attah came to tell him that Mr. Thayer wanted to see him, Johnnie felt for a paralysed moment that he could not walk down the hall to James' office. What if Cameron Sheppard were there? He could not talk to either man in the presence of the other. But when he entered the Manager's office, James was alone.

The Squire was standing at the window, looking out with fixed concentration, as though he had not seen the same noisy throng of Africans every day for years.

Johnnie waited, and finally James turned around. Johnnie was startled at his appearance: the Squire's face was an unhealthy grey and the skin was puffed into dark pouches under his eyes. He blinked repeatedly, like a dun-coloured mole trying unsuccessfully to penetrate the daylight.

'Oh — Johnnie. Mr. Sheppard — ah — goes back to London tonight?'

They both knew he did.

'Yes.'

'Then I suppose you'll be taking him to the airport, as he's staying at your place? Or do you want to arrange transport?'

'I'll drive him myself.'

'Oh —' again the vague worried blinking, 'you're sure it's no trouble?'

'None.'

James coughed and rustled some papers on his desk. Then he appeared to make his decision. He leaned against the desk and gripped it with both hands.

'Johnnie — has he — discussed this Africanization business with you?'

Johnnie felt his face grow hot and scarlet.

'A little,' he evaded. 'Why?'

James did not reply at once. His fingers again sought and found the letters on his desk. He kept his eyes averted, and Johnnie, hazarding a quick glance, was able to see why.

Horrifying in their absurdity, the tears rolled slowly down the Squire's face. James could not speak because he was crying.

In a moment, James had himself under control, although he took care to turn once more to the window so that Johnnie could not see his face.

'It's preposterous —' James' voice sounded more surprised than angry, 'but he won't let me explain my point of view at all. He talks and talks about the necessity of having Africans in top posts, and when I try to explain that whitemen will never be able to work alongside blacks, not decent whitemen, anyway — then he simply ignores me. He acts as though I haven't said a word, and goes right on outlining his own theories. Why, Johnnie, I knew Sheppard when he was a mere youngster, scarcely out of school. And now——'

James brought one fist down on the windowsill, in an impotent and meagre gesture of rage.

'Now —' he cried, 'he treats me as though I were a schoolboy, as though my opinions and experience didn't count for a thing — almost as though he didn't even know it's my department — the department I've made——'

James did not seem aware of the extent to which he was exposing himself to another's eyes. But Johnnie, shocked into sharp vision by the Squire's tears and by the pain in the old man's voice, saw for the first time what James' true position here had been. Bumbling and pompous, the Squire would likely have spent his life as a mole-like ledger-keeper, had he stayed in England. But here — here he had walked on Mount Olympus. He had dispensed justice as he saw it — rewards for the compliant ones, punishments for the unruly. A frail and balding Jupiter, he had paced his temple in time of riot, waving an old army rifle, subduing and chastening his erring children.

The Squire had spoken as a god might speak, who had created a world only to have its creatures mock and finally destroy him by their disbelief.

Then James swung around, and his eyes, meeting Johnnie's, were both apologetic and eager.

'I was wondering, Johnnie — would Miranda mind not going to the airport? You'd have some time alone with him then. You're young. You speak in his idiom. You're a convincing talker. Maybe he might let you explain our point of view, the way we feel, out here, about Africanization. All the things the London office doesn't understand — the impossibility of the whole idea. He might listen to you. Would you — would you try, Johnnie?'

Johnnie felt unsteady, as though he were very drunk, and his own voice sounded strange to his ears.

'All right,' he heard himself speak the lie. 'I — I'll try, if you like.'

James reached across the desk and held out his hand.

'Good. I knew you would. You've been a great help to me, Johnnie. I won't forget it.'

Dazed, Johnnie stared. The pattern of events seemed to have shaped itself, without his volition, yet that was not so. He could still turn back, at this moment. But would that alter anything? The wheels had been set in motion, and they would keep turning now, whatever he did. And anyway, he was not going back. That was the one immutable concept to which he must hold.

Automatically, and because there was nothing else to do, Johnnie took the Squire's extended hand.

★ II ★

JACOB ABRAHAM's office was in startling contrast to the rest of Futura Academy. Where the classrooms were wood-and-plaster skeletons, mouldering into dust, the sanctuary was sleek and shining, in the fat of life.

The massive desk and the chairs were in 'ofram', a pale wood handsomely streaked with black, an expensive wood. A blue and plum-red Indian wool carpet caressed even shod feet. The bookcases, too, had a look of plumpness, bulging with Encyclopædia Britannica in fine bindings, several costly Atlases, and numerous fresh and apparently virginal text-books on subjects far beyond Futura's scope. Jacob Abraham had great faith in appearances, as though the simple act of placing a book about calculus on his shelves would impart to him, in some mystical fashion, the knowledge within those pages.

Sitting now behind his desk, his mammoth dignity was draped in fawn gabardine of fine quality and good cut. Who but he could wear a tie in this weather? His was blue and gold, Italian silk. Nathaniel knew it was Italian silk because Mensah had told him. Also its price, which was two guineas.

Nathaniel felt the injustice of his own khaki slacks and his cheap cotton shirt, threadbare at the collar. Why did he not ask Mensah for more money? He could do it, here, now, in this room. Ask him, ask him now. Nathaniel's palms were wet and his throat was dry.

'Well,' Jacob Abraham said in his syrupy voice, 'what is it, Amegbe?'

Nathaniel adjusted his glasses with a quick, nervous gesture that did not escape the big man.

'About the senior students——'

Cautiously, he told about his interview with Johnnie Kestoe, deleting and adding a little for the sake of his own status. He told it hesitantly, wondering as he did so if there was any offence in it. To his surprise, Jacob Abraham was delighted.

'Jolly good,' he said. 'Jolly good, Amegbe.'

Nathaniel winced at the phrase. Englishmen said it, and it sounded all right. But in the mouth of this man it was an affectation. Like the room, he now saw, or the suit or the tie. And behind it there were only dreams and the substance of dreams.

'You don't mind, then?' Nathaniel asked.

'My dear fellow,' Jacob Abraham replied, 'of course not. I am in approval. That is definitely so. I greet it with acceptance and pleasure. What could be better? A place found for our most deserving graduates — well, well——'

Nathaniel realized he had not mentioned his intention of finding jobs for the boys who had failed. He did not dare mention it now.

Mensah fixed Nathaniel with an appraising glance.

'It might prove itself useful. Contacts, you know, Amegbe — if you have contacts that is a beneficial thing.'

Nathaniel could not see what the big man was hinting at, and he could not bring himself to ask. Humbly, he waited.

'What would you say,' Jacob Abraham continued, 'if we make this a — a permanent feature? Places found for deserving boys, eh? I have just had the idea this minute. It has possibilities, don't you think?'

'No,' Nathaniel said impulsively, and, as he realized a second later, foolishly.

He knew what Mensah's scheme would become — a sideline that could profitably be kept going as long as the charge to ambitious parents exceeded the bribes given to anyone influential with prospective employers.

'Why not?' Jacob Abraham's voice was harsh.

'I mean — it would take a large clerical staff to deal with it,' Nathaniel stumbled.

Jacob Abraham was a giant and a clown, a dreamer and perhaps a knave. But he was not a fool.

'Nonsense,' he said. 'You know that is nonsense.'

They paused, each trying to see how far the other could be trusted.

'You think about it, Amegbe,' Jacob Abraham said finally. 'We do not have to decide this minute. Think about it. It would sound fine, would it not, when we apply for government acceptance and aid, if we had a little bureau which attempts to find posts for suitable graduates——'

'Yes, sir,' Nathaniel replied without expression.

It was true. It would sound fine.

And now, the way the conversation had gone, how could he ask for more money? But Nathaniel knew that if he did not do it now, he never would.

'Mr. Mensah——' he began. 'Please, sir, there was something else——'

His voice trailed off into a stutter.

'What is it?' Jacob Abraham spoke curtly; he was now the man of business, shrewd and suspicious.

'I have been here for six years,' Nathaniel blurted out, 'and I have only had one rise in salary. I — I thought——'

Jacob Abraham smiled kindly at him.

'Oh —' he said, 'you thought, did you? You have forgotten, I think, our little conversation just before the end of term? I said then that men with their School Cert were easier to find nowadays, did I not?'

'I have not forgotten,' Nathaniel said dully.

The headmaster waggled a playful finger at Nathaniel.

'Too much thinking about reward,' he said, 'it is not beneficial, Amegbe. No, indeed. Someday, no doubt — we will see. In our own good time, as they say. But for this time, I would advise you to think about something else.'

Nathaniel thought about something else. He thought about Aya and his child. The waiting forest on one side, and on the other, Ghana. His classroom was a foothold on a steep cliff. There were not many footholds. He was not sure he could find another.

'Yes, Mr. Mensah,' Nathaniel said. 'Yes, sir.'

> *'Les' you break my heart forever,*
> *Come and never go forever,*
> *Come and never go forever,*
> *Come and never go——'*

The voice broke off into a snicker, then resumed its plaintive moan. Feet scuffled the rhythm on the hard clay floor, and a wooden table served as drum to a dozen hands. Then a yelp of laughter, a tossed book missing its target and slamming against a wall, voices clattering in argument.

Nathaniel was thrown off balance by the normality of the sounds coming from the classroom. He hesitated outside the door. He had expected the boys to be more subdued. And he had not anticipated the arrival of so many.

He had written to the boys who had failed the examination, asking those who were interested in jobs with a commercial firm to meet him at Futura today. Nearly all the boys in his last term's senior class seemed to be here.

They were waiting for him, perched cockily on his desk or sprawling on benches too low for their long legs. They had the lanky loose-jointed appearance of the young whose strength does not yet measure up to their height. They had shed their tattered khaki school clothes like lithe snakes slipping from old skins, and now they were gaudy and new in bright cloth, casually draped around them, and shimmering nylon shirts.

Nathaniel wondered how he could possibly do anything for them. These were not the hurt bewildered faces he had seen after the examination. Failure had been assimilated. Now they seemed as brash and optimistic as they had ever been.

Nathaniel remembered his own failure. There were not many years between these boys and himself. But they were very different. A decade, and the breed changed. He had been foolish to strain after similarity. He had been foolish to try this at all. They had come here only out of curiosity.

The skin of his face began to itch and burn like prickly heat, and he knew he would stammer when he spoke to them.

Then they saw him, and miraculously they grew quiet at once. Peering apprehensively at them through his thick lenses, Nathaniel was startled to see the unconcealed eagerness in their faces.

'Good day, sir. Glad to see you,' they cried.

Nathaniel adjusted his glasses.

'First of all —' he only stammered a little, 'first of all, as I explained in my letter, there are not many posts available with this particular company right now, so I want only those who are really serious about it to apply. Would — would you boys take jobs as clerks?'

There was a silence.

'Yes, sir,' a voice replied finally, and heads were nodded in agreement, 'it would do to begin.'

To begin. Oh, fine. Nathaniel had the discouraging conviction that these boys would have been better to train as mechanics or masons or scientific farmers. In twenty years Africa would be swamped with white-collar men and nobody would know how to produce anything except more children. He pushed the thought from his mind. It was not his concern. He could only try to do something with the material at hand.

'A European I know —' he felt a sudden hesitance at saying it, 'a European with whom I am acquainted — he is looking for boys to train as clerks. He wants boys who will stay and learn the business, work up in the firm. It is a big firm here. You all know it. This firm has decided recently to expand their Africanization programme and they want to train local staff to take over from expatriates. It is a great opportunity. He would only take a few boys now, but if these did well, there might be room for others later.'

Their faces were solemn and rapt. Nathaniel felt unaccountably dismayed. They saw themselves as department managers already. Were they thinking of offices like Jacob Abraham's, the big desk, the fine carpet, the impressive bookcases?

'It would take a long time to reach the top,' he snapped at them, 'and you would never reach it unless you were very good and worked hard. Do you understand that?'

'Oh yes,' they chorused obediently, 'we understand.'

Did they? Did they?

'I want you to think about it carefully,' he said. 'Unless you really want to go into the commercial field, there is no use applying. I will only send two boys to the first interview, so some of you are bound to be disappointed. However, if more applicants are required, I shall select another two, and I will let you know. You see this box on my desk? Those who want to apply for these jobs please write their name and address on a slip of paper and put it in this box. There will be time for you to think about it. I will come back tomorrow and collect the applications, and I will contact the boys I select for the interview. Is that clear?'

They nodded, and Nathaniel rose to leave. As he was going out, a number of voices, impulsive and earnest, held him.

'Thank you, sir. You are very kind.'

Nathaniel walked away, his heart warm. His first impression today had been wrong. They were serious underneath. There was nothing wrong about being self-confident. A man should have faith in himself. They would need that faith. It would help them. They would not be awkward and embarrassed as he would have been at their age and in their place. A new breed.

They were good boys. Some of them were very bright. Dodu, for example, and Inkumsah and Etroo. Very bright, quick to learn, keen. They would be all right.

Kestoe would be grudging about his praise, of course. But he would be forced to admit that the boys showed promise. It would do the school's name a lot of good. How could Mensah hold back after that?

Nathaniel walked out into the sunlight, and the frown lines between his eyebrows had disappeared.

The air was sticky and thick with unshed rain when Nathaniel went back to Futura. He wondered once more why he had chosen such a relatively complex way of selecting two applicants. Surely he could have picked them at the time. He had felt in some vague way that it should be like a secret ballot, so there would be no jealousy of those who succeeded. But what did it matter, since they were no longer at school together? Perhaps he had wanted, also, to impress the boys with the seriousness of the venture.

Nathaniel opened the box and leafed through the applications. There were ten. Several of them had pencilled remarks and pleas. 'I promise to do all my most accomplished'; 'the Good God will bless you forever if you should select your humble and most needful servant, J. Owusu'; 'my sister is ill and I have no rich uncle for obtaining employment, so I beg you give me highest consideration.'

Perhaps they were not as confident as he had thought. Under the brash manner was the fear that there would be no place to go, no place that needed them, the dread — hardly expressed even to themselves — that their proud education would not be the golden key that was to have opened all doors.

Nathaniel leaned his head on his hands. He did not know how he was going to select two out of ten. Etroo and Inkumsah? Yes——

'Please, sir——'

Nathaniel swung around. Two boys stood in the doorway.

Kumi's pinched-up, rodent-featured face seemed almost to be twitching with his nervousness. He chewed his lip, and his sharp little eyes darted from Nathaniel's face to the applications on the desk. Behind him, hulking Awuletey stood awkwardly, grinning and frowning and grinning again, as though he could not make up his mind which was suitable.

'What is it?' Nathaniel asked irritably. 'I told you I'd let you know if you were selected for the interview——'

'Oh yes,' Kumi breathed. 'But please, Mr. Amegbe, we wanted to see you about — some matter——'

'Be quick about it, then.'

Kumi sidled up to the desk. Awuletey still stood in the doorway, smiling foolishly.

Kumi drew a deep breath. He had obviously prepared a speech.

'I hope it will not be offence to you, sir,' he said, 'but we were thinking yesterday of the great good you are doing us. All the time you are spending on this matter, and money for stamps to send the letters to us, and talking with your European friend for our consideration. Etcetera, etcetera, sir. We are grateful for your help. And I said to Awuletey, when a chief spends his time for you, and judges your case, you show some thanks to him.'

In the doorway, Awuletey was bobbing his head up and down to endorse his friend's words, and for the first time Nathaniel noticed a package held delicately in one of the broad hands.

Kumi coughed politely for attention and Nathaniel looked once more into the small pointed face. But now the boy's eyes did not seem probing and metallic. They were humble, beseeching, and Nathaniel found it anguish to look at them.

'So we think we should bring you some small things,' Kumi went on, 'only to show our thanks for your time and how thoughtful you are for us. Please accept them. It is a small thing.'

He hesitated, one hand digging into his shirt pocket.

'And we pray our cases meet approval for selection of these posts,' Kumi finished.

Nathaniel did not speak.

On the desk-altar, Kumi laid his offering. It was a gold necklace, made locally of yellow Ashanti gold, beaten links decorated in the traditional geometric designs.

Nathaniel could tell at a glance, from its colour, that the gold content was high. Instinctively, he tried to assess its value. Not less than ten or twelve pounds, surely. Maybe more.

Awuletey shuffled forward then and laid his package beside the other, neatly undoing the wrapping paper and exposing the contents.

Two silk shirts. Nathaniel felt his fingers tingle with desire to touch. One was a pale gleaming green and the other the colour of rich cream. At least three pounds ten apiece. A muscle jerked in Nathaniel's hand, but he did not move.

Kumi and Awuletey waited. They were in no hurry. They seemed to understand his need for time.

Nathaniel's mind willed his eyes to move from the objects on the desk, but his eyes refused to obey.

The only sound was the fretful clucking of chickens in the compound. The wind was holding its breath, and the air was heavy and still. Nathaniel could feel the sweat welling up on his temples and beginning to make little rivulets down his cheeks. But he did not move or speak.

Gold, colour of the sun, colour of the king. Ghana, ancient city, city of gold. The king of Ghana had a golden nugget that weighed a ton. Ghana was an empire of gold. And in Asante, in olden times, at high festivals the chief's body was sprinkled with gold dust. No wonder. Life was in it, and it was a symbol of life.

Old empires, ancient darkness, the days when men were warrior-children, when men were bought and sold as though a man were a thing that could be owned by another. Perhaps, in those times, if a man sold himself for gold or silk, there would be no damnation in it, for he had not looked on the evil face, nor called the whore by her name.

But the new land — that was a different matter. A man could not say 'I did not know.' He knew. Nathaniel knew. He knew the face of evil. He was a modern man, and knew many things. Too many, for his own peace.

Could health grow from disease? If the cocoa tree was diseased, it had to be cut away. The government was always giving this advice to the cocoa-farmers. The sick tree may infect the whole plantation, so the sick tree must be destroyed. The new way. And so it must be in all things.

And yet — and yet——

Was he a fool, the object of clever men's laughter? Other men did not resist. Mintah the contractor, whom Adjei had talked about — he was a respected man. There were many others, men in high places, important men, officials.

He had often thought that if he could afford to dress better, his classes would show him more respect.

It occurred to Nathaniel that Johnnie Kestoe believed he had taken a fee already. The whiteman would never be convinced that an African would not insist on some fee. The thought angered him. If he was believed to be a taker of dash, he might as well profit from it.

Still he did not speak.

The boys' subtle flattery, that of placing him in the same category as a chief, had not escaped him. He knew it for what it was. And yet it was true. Strangers might have their own customs. But here, you would not claim even a man's time without bringing some token of appreciation. It was courtesy. It did not mean Kumi and Awuletey expected any further return.

Three pounds ten plus three pounds ten plus — let us say — twelve pounds. Equals nineteen pounds. Who would not expect a further return, for that? How could they have afforded it? Relatives, most likely. It was thought of as a worthwhile investment.

They were intelligent as most, weren't they? All they needed was opportunity.

The sweat trickled down Nathaniel's nose and around the rims of his glasses, steaming the lenses until he was looking at the objects on the desk through a blur of mist.

So many voices. 'How many nights I weep and pray and still you never come or send Some Small Thing for help——' 'Again he refused you more money and yet you stay with him — are you his slave?' 'There are good pickings here now — you're crazy, Wise-boy, always broke.'

And others. I will be somebody. Not a fish, not a spider on the wall, but a man among men. I will do something — you will see. Rise up, Ghana. Free-Dom.

He could sell the necklace. That would be Kwaale settled for a while.

He had only two shirts good enough to wear to work. Both were cheap cotton, and both were mended.

Nathaniel glanced up at the boys. Their faces were patient, impassive.

Then, slowly, he reached out one hand and placed it on the necklace and the shirts.

'I thank you,' Nathaniel said quietly.

When they had gone, he picked their applications from the pile. The others he tore into small pieces and burned.

'Hey, Nathaniel!' Lamptey greeted him. 'Hey, Wise-boy, what's all this I hear? You gonna be some competition for the Labour Exchange?'

'Who told you?' Nathaniel asked sourly.

Lamptey jigged up and down in the street, loosely clenching his hands as though they held sticks, while he beat out a rapid rhythm on air.

'Talking drums,' he said. 'You know those things.'

'No,' Nathaniel said obligingly, 'never heard of them.'

Lamptey shrieked with delight.

'You know — like a telephone, only you can't hang up. I'm a true African. Yes, man. Get all my news that way, didn't you know?'

'Who told you?' Nathaniel repeated.

'You really want to know? Why, the old bastahd himself. Who else?'

Nathaniel was relieved. It didn't matter, of course. It didn't matter at all. It was nothing. But all the same he was glad that Kumi and Awuletey hadn't been talking to Lamptey.

'Sa-ay, how about getting me a job there, too?' Lamptey went on. 'Futura's not getting any better, that's sure. What if it folds?'

'I thought you had another line.'

'Now what line could that be?' Lamptey grinned. 'I don't know any other line. If you mean I like going on the town sometimes with the boys, why — sure, sure. But I'm no big boy, man. No capital. Couldn't start my own business. I'd miss my students if this place folded. It would ruin me. No more happy time then. No soul to show the sights and the lights, man. What I do then?'

'You wouldn't starve, don't worry,' Nathaniel said. 'You'd find another line. How's business?'

Lamptey sighed, throwing his head back and hissing the air out through his teeth.

'I tell you, true as God, business never been worse. Most boys gone home. And the ones who stay — whasamatter with these youngmen? Not interested in geography this time.'

'They're just keeping the gun loaded for Independence night,' Nathaniel suggested.

'Lord God,' Lamptey said gloomily, 'it won't be no gun by then; atom bomb more like it.'

When they had stopped laughing, the Highlife Boy pulled at Nathaniel's arm.

'You come along one of these Saturday nights, Nathaniel? You live too quiet, man.'

'I got no money, Highlife Boy.'

'Sa-ay, what's that stuff?' Lamptey looked offended. 'For you, Nathaniel, not one penny. Everything arranged. Not one penny for you, my friend. Except the young lady, of course. Say, I know a man who's got ten girls from the north coming down next week. I tell you true, man. New ones. Hand-picked desert flowers, I been told. How about it?'

Nathaniel hesitated. He had kept the necklace with him, looking at it from time to time. He could not bring himself to part with it yet. But soon he would sell it. He could use some of the money. He need not send it all to Kwaale. He owed himself a celebration. What would those desert girls be like? Very young — almost children, probably. Young and stupid, cow-eyes blinking at the lights, the highlife, the city. Bodies ripe and tender, untouched. No. Not for him. He wanted a city girl. A girl wise in the rites. Perfume, nylon, knowing laughter. A lovely drunken girl in high heels.

'No bush-girl for me,' he said laughingly.

'Wait till you see them,' Lamptey said. 'Anyway, something fine I can fix. I swear I'll do well for you. So? You gonna come along?'

'Well——' Nathaniel said. 'Look, I'll wait and see how the boys get on. If they get the jobs, we'll celebrate, Lamptey, you and me. How's that?'

Lamptey thumped him on the shoulder.

'Never thought you'd do it, Nathaniel!' he cried. 'Hey, that's good, that's fine!'

Nathaniel grinned self-consciously. He felt happy. Well, why not? Why shouldn't he? He had lived frugally here all these years. He had had to. Now, if only for a little while, he would be a proper city man at last. He would put on one of the new silk shirts and go with Lamptey.

— I am the City, boy. Come and dance.

— Sasabonsam, you lie. Lucifer, you lie.

At the head of the parade there was a girl. She must have been about sixteen and she was beautiful. Her hips undulated and her breasts bounced gently to the hymn's jazz rhythm. In her hand she held a ribbon attached to the church banner — white and purple satin fringed with gilt, carried by two younger girls. The banner billowed out like a sail without a boat, and the lead-girl tugged lightly on the ribbon while she nodded and smiled to the street crowds like a young queen honouring her subjects.

After the banner came the girl children, thirty or forty of them, bony little hips swaying imitatively. And behind them charged the ranks of women, four abreast, all wearing the same blue mammy-cloth, the fishes and the sea nightmares leaping as the hips like wheels spun round and round and the soft brown shoulders lifted.

The music, shrill and deafening, came from the fifes and drums of the boys' band. Reborn, the old hymn tunes had a syncopated beat, a highlife beat, compelling as night drums, the voice of darkness now strangely calling the words of Light.

The parade flowed unevenly down the street. Mammy-lorries pulled to the side of the road and the passengers watched and laughed and clapped their hands. Cars bearing exasperated tense-faced Europeans honked and honked to get past. From the streets, from the gutters, from shacks and shops, the children tumbled out to join in the excitement, hopping around the parade like ragged moulting sparrows, prancing and contorting their skinny tatter-clad bodies to the music.

The sun poured its lava down upon earth; the palm trees dropped in the breezeless heat; the fife players sweated and tootled; the city shouted and the women danced before their God.

Nathaniel tried not to look for Aya. But his eyes refused to stop searching. Then he saw her. She carried the weight of her body easily, almost gracefully. She did not look grotesque. Her new cloth swathed her, and her face showed an exaltation that made Nathaniel ashamed of his embarrassment. He turned to go.

It was then that he saw Miranda Kestoe. She was pointing to the kerb, instructing her driver to pull up the car. Nathaniel tried to slip away into the crowd. A few paces away was the Paradise Chop Bar. Sanctuary. But she had seen him. She leaned out of the car window.

'Hello!' she called. 'Isn't it wonderful?'

'Wonderful,' Nathaniel said with a sinking heart.

'I love these parades,' Miranda continued happily. 'They're so colourful, aren't they?'

Nathaniel felt an overpowering desire to spit. He managed to swallow the flood of saliva.

'Yes,' he said without expression, 'so colourful.'

He wondered what she would think if she knew one of those jiving women was his wife. She would probably think it was very interesting. Everything was interesting to her. She was crazy about quaint customs — she collected them like postage stamps. If this parade had been a pagan one, now, Mrs. Kestoe would have been in ecstasies.

'I'm glad I happened to see you,' Miranda said. 'I've been wanting to tell you how glad I am that you saw my husband about those boys. They're going to see him to-morrow, aren't they?'

She knew they were.

'That is what I have arranged.'

She looked at him gravely.

'I do hope it works out well,' she said. 'I'm sure it will.'

'Your husband,' Nathaniel said on impulse, 'he is not so sure, I suppose?'

She flushed.

'He's not doing it as a favour to me,' she said emphatically. 'He's very much hoping that they'll be all right. He told me so.'

'You did not tell him I was going to see him,' Nathaniel said abruptly.

She twisted her hands together, and her eyes betrayed her anxiety to please.

'I — well, no, I didn't. I thought you might prefer it if I didn't.'

Nathaniel wondered if she had expected him not to tell Johnnie Kestoe who it was that had prevailed upon him to go. She wanted it both ways. If her husband was impressed, then she would take the credit. If not, then she hadn't had a thing to do with it.

'Really, I thought you would tell him,' he said.

'I'm terribly sorry,' she stammered. 'I — I never thought — I guess it was stupid of me — I'm so sorry——'

There was no limit to their self-humiliation, these broad-minded whitepeople. They thought they could gain a man's trust by grovelling.

'How many boys are you sending?' Miranda asked timidly.

'I have selected two.'

'Good — I'm sure they'll be keen and bright——'

'Naturally they are bright,' Nathaniel replied rudely, 'or I would not have selected them.'

For an instant the gold necklace seemed to burn through his shirt pocket onto his skin, a tiny irritating scorch-mark.

'Oh — of course,' Miranda said apologetically. 'Well — I do hope it works out all right.'

How many times had she repeated that? Couldn't she think of anything else to say? All at once Nathaniel felt compelled to say the exact opposite.

'It may not work out,' he said. 'It probably won't. He will think my students are no good.'

Purposely he emphasized the work 'he', implying a blindness on Johnnie Kestoe's part.

'Don't say that,' she begged. 'I'm sure he won't think that.'

'Yes he will,' Nathaniel was by now more than half convinced by his own words. 'It is quite likely. Extremely likely. He will probably think I am no good, too——'

She looked upset. Then she smiled and reached out to touch him on the arm.

'Don't worry about it, Mr. Amegbe,' she said. 'Even if he does think that, I won't. Honestly.'

Nathaniel looked away, too full of loathing and self-loathing to speak.

'Thank you, Mrs. Kestoe,' he said finally, slowly, dutifully.

'Oh — that's all right,' she said naïvely.

Nathaniel suddenly threw back his head and burst into laughter. It cleansed and purified him. He waved at her gaily.

'Yes,' he cried, 'thank you, Mrs. Kestoe! A thousand thanks!'

Miranda looked at him in astonishment. As the car drove off, he saw her puzzled frown.

The parade swayed in its slow dance along the street.

— Oh my people, who dance in joy, who dance in sorrow.

KUMI AND AWULETEY had promised to get in touch with Nathaniel immediately after the interview. He waited in his office until six that night, but they did not come. Finally he went home.

'What is it?' Aya asked, as soon as she saw him.

'It is nothing,' he mumbled.

'Something troubles you. I can tell.'

'It is nothing,' he insisted. Then, impatiently, 'You trouble me when you keep asking stupid questions.

Offended, she turned away and would not speak to him all evening. Akosua made gloomy reference to the dangers of upsetting pregnant women, until Nathaniel, tired and on edge, went out to Obi's Friendly Chop Bar and drank too much palmwine.

The two boys were probably out celebrating. There would be no room left in their thoughts for anything else. When they settled down in their jobs, they would let him know. That must be it.

He knew he would not be able to contain his aching curiosity. He would get in touch with them. But how?

When he sent out letters to the boys who failed, he had borrowed the list of addresses from Mensah. And Mensah was in Ashanti now, touring the villages, spouting the Great Promise. Futura Academy did not boast a registrar. There was one clerk, an old man who Nathaniel suspected was a feeble-minded relative of Mensah's. But he did not know where the old man lived. The two boys' addresses had been on their applications, but Nathaniel had foolishly destroyed these.

At last it became clear to Nathaniel that his only point of contact with Kumi and Awuletey was, ridiculously, through Johnnie Kestoe.

The next morning Nathaniel had a headache and complained about his digestion until Akosua snapped that no one had found her cooking at fault before.

'It's not your cooking!' he shouted. 'I've got worries, troubles——'

'Worries, troubles,' Akosua mimicked. 'What has your wife got? She'll have a bellyful of pain any day now, and you talk about your troubles. Do something, then.'

Aya sat silent and miserable while they bickered, her eyes large as a child's that has just finished crying. She wanted only for them to be quiet, he knew, whatever they felt.

'Akosua, Akosua, my sister — please——' he hated his conciliatory tone and for a moment he hated this spare competent woman who had taken over his house.

Akosua was pacified.

'I will make some more tea.'

'Fine, fine,' Nathaniel said hopelessly. 'Some tea. That will solve everything.'

The two women looked at him uneasily, as though they thought he had some strange affliction of the mind.

It was then that Nathaniel decided to go and see Johnnie Kestoe.

The office was busy but not impressively so. Nathaniel walked through the outer office where the clerks sat, and his eyes searched among them. But neither Kumi nor Awuletey was there. He had to wait on a bench in the outer room for some time before he could see Johnnie Kestoe.

Nathaniel wondered if he were being kept waiting purposely. People did that. What a comfortable sense of power it must give, to be able to keep people waiting outside your office, until the moment you chose to say 'now'.

'Mr. Kestoe will see you now,' someone said.

Nathaniel blundered in. Why had he brought his brief-case? Obviously, Johnnie Kestoe would think it unnecessary. Probably he would be amused. Nathaniel could hear him recounting it — 'this fellow came into my office, lugging a dirty great briefcase — nothing in it, of course——'. A book of Gold Coast history was in it, several old essays, that day's newspaper and a wadded-up handkerchief. Nathaniel longed to throw it away, to drop it. He considered going out again and leaving it on the bench. But the clerks would laugh.

'Good morning, Mr. Kestoe.' He spoke more loudly than he had intended. 'I happened to be passing by, and——'

Johnnie Kestoe's eyes were cold.

'Indeed? I didn't think you'd venture to show your face around here — now.'

Nathaniel felt the sweat forming under the bridge of his glasses. Soon it would run conspicuously down his nose.

'I wondered——' he began again uncertainly. 'I thought I'd enquire — did you see those boys yesterday, Mr. Kestoe?'

'Yes,' Johnnie Kestoe said. 'I saw them. Didn't you gather that?'

'Oh. You interviewed them?'

'Yes. I interviewed them, Mr. Amegbe. Are they the best you could do?'

'Well——'

Johnnie leaned forward across the desk. He was breathing

rapidly and his nostrils flared. Nathaniel could see now that the whiteman was very angry.

'Do you want to know what happened? I'll tell you. The little chap——'

'Kumi.'

'Yes. He did a lot of talking. I should think that's about all he can do. Said he'd had a lot of experience as a clerk. Said he could type——'

'He studied typing. They all did.'

'Who taught it?' Johnnie asked rudely. 'An imbecile? I gave him a test. What a farce.'

'He would be nervous——'

Nathaniel could see him, typing to dictation from this man, at an unfamiliar machine, the clerks giggling in the background.

'Perhaps so,' Johnnie said dryly. 'That's hardly my business, is it? I assure you, there wasn't one correct word in the whole thing. I didn't even test his speed. I could tell it was hopeless.'

'I see.'

'He begged and implored for a job,' Johnnie went on. 'He didn't speak English too badly. So do you know what I did? I told him he could come in on two weeks' trial as a filing clerk, and I'd see if he was capable of picking up anything.'

'He is an intelligent boy,' Nathaniel said. 'He should not have told you he had experience. But he is an intelligent boy. I know that, Mr. Kestoe.'

'What you call intelligent, Mr. Amegbe, and what I call intelligent must be two different things. Do you know what young what's-his-name said then? He said he would accept the job, but he wanted to know first how soon he'd be promoted, because he thought an administrative post would suit him. He thought it would suit him! Of course he never bothered to ask himself how he'd suit it. So I told him to get out. Naturally.'

'He did not mean it the way it sounded to you, Mr. Kestoe,' Nathaniel said stubbornly. 'He is ambitious, that is all. What is the harm in that?'

'Harm!' Johnnie shouted. 'I'll tell you what the bloody harm is! I get youngsters in here every day, looking for an easy leg up. I've given some of them a try-out, and I know what they're like. They sit on their fat behinds and read magazines all day, and feel hurt because they're not branch managers in a month. I didn't think you'd waste my time sending me that sort of boy, Mr. Amegbe.'

'They are not like that,' Nathaniel said slowly, tenaciously. 'Kumi — he is not like that. It is just the way he talked——'

'It's the way they all talk. How you people can prattle about Independence——'

Nathaniel stood silently, not daring to speak because if he did he would shout and shout and keep on shouting.

He hated Johnnie Kestoe. He had never felt it so explicitly before. There were Europeans he had disliked or despised, and sometimes he had hated them in general. But now he hated this one, this individual. Nathaniel's hatred numbed him like a narcotic. He felt almost drowsy with it, as though in a dream he could take a step forward and kill this man. But he did not move.

'What about the other boy?' he asked finally, his tongue thick and heavy.

Johnnie had turned back to his desk. He gave Nathaniel a bored glance, and his voice was casual, but it was only a mask — the anger was still there and still close to the surface.

'Oh — him. Biggish chap, pretty clueless. I nearly hired him.'

'I beg your pardon?'

'I told him he could have a job,' Johnnie Kestoe said, 'as a messenger.'

Nathaniel could hardly believe what he had heard.

'A messenger——'

'Yes. But when I told him what his work would be, he turned it down. Said it wouldn't suit him. It wasn't the sort of job he'd expected.'

Big, easy-going Awuletey, with the quick grin and the loping walk. He was not brilliant, not even very clever, perhaps, but he was earnest and he worked hard. Nathaniel could see him in a messenger's khaki, scarcely distinguishable from his school khaki, sitting outside this office, waiting for someone to give him an errand to run.

After the dream, the bitter morning, and no further dreams to allay the craving.

'Of course he turned it down——' Nathaniel cried. 'He didn't want to be a messenger!'

Johnnie Kestoe looked at him with raised eyebrows.

'What else could he be?'

For a moment, silence — even within Nathaniel's mind. He wanted to protest, but he could not. He raised his head slightly, and what he saw in the whiteman's eyes frightened him.

'Mr. Amegbe,' Johnnie said quietly, 'what made you think I would hire boys who had failed their School Certificate? My wife must have told you that those particular posts might lead to advancement in the Firm. Did you really think I was as stupid as that?'

Nathaniel could not sweat now, that was the terrible thing. His skin was parched and burning, like a man whose life is being shrivelled up in a fever's fire. He rubbed his palms together. They were dry as charred grass.

'I — I — I d-did not——' his stammer had returned and his voice was like a hammer that never succeeded in driving a nail, 'I did not think you were stupid. It was — not like that——'

'Oh? What, then?'

'They were — they wanted jobs — they needed — I thought——'

He realized with nausea that he would not be able to explain. If he told Johnnie Kestoe that the boys were not really failures, that they had not been adequately taught, it would reveal the true quality of Futura Academy. And what would it seem to imply about Nathaniel Amegbe, schoolmaster?

He was trapped. He could not say anything. His skin itched and burned with its fever.

'They needed jobs——' Johnnie Kestoe repeated. 'Isn't that nice? So you told them it could be arranged — at a price——'

Nathaniel stared.

'Yes,' Johnnie Kestoe said, 'they told me. They told me there must be some mistake. It had been arranged, they said, and they'd invested over twenty pounds between them to get the posts——'

They had told him. They had told him. They were baffled and angry about the jobs, of course. And so they had told him, probably not even realizing how it would sound to him.

After the dream, the sick dry-mouthed awakening. Nathaniel knew now that the dream addict had been himself.

'No! I — I swear to you——' he choked, 'it was not like that — you do not understand——'

'I understand quite enough. You accepted bribes to do

something it was not in your power to do. You don't even give value for money, do you?'

Nathaniel could not reply. To speak would be like straining to make your voice heard across an ocean.

— Among my people, when a man asks for another man's time, or thought, or consideration, he does not come empty-handed. It is a custom.

— 'Mastah, I beg you, you go dash me one penny'. And the voice of the white priest echoed, scathing still, in his ears — 'Beggars! Beggars! Shame on you!' Never, never again had that boy begged dash from whitemen. Never. If you want to take dash, go do it from your own people. I suppose that makes it all right.

He had no words that would rise beyond his throat.

'I'm going to report the whole matter to the police,' the whiteman said. 'What do you think of that?'

Then the sweat broke out on Nathaniel, fear made visible.

'Please — please, sir,' and through his panic he despised himself as much as if he had knelt, 'please — if you would allow me to explain——'

The whiteman leaned across the desk.

'You couldn't explain,' he said softly, venomously. 'Not to me. What a fool I was, to imagine——'

Abruptly, he broke off and turned away. Without looking at Nathaniel, he jerked one hand in a short contemptuous gesture towards the door.

'Get out of here. Go.'

Stumbling, half sobbing, Nathaniel went, his briefcase clutched in his hand.

Nathaniel walked.

From his prison, he could not see the streets or the people who moved close beside him. Automatically, he put one foot down after the other, a short stolid figure, his wide face expressionless.

The police. They would come, sure as death. African police, but they would believe the whiteman's side of the story, not his. Kumi and Awuletey would give evidence. And that would settle it. For Nathaniel Amegbe, teacher of History, everything would be finished.

When he returned to his village, he could throw away his spectacles. What was there to see in that place, anyway? He could throw away his books and his briefcase — he would not need them.

The table, the chairs, the second-hand wireless, the bed with mosquito net — he would have to sell them. Strange, it was the thought of selling the big brass bed that bothered him most of all. Only somebody who was Somebody could sleep in a bed like that.

Kwaale would not get the money for her case now. She would have to send him money for his. What a laugh.

He could never explain, that was the worst. He could never explain to anyone. He could only walk away.

So many desires. Kumi and Awuletey's desire to have jobs that were big and important. Nathaniel's desire to create a place of belonging for those who had no place. The desire to do something, be somebody. The desire to be God and the desire to wear a silk shirt.

How could the whiteman know? He could not know. He had everything. For him, tomorrow was now. How could he know what it was to need a mouthful of the promised land's sweetness now, now, while you still lived?

Hatred ran like a fever in Nathaniel's blood.

— You whitemen. You Europeans. You Englishmen. You whom we used to call masters. You whom we do not call master any longer. You who say you come only to teach us. You would like us to forget, wouldn't you? You forget — it is easy for you. But we do not forget the cutting down of the plant, the burning of the plant, the tearing up by the roots.

— How many centuries' clotted blood lies between your people and mine?

— I was there. I saw it — I was there. And the blood trembled in my heart.

— Doom along the Niger and down to the sea. Doom along the Congo and down to the sea. Doom to all the ports of golden Guinea.

— The slavers came. They came for gold and they came for men. They stirred the fires of tribal hate. They promised us help against our enemies. So we fought. Oh my children, we fought. We fought and we sold each other. We thought we were clever. We did not see it was only ourselves that we killed, only ourselves we sold into bondage. Tribe fought tribe and tribe fought tribe. And no one won but the slavers.

— Our states broke. Our tribes broke. Each village turned in upon itself, like a man hugging his secret, afraid, afraid, afraid. Who trusted his neighbour? Who could trust even his brother? Oh my ancestors, my children, why did you not see whose face it was behind the mask Fear wore? Oh my people, innocent and evil, forging the links for your own chains.

— And the slavers smiled. 'These are not men, but animals, my brethren, have no remorse.' They did not offend their God. Their God was happy at the haul of black ivory. Their sleep was calm, their gold unstained. They were bringers of mercy. In return for our lives, they were willing to share their God with us. What generosity! 'How Sweet

The Name Of Jesus Sounds' — yes, how sweet it sounded to the man who wrote that hymn: a commander of a slave ship.

— I saw Elmina Castle, with its great stone walls. Stone on stone up to the parapets where the cannon were mounted. Stone on stone down to the cells beneath the ground. In went the bodies, and all of them alive. But not next morning. Not all alive then. The stench of death is in our nostrils and the taste of death is in our mouths. We called on our gods and our gods did not reply. We screamed and tore at each other in our madness. But the slavers were contented, for were they not our souls' salvation?

— Then the black ivory market, deep in the castle, the market where the sea-captains bid for us. And the underground passage, out to the sea and the waiting ships. Many common men went that passage, and many princes. Many kings went that passage, and their sorrow was the sorrow of kings. Colour of the sun, colour of gold, colour of the king. And for gold, their emblem, the kings were sold and the sun, although it shone in the sky, had gone out.

— Oh my ancestors, my children. Chained in pairs, in the ship's bowels. Chained to typhoid and to blackwater. Chained to madness and to death. Chained and made to dance. Yes, even that. Hauled to the deck and made to dance. Nothing spared. Made to dance. My people, who dance in joy, who dance in sorrow.

— Dance, black man, dance.

— Hate is a fire. Hate is a fire. Hate is a fire that consumes my soul. Once long ago I heard my father beat upon the Fontomfrom the song of hate——

'*As we pass here, Hate!*
Hate would kill us if it could.

As we go there, Hate!
That Hate came forth long ago.
Hate came from the Creator.
He created all things.'

— Did He create the whiteman, did He create the
slavers? Yes, He created all things. Creator, what was the
matter with Your mind on that day?

— After the slavers, the soldiers. Our land — overnight,
it seemed — became not ours. Oh, it was paid for. Do not
say otherwise. We were paid a few bottles of gin for our land.
What did you pay us for our souls?

— We fought. Our kings were warriors, and our people. Oh
yes, we fought. Year after year until it was over. We fought
with spears. They fought with Maxim guns. Then it was
over.

— The graves of our kings were destroyed. Casually,
as one might kindle a fire to drive away the black-
flies. The graves of our kings were holy. The gold-joined
bones of our kings, oiled with sweet oil — they were holy
and their spirits cried out to be cared for. Our holy
duty was to tend them, then and forever. Casually,
lightly, they were shattered, as the jaws of the dog splinter
bone.

— And the whitemen tried to steal our soul. They tried to
steal the Great Golden Stool, wherein lay the soul of Asante.
But we were as fire then. It was enough. We said NO. We
hid the nation's soul. But many men could not hide their
own souls so well.

— 'Take the gold from golden Guinea. Take the gold and
bring them to the Lamb. Take the timber and let the light of
Holiness shine upon them. Take the diamonds and be sure
their souls are saved. Tut, tut, our black brethren, surely you

do not want to lay up riches on earth, where moth and rust doth corrupt?'

— Nathaniel, it is not good to hate, for it corrodes a man's own soul. My people wash their souls to keep them from harm, to keep them from hate. My people wash their souls to keep them whole. Wash your soul, Nathaniel, wash your soul.

— I cannot. Hate is a fire.

— Wash your soul, Nathaniel. Your King commands it. Why do you hate? Why do you blame? Because it absolves you from blame?

— I cannot think of that. Not yet. Not for a while. Let me hate in peace.

— Wash your soul, Nathaniel.

— I cannot.

Nathaniel discovered that in his blind walking his footsteps had turned towards Futura Academy. As though some deep-buried need had led him there, he was standing outside the dwelling of Highlife Boy Lamptey.

Even during the holidays, Lamptey kept his room in the filthy tin-roof shacks known as the school residence. It was cheaper that way for him, and his own business demanded that he remain in Accra. In any event, he would never have returned to his home to visit. His village would have bored him to distraction within a day. He was a city man. The only life he knew and understood was here.

Nathaniel entered. Lamptey had just wakened. He was perched naked on the edge of the narrow iron bed, his blankets a stale-smelling tangle around him. In his fingers he held chunks of cold kenkey, which he was chewing with distaste. He pointed towards two bottles of beer which stood among the litter of magazines and downflung clothes on the rickety table.

'Can't find the bottle opener,' he cried, 'and my teeth aren't so strong any more. Gettin' old, that's it.'

After a few tries, Nathaniel knocked the bottle tops off on the table-edge. Lamptey seized one bottle gratefully.

'Ahaa! My friend! You take the other one. Here, I got some cigarettes somewhere — look in that shirt pocket. No? Let's see——'

Lamptey wriggled to his feet and wrapped a thin cotton blanket around his waist for decency's sake. He pranced about the room, whistling softly to himself, his body looking weirdly thin and slight without its protective covering of gaudy loose-fitting shirt.

'Here y'are, Wise-Boy. Only the best for a friend. Sit on the bed.'

Nathaniel did not know how to begin, so he put it off.

'I'm surprised to find you alone.'

Lamptey's shrill titter seemed to fill the room.

'Hey, how d'you like that? Say, boy, whatever I do before I sleep, I go to sleep alone. What's a woman, Nathaniel? Fine to play with, very terrible to sleep with. She never gets enough. She lies so close you both sweat like you're sick to death. All the time she's breathin' in your ear and if you say "Move over, woman", she's mad as hell. Not for this boy, wha-at?'

But Nathaniel's laughter would not come, not this time. Lamptey looked at him suspiciously.

'Why you come to see me, Nathaniel? What you doing here, eh?'

Here it was. Nathaniel tried to look casual.

'What about tonight, Lamptey? I said I'd go with you some night. Tonight all right?'

'Sure! Tonight's fine. We'll go to "Weekend In Wyoming", eh? Spider Badu's band — that's the Teshie Sandflies — they're on tonight. Saturday today, eh? "Everybody Likes Saturday Night" — da da da da DUM da da daah — that was a fine highlife before the Europeans decide they like it — man, no one play it now — at all. Yessir, tonight. You know Spider Badu?'

Nathaniel shook his head.

'He's great, man, great.' Lamptey broke off suddenly and gave Nathaniel an odd glance. 'Say, you sure you want to go?'

'Sure,' Nathaniel said quickly. 'Of course. Why?'

'Well — ' the Highlife Boy said, 'you sure as hell don't look happy, Nathaniel.'

Nathaniel choked down the fear that rose like bile into his throat.

'All I need is a few drinks, that's it,' he cried, 'and I'll be happy tonight — true as God, Lamptey, I'll be happy tonight!'

The bungalow was always hot; today it seemed insufferably so. Johnnie poured himself a beer and wondered who would live here next. Miranda would be sorry to leave this house. She even liked the plain, crude, locally made furniture, because it was solid mahogany. But most of the furniture in this country was mahogany — it was the cheapest wood. Miranda had outdone herself with the livingroom. On the floor, a Hausa rug, coarse wool, dirty white, patterned in black and a red the colour of dried blood. On the bookshelf, an ebony head, an ivory crocodile, a clutch of mauve and white seashells. For ashtrays, small brass bowls that Whiskey polished with lime juice. Miranda said the Braque prints on the walls harmonized with primitive art.

'The sooner the better,' he said aloud. 'The next 'plane would suit me.'

Miranda was standing in the doorway, sleek-haired, swollen, her eyes anxious.

'Why do you say that?'

'Don't you know why?'

'I don't understand it,' she said. 'He must have had better students than those. There must be some reason——'

'There is. He selected them because they paid him well to do it. What do you think of that? I wanted to be certain before I told you. I'm certain now. I saw him today. Your black friend has been doing rather well on bribes.'

Miranda's eyes widened.

'I — can't believe it.'

'I still have the boys' addresses. Would you like to hear it from them?'

'No,' she said in a low voice, 'that won't be necessary.'

The sullen triumph receded like a wave returning to sea, leaving him empty as a beach.

'I'm sorry, Manda. But you might as well realize it right now. They're all the same.'

'That's ridiculous. You know they're not. You told me Kojo could do Bedford's job.'

'All right, so they're not all the same. The odd one here and there might possibly do. But how am I going to find them? Time's running out.'

'What do you mean — time's running out?'

'Cameron Sheppard,' he said impatiently. 'He needs his showpieces quickly, to dangle in front of the Board, before he'll be given a completely free hand here. The whole thing's got to be done before Independence. What the hell will I tell him now? What'll he think? It makes me look like a fool——'

'You'd better go back a bit, and explain. There seems to be a lot that I don't know.'

He hadn't intended to tell her about his arrangement with Cameron, but once he began, it was almost a relief to speak it. Only one thing he did not mention. He did not say where Cameron had obtained his information about the Thayers and Cunninghams.

'I see,' Miranda said. 'The Africanization issue was merely a lever to get James and Bedford out of the way.'

He took her face between his hands, not gently.

'What would you have done, then?'

She twisted away.

'James has — nothing else. Only this. You've said so yourself.'

It was a release, to be able to feel uncomplicated anger towards her.

'I tried——' he said. 'I did try not to say it. But God damn it, you're going to hear it now. You know who had the idea in the first place, for me to start my own Africanization scheme. This is a fine time for you to get squeamish. You weren't bothered about it before, were you?'

Her handsome face, the beauty of its bones, hurt him now with its uncertainty.

'I didn't know —' she said, 'I didn't know at all what it would mean——'

He put an arm around her.

'I know,' he said tiredly. 'I know you didn't. But I did. And I'm not making any excuses, either. I tried to save my job, that's all. But after what's happened now, I can see it isn't the slightest bit of use. James was right — Africanization may be fine in theory, but it won't work. It's going to cost the Firm a packet to find that out, and by the time they do, it'll be too late to do us much good.'

The anger that he had locked into himself ever since Nathaniel's visit now beat again like prisoners' fists.

'If I could only see that bastard Amegbe in jail — do you know, I can't think of anything at this point that would make me more happy——'

'Johnnie — don't. What's the use?'

'Just to see him there, blinking behind those ridiculous spectacles, blinking and saying if they'd only let him explain. And all the time, the sweat bubbling out onto that squat face of his——'

Miranda had drawn away from him.

'Is that what it was like in your office? Is that what he said to you?'

'You should have seen him, sweating and stuttering when he knew he'd been found out. By God, I really wish you'd been there. It would have finished you with the whole damn lot of them, once and for all.'

'You didn't let him explain, did you?'

He turned on her.

'Don't tell me you're going to start defending him.'

'I persuaded him to go and see you in the first place,' she said dully. 'I don't believe he'd ever have gone, otherwise. So who's really responsible for what happened? Perhaps we all are.'

'Like hell we are. Look at the use he made of your friendship. Isn't that enough to show you what he's like?'

Miranda was looking at him with a curious detachment.

'I don't know,' she said. 'I don't know how much is enough to show what anyone is like. That night when you and Cameron talked so late, I wakened. Voices carry, with all the windows open. I wasn't awake for very long. But it was long enough. You had just started on James and

217

Cora. I didn't understand, then, why you were doing it, but I know now.'

Johnnie did not speak.

'All the things Cameron needed to know,' Miranda finished. 'All the things he couldn't have found out himself, because people only reveal those things to someone they think they can trust.'

Johnnie turned and walked out of the bungalow.

He started the car too quickly, with a clashing of gears. He drove through the city, through a maze of sidestreets. Finally he noticed that he was approaching the 'Weekend In Wyoming'. He drew up the car in front of the night club and got out.

The 'Weekend In Wyoming' was crowded and noisy. Spider Badu's band was playing 'Akpanga' and the dancefloor was a tangled forest of shuffling feet, jerking shoulders, swaying hips.

The moment Nathaniel had walked in, trailing self-consciously behind the Highlife Boy, he caught the excitement. It grew like a germ in the blood, spreading through every vein. Involuntarily, his shoulders began to move with the music.

Tonight would be the last time. Tonight he would take everything that came his way. Tonight he would be happy.

He wore one of the silk shirts, yellow-white as rich cream. It was smooth and cool like a girl's skin on his.

The only lights in the place came from behind the bandstand, and when the floor was jammed with people even this light was half obscured. The little tables, sprinkled around the dancefloor's edge and in every corner of the big compound, were so surrounded by dark that you had to step carefully to find your way. Lamptey sauntered among them with ease, though, like some strutting tom-cat whose eyes were best in the gloom. Nathaniel followed obediently.

Lamptey hesitated at a table where a group of club-girls were giggling and re-painting their mouths, waiting to be chosen. He bent down swiftly and whispered to one of them. She nodded and Lamptey walked on, darting around people, screaming greetings, waving frantically to acquaintances beyond earshot.

Finally he settled. Their table was a long way from the dancefloor, in a corner.

'O.K., Wise-Boy? This O.K.? What's yours?'

All at once Nathaniel felt gauche. He would never be casual, flippant, like the Highlife Boy, never if he lived to be a hundred.

Then the deep insistent rhythm of the music entered into him once more, and he did not care about anything else. He felt the tremendous pressure of excitement in his heart. Tonight, tonight——

There would be only one night like this, all his life. To-morrow the fear would descend again, and the long process of humiliation would begin. But just this once he would belong in the city and to the city, heart, muscle and soul of him.

They had scarcely finished their first drink when the two girls arrived. One was short and perky, mouth scarlet as a jungle lily, slanted eyes laughing and wise, hair carefully straightened and held with a blue satin bow. She wore a tight blue skirt and a transparent pink blouse with pink lace around the collar. The brassière she wore was transparent, too, and her breasts showed pink-brown with dusky rose nipples. She hugged Lamptey.

'How's my Money Man? Love me? Stay forevah, boy. Comfort, she say you ask for me and the other one. So

219

here I am and here she is. Gin for me. She — her — that one — she nevah done much drinking, Lamptey. Sure you got the right one, man? Joe-boy said——'

Lamptey pulled her down onto the chair beside him.

'Never mind what Joe-boy said,' he replied, his voice shrill with annoyance. 'My friend here don't want to listen. Christ, Nathaniel, women talk a lot, don't they? You got a pretty little mouth, Sue-Sue — why don't you shut it sometime? That's all right, my baby, don't be mad. Nathaniel, this is Sweet Sue. The other one is — now what was it? — oh yeh, Emerald. Emerald — that's her.'

Nathaniel turned to the other girl. She was tall and slender and she wore traditional dress. Her cloth was bright green with yellow moons and stars on it, and her head was bound with a yellow scarf of shiny satin. She wore lipstick, but clumsily, as though she were not used to it. Her face was quiet and Nathaniel took this to be composure until he noticed that she was watching him, unobtrusively, her eyes flickering away and then back again.

'This lady,' Lamptey was saying, 'is one of our northern beauties, Nathaniel. I don't know where the hell she comes from — somewhere up past Tamale, some place nobody ever heard of, I guess. I couldn't get her name, man, at all. Those northern people got some wicked names — sounded like a sneeze, I tell you true. Joe-boy named her Emerald and I went and told Sue-Sue she should get a green cloth for her. Emerald — green, how you like that, man?'

He neighed with mirth and slammed his hand down on the table until the glasses danced.

Nathaniel held out his hand to the girl, and she took it, gravely.

How had she come here? He wondered if it was her own choice — the land was poor and the people lived poor lives where she came from. Or had her father or uncle made the deal? What kind of contract bound her and who was Joe-boy? Nathaniel would never find out. It was not intended that he should.

What did it matter, anyway? He shouldn't be thinking this way. He shouldn't be thinking at all. What did it matter to him, who she was and where she came from? The thought wouldn't have entered his mind if she'd been a city girl.

Had Lamptey thought he wouldn't feel at ease with a city girl? Hadn't he seen that was what Nathaniel wanted above all else? Or had this one merely been an extra, someone who could be spared? He, Nathaniel, didn't have much money — Lamptey knew that. Why waste a city girl on him?

He glanced over at Lamptey, and his rage became a helpless thing that could be directed only against fate. The Highlife Boy was grinning at him proudly, genuinely. Lamptey thought he was doing a real favour to a friend.

And Nathaniel knew that he could not take her, that if he tried he would shame her and himself by failure.

He finished his drink in one gulp, still staring at Lamptey. Then he threw back his head and laughed, long shuddering gasps of laughter.

'What the hell?' Lamptey sounded confused.

'That's right, man!' Nathaniel shouted. 'What the hell?'

They drank and danced and drank again. Soon the music and the gin numbed Nathaniel. He moved in a dream. The writhing bodies of the dancers blended and merged, became his body. He laughed, sweated, shouted, thrust his every muscle into the music's fire and was consumed but whole.

Halfway through the evening, Nathaniel staggered off to find the lavatory. He was not as adept as Lamptey at snaking his way through the maze of people and tables. He kept bumping into people, grinning apology, moving on. Finally he lurched against a table. It was a table in the opposite corner of the compound, and it was in virtual darkness. Nathaniel glanced at the sole occupant, an apology on his lips. Then he stopped dead.

The man sitting at the table was Johnnie Kestoe.

'I can't seem to get away from you, can I, Mr. Amegbe?'

The sweat-fear broke out on Nathaniel's skin. He could feel it drenching the cream silk of his shirt. The sweat poured from his armpits down his sides. His body itched with it. His throat felt tight, the muscles of it clenched like a fist.

Tomorrow, tomorrow. Tomorrow was now. The lifted telephone, the voice of the whiteman speaking destruction, one man's worth crushed casually and tossed into the nearest wastepaper basket.

'Well,' Johnnie Kestoe said, 'what are you waiting for?'

What was he waiting for? Suddenly Nathaniel knew.

He leaned over the table. He thrust his scowling tormented face close to the other's.

'Damn you,' Nathaniel said. 'Damn you, whiteman.'

Johnnie Kestoe pushed his chair away and stood up.

'All right. That's enough——'

Nathaniel scarcely heard. Inside him, he felt the pressure released, like the pressure of love. Only this was the pressure of hate.

'Go get the police, whiteman. Go get them. Go get anybody. I spit on you. I piss on you. Whiteman.'

'Get out of here,' Johnnie Kestoe said. 'Get the hell out of here.'

'No,' Nathaniel said slowly. 'Get out, you. You go 'way. Who want you here? Go 'way, you.'

'So that's how you really talk,' Johnnie Kestoe said. 'Pidgin English. That's your level. You're no teacher. What's your real job? Stewardboy?'

In a dream, Nathaniel moved forward, his head thrust out, his arms dangling but ready. He could have strangled him then, in that moment, the moment of hate made flesh. But he did not. Carefully, drunkenly, he called back his muscles from their search. Controlling them now, Nathaniel lifted his arms, palms outspread. He did not hit Johnnie Kestoe.

He reached across the table and pushed against the whiteman's chest. And Johnnie Kestoe, caught by surprise, lost his balance. The whiteman's legs skidded forward and he sat down with a crash on the mud floor. Silly and spraddling, Johnnie Kestoe crashed onto his rump.

Nathaniel wanted to laugh, but he held himself quiet.

Johnnie Kestoe struggled to his feet. And Nathaniel saw his own hatred mirrored in the other's face, that bleak white face with its burning eyes.

'Goddamn you,' the whiteman said in a low voice. 'Goddamn you.'

For a moment Nathaniel thought and hoped that the other man was going to strike. Then it would have gone on to some conclusion, even if the only conclusion was the destruction of them both. But some obscure discipline, some awareness of time and place, held Johnnie Kestoe back, even as it had held Nathaniel.

'No,' the whiteman said deliberately. 'I've got a better way. This'll clinch the case against you. Assault. It's all I needed. Thanks very much.'

'You can't prove anything,' Nathaniel heard himself saying.

The whiteman's smile flickered on the thin mouth.

'I can find witnesses here who'll give evidence, if I make it worth their while.'

He was right. Even through his dream, Nathaniel knew it. It would not be difficult to find witnesses, and Johnnie Kestoe could easily make it worth their while.

Without a word, Nathaniel turned and walked away.

He had been shocked into momentary sobriety. His head was splitting, and nausea churned his stomach. He found the lavatory and used it. Then he walked back to Lamptey's table. Sue-Sue was kissing the Highlife Boy, her tense little breasts jiggling with delight. Lamptey broke away when he saw Nathaniel.

'Man, I thought you got lost.' His face was worried. 'What happen?'

All at once it did not matter to Nathaniel to conceal it. He told Lamptey everything.

'And now,' he finished almost in a whisper, 'now I've really done it, sure as death.'

He jerked his head up and looked at Lamptey desperately.

'What'll I do?' he cried. 'What'll I do, man?'

Gently, Lamptey unwound Sweet Sue's arms from his neck. His sharp-featured face was anxious. Absentmindedly, he stroked Sue-Sue's arm. He looked at Nathaniel, vulnerable and shivering beside him. Then, thoughtfully, he gazed at Emerald.

In Nathaniel's absence, they had begun to instruct the young northern girl. Silently she was sipping at a gin and tonic, and her long fingers were twiddling with a lighted cigarette. She seemed to accept her role without question. She did not look resentful. Only bewildered. She was anxious to please, but she did not know how.

Lamptey turned back to Nathaniel.

'I'll fix him,' he said. 'Don't you worry, boy. I'll fix him proper. You'll see.'

Nathaniel watched the Highlife Boy walk away, jiving to the music as he went.

Sue-Sue was watching, too.

'That Lamptey—' she said finally, 'that boy. He no good, but you know — I like him.'

And Nathaniel, strangely, was comforted.

It was a full half-hour before Lamptey returned. He sat down beside Nathaniel and slapped him on the shoulder.

'All right,' he said. 'It's all right now. He's fixed — proper.'

Nathaniel looked up with dull unbelieving eyes.

'What did you say? What did you do?'

Lamptey grinned.

'Easy,' he said. 'I tell him, my friend he got himself in trouble, small. And I say to him — look here, you forget the whole thing. Forget the police, forget tonight, forget everything. If you do, I say, you won't be sorry. I can make some nice arrangement for you. He knows what I mean. So he says — what if I do? So I say — if you do, man, you better stick to it or true's God your wife gonna know every single thing.'

Nathaniel stared at him.

'So?'

Lamptey patted him on the shoulder again.

'He thinks for a while, then all of a sudden he laughs like he's crazy. Then he says — fair enough. That's all.'

— That's all. So simple. A fair exchange. Nathaniel Amegbe is set free, and Johnnie Kestoe gets what he's wanted for a long time. Oh, very simple.

Lamptey was looking at him shrewdly.

'About the money,' he said awkwardly, 'for the lady. Don't worry, Nathaniel. Pay me sometime.'

Nathaniel sat silently, his head lowered.

Then, dimly, he heard Lamptey whispering to Sue-Sue, and a moment later, the two women whispering together.

He looked up to see Emerald walking away.

She was walking towards Johnnie Kestoe's table.

'I'm sorry, man,' Lamptey was saying apologetically, 'I'm sorry to spoil your fun. But she's the only——'

Hysterically, Nathaniel began to laugh.

When he looked up again, Victor Edusei was standing there.

'I never thought to see you here, Nathaniel. What're you doing here?'

'What?' Nathaniel struggled to think.

Victor frowned. Then he looked at Lamptey, who was busy avoiding his glance.

'And what're you doing with — him?'

Scorn poured out in Victor's voice. He detested Lamptey. The Highlife Boy, hearing it, edged away. Lamptey was afraid of Victor. No wonder. Victor was about twice his size and would have welcomed the chance to beat him.

Nathaniel raised one hand like a priest giving a benediction, and the chaos began to recede from his mind.

'No——' he said. 'Don't, Victor. Don't be mad at Lamptey. He's just kept me out of jail, maybe. He's just done for me what — what no other man could have done.'

It was true. He could see Lamptey smirking at Victor's puzzled face. And yet — it was true. Of all the people he had ever known, of all the people who had ever cared what happened to him, only the Highlife Boy could have saved him then. And in that way. In that way. With that one girl, out of all the girls who ever walked the streets. It seemed to

Nathaniel that she was a human sacrifice. And he had allowed it. He had been relieved that there was someone who could be sacrificed.

— Here, Kyerema, here is one more skull to decorate your drum, for I have embraced what in my ancestors I despised.

He was Esau. He had sold his birthright and now could not take up his inheritance. Independence was not for him. Free-Dom was not for him. He would not go to prison. But what could gain him his release from the prison of himself?

How had it happened? He did not know.

— The Drummer's bitter voice thudded like 'ntumpane' in his head. Other men, in their anguish, might burn or slay. But not you, Nathaniel. For you, only a mouthful of spittle on a plaster face. For you, only a shove at the body of an enemy, a little shove, palms outspread, woman's way. Your sister would have done more. That leopard would have gone magnificently to the cage, clawing her hunters.

Nathaniel looked up at Victor and began to stretch out his hands. Then he drew them in to his sides as though he had no right to seek his friend.

'Victor —' he said, 'I'm going back.'

Victor forgot to mock. His eyes were troubled.

'You're crazy, man. Going back where?'

'You know where,' Nathaniel said. 'This isn't my home, this city of new ways, this tomorrow. You know where I belong. The village — back there, far back, where a man knows what to do, because he hears the voices of the dead, telling him. Here, I spoil everything. And I don't know why——'

He could not go on. His body slumped in the chair and he buried his head in his arms.

Spider Badu's band still beat out the highlife. But Nathaniel, although he was conscious, no longer heard.

The girl hesitated at the top of the stairs, then walked slowly into the room. Awkwardly, Johnnie Kestoe followed her.

She seemed no more sure of her surroundings than he, as though the room were unfamiliar to her, too. Her uncertainty irritated Johnnie. He wanted her to mock him with herself. Like Victor Edusei's girl, the one he had danced with that time. Or like Saleh's serpent-eyed daughter, laughing at his unacknowledged desire.

Johnnie looked quickly around the room. It was no more than a cell. A look of utter impersonality characterized it. Many people had used the room, but none had lived in it.

The air was laden with the smell of former brief tenancies: the coarse woodsmoke-and-sweat smell of bush Africans; the cloying memories of two-shilling perfume. Beside the iron cot stood a wash-stand with a basin half full of swampy-looking water, chiefly for the benefit, no doubt, of visiting Muslims. Johnnie regarded it with distaste, wondering how many conscientious sons of Islam had to perform their post-love ablutions there before the water would be changed.

Christians were catered for, too. On the table lay a stout black Gideon Bible. In case repentance should be immediate, the demands of the spirit as suddenly urgent as had been the demands of the flesh? The Book's incongruous presence made Johnnie want to laugh. And immediately he felt fine, strong, capable, uncaring.

The room's squalid quality no longer bothered him. Dust-streaked, mauve and faded orange mammy-cloth curtains fluttered in the feeble night wind. The one chair was broken and lame-legged. The ashtray on the table had not been emptied for some time. The white enamel chamber pot under the wash-stand was encrusted with sulphurous yellow. In the ceiling, one bulb glared, dispelling shadows.

A framed picture in full colour decorated one wall. It was a portrait of Nkrumah, and the caption consisted of one word: 'Freedom.'

The girl waited. Johnnie's appraisal of the room had taken only a minute, but now he felt as though he had been looking at it for hours. Did she think he was stalling? He turned towards her angrily. She smiled at him but she did not move.

She was waiting to be told what to do.

Her supple brown fingers sought the cover-cloth draped over her shoulders. She pulled it tight around her, as though, like a prisoner with his blanket, it was her sole home. Then, seeming to fear that Johnnie would misinterpret the gesture, she let the cloth drop to the floor.

It occurred to Johnnie that he might be her first whiteman. Perhaps, like Whiskey's child-wife, she wondered if whitemen were like black in any way at all, even this way. But this girl could not refuse him.

She was very young, not more than sixteen, he guessed, perhaps younger. He wondered what her experience had been and where she had come from.

No. None of that was his concern. She was an African whore. That was all he needed to know about her, all he wanted to know.

If only she weren't so quiet. He took a step towards her and grasped her shoulders.

'What's your name?'

Why bother to ask that? What did it matter to him, her name? She was an unknown brown girl in the anonymity of this room, on a night that would be conveniently forgotten.

Her eyes questioned him. She frowned and shrugged. Her soft laughter was that of embarrassment. Then she said a few words in her own language.

Johnnie was startled, then he understood. She did not speak English, not even pidgin English.

The drape-suited spiv hadn't given him much of a bargain. A little brown duiker of a girl. Johnnie felt cheated. All at once he became positive that Nathaniel Amegbe and the spiv had arranged the situation. This was Nathaniel's revenge — to find the most stupid, the most cowlike street-walker in all Accra, an animal, a creature hardly sentient, a thing. And they would be sitting downstairs now, laughing their hoarse laughter while the highlife blared and moaned.

It seemed to Johnnie then that his ears were filled with the sound of blackmen's laughter. Victor Edusei's deep raucous laugh, daring him to be angry. The tittering clerks in the office. The breast-heaving laughter of the big trader-mammies at the newness of a whiteman who could not tell whether they were joking or not.

He drew the girl close to him and twisted her body against his own. Under her voluminous green cloth, her breasts and hips were full and rounded. Deliberately, he released her.

It occurred to him that she might be in on Nathaniel's game, that her silence and her seeming uncertainty might be only an act, a role in which she had been carefully instructed.

Roughly, he pulled at her cloth. The length of material that served as skirt, reaching from her waist to her feet, came away in his hand. The blouse, only cobbled together, tore easily. Her eyes widened, as though she were horrified by such a waste of material. But she made no move to stop him.

She stood before him naked. For a moment he could only look at her. She showed neither shame nor wantonness, neither skill nor the lack of it. Her face was expressionless, and her body, beautiful and young as it was, was blank. It spoke nothing — not desire nor coldness; not violence nor simulated tenderness; not even the professional hope for further payment.

Involuntarily, Johnnie glanced at the iron cot. Without a word, she walked over to it and lay down.

Her easy acquiescence became to him something detestable. She lay spreadeagled, sheeplike, waiting for the knife. She might as well have been drugged, lying there, or dead. The laughter of Africa sounded again in Johnnie's ears.

As he took off his own clothes, a tremor passed over her body, a rippling of the dark skin. Her eyes were blank no longer. In them was an inexplicable panic.

She was a whore — why should she look like that? But he was glad she did. Her slight spasm of fear excited him. She was a continent and he an invader, wanting both to possess and to destroy.

It was then that he discovered the fantastic truth. If there had been a trick, it was not hers. Her doubt was not a studied role. She was, quite simply, a virgin.

The stark shock of it, the ludicrous irony, almost unmanned him. Then, suddenly, he did not care. The dark skin was warm against his in the warm night. Sweat made slippery their bodies. His urgency returned. And something else.

There was no challenge in her, but now it did not matter. Now he knew how he could hurt her. And he did.

Then it was over. All the time, the girl had not moved. Once she had cried aloud with pain. That was all. Johnnie got up, lit a cigarette, and began to dress. A black girl. For a moment he could think of nothing but that. A black whore. But he'd sold himself just as much. To the spiv — for this.

No. He had wanted to frighten Nathaniel, and he had wanted to imagine Nathaniel in jail. But even in his most intense anger he had known it was unrealistic to think of going to the police. They were Africans. They would take Nathaniel's word against his any day. The schoolboys would be unlikely to give evidence against a fellow African. And as for tonight — he could not afford the luxury of bribed witnesses. He had realized it even before the spiv came up and whispered to him. So there had been nothing to sell.

But Nathaniel hadn't known that, when he sent his emissary.

Johnnie finished dressing and stubbed out his cigarette in the crowded ashtray. He did not want to look at the girl again. He started towards the door, but some vague uneasiness made him turn.

She lay as he had left her, her body limp. Her eyes were open, but she seemed not to be aware of his presence. She began to speak in her own tongue, a low rhythmical keening sound. Her voice rose for an instant and then shattered into incommunicable anguish. Frightened, Johnnie stared at her. It was then that he saw the blood, seeping into the quilt. A clot of blood on a dirty quilt. He closed his eyes, and the sight was momentarily blotted out, but not the memory.

Johnnie retched. Then panic. Why should it be like that — and so much? He forced himself over to the iron cot. Now that he was close to her, his nausea subsided, and he was able to examine her almost clinically. The reason was not hard to discover. He remembered having heard that some tribes still practised female circumcision. It was one of those scraps of information about Africa that every whiteman picks up. He had always thought it exaggerated. But it was not. Among certain peoples, the clitoridectomy was performed at puberty. By a bush surgeon — some fetish priestess, perhaps. Some of them were said to use the long wicked acacia thorns as needles. The wounds often became infected and did not heal for a long time.

The scars had opened when he savaged her.

He understood now the reason for her fear. He did not want to think of what the pain must have been like. Yet she had cried out only once. Perhaps she was afraid of displeasing him.

He knew nothing about her, but she no longer seemed anonymous to him. He noticed for the first time that her face was fine-boned, her hands slender and smooth as though they had not been coarsened by too much heavy work. Had she been sold by her family, or stolen, or had she elected to come here? He would never know. He could not speak to her. They had no language in common.

But it did not really matter who she specifically was. She was herself and no other. She was someone, a woman who belonged somewhere and who for some reason of her own had been forced to seek him here in this evil-smelling cell, and through him, indignity and pain.

He looked down at the girl. Her eyes pleaded with him. She knew she had not been skilful, and she was afraid that he was not pleased. She begged him, silently, not to betray her to her employer.

She saw from his face that she had nothing to fear from him now. She looked again, more closely, as though surprised. Then — astonishingly — she reached out her hand and touched his. She smiled a little, her eyes reassuring him, telling him she would be all right — it was nothing — it would soon heal.

233

He took her hand and held it closely for an instant. Then he stooped and picked up her crumpled green cloth from the floor. Very gently, he drew it across her body. It was all he could do for her, and for himself.

He drove his car to the edge of the city, beside the lagoon, and parked it in the grove of coconut palms. He put his head down on the steering wheel and sobbed as he had not done for nearly twenty years.

★ 13 ★

THE COCKERELS crowed the brash dawn, and Johnnie wakened. He lay very still and listened to the morning. The slow rusty groan of a door, then Whiskey's hoarse and irascible muttering as he cursed at his two wives for his own sterility. Bare feet shuffling across the compound. A key rattling in the lock, as the old man entered the bungalow kitchen. A cymbal-clashing of angry sound — Whiskey attacking the kerosene stove, daring it not to burn. And all the while the low reiterated mourning — 'Why God give pickin for all man and me He give none? Why God do so to me?'

From the servants' quarters came the clunk and thud of earthen bowls being unstacked and charcoal placed in the burner. The shrill quaver of the old wife as she scolded and nagged at the young one. Then the girl, taking the water bucket to the outside tap and singing to herself in a high clear voice, patient and lonely, like a single bird lost from its forest.

Johnnie closed his eyes and tried to sleep again, but he remained awake.

Then Miranda was bending over him, her dark hair loose around her shoulders.

'You must have come in late last night,' she said. 'I didn't hear you.'

He reached out a hand tentatively to her face.

'Are you still speaking to me?'

'Yes. Are you to me?'

'Manda — I shouldn't have walked out like that. You weren't wrong. James did trust me, and I——'

'Never mind,' she said quickly. 'It's over. Don't think about it. I had no right to cast it up to you.'

He gripped her hands tightly, and she looked startled and apprehensive.

'Listen, Manda —' he said urgently, 'after I left the bungalow——'

She drew away one of her hands and placed it on his mouth.

'I don't want to hear,' she said. 'Please, Johnnie, whatever it is, I don't want to hear it.'

She lowered her head to his. Her long hair brushed across his body.

'I don't want to probe any more. Just to accept.'

And because he had wanted this gift from her for so long, he could scarcely refuse it now.

After the rains, the Cunninghams' garden looked more unkempt than ever. The bougainvillaea was a matted crimson forest. The thin branches of the Pride of Barbados bent under their red-gold flowering. Dark leaves of the castor-oil plant were like giants' outspread hands. Clumps of prickly pear shone lime-green and needled. Huge zinnias, mauve and yellow and ferocious pink, grew rank as weeds. Unhurriedly, the garden-boy with his machete chipped away at this wilderness like a sculptor at a marble mountain.

Helen was sitting on the stoep, keeping a nervous eye on the children playing in the dust below.

'Brian — what have you got there?' Her voice, as so often, was on the verge of panic.

'It's only a toad.'

'Are you quite sure?'

Johnnie knew that if anyone were to mistake a scorpion for a toad, a snake for a lizard, it would certainly not be Brian.

'Of course I'm sure,' the boy said. 'Silly.'

'Well, dear, it's just that — oh, hello, Johnnie. I didn't see you. I know I must seem a terrible fusser, but I can't help it. Would you like some orange squash? Take that chair — the other's broken and no one ever gets around to mending it.'

When the steward brought the glasses, Helen leaned over the low stoep wall and handed one to each of the children. Kathie drank hers, but Brian's attention was still fixed on the toad.

'Come on, dear,' Helen said, 'you really must. You need it.'

She turned to Johnnie.

'It's a constant struggle to get enough liquid into him. I always think of cystitis. He had it once, and he was in agony. Of course, that fool of a doctor did virtually nothing; sometimes I think he only knows of two remedies, whatever ails one — quinine for the inside, and gentian violet for the outside.'

'Miranda seems to like him.'

'Oh, I daresay he's all right. Don't pay any attention to me. I'm not in a charitable mood.'

She gave Johnnie a sharp glance.

'Did you come over to commiserate with us?'

'I wondered if Bedford was sick, that's all, as he wasn't at work this morning. What do you mean — commiserate?'

'He got his notice,' Helen said simply. 'Yesterday.'

'Oh. I didn't know——'

'Yes,' she said, 'it's all over but the shouting, and there'll be precious little of that. We knew, of course — we've known it would come——'

She sat down, clumsily, her cotton skirt bunched between her thighs. Johnnie thought she was going to cry, but she did not. Her eyes were blank as blue glass.

'It's odd, you know,' she said, 'when a calamity actually happens, one is always so much more calm than at any point beforehand. I think Bedford was afraid I'd stage hysterics. He was so relieved when I didn't.'

'Where — ' absurdly, Johnnie's voice was nearly a whisper — 'where will you go?'

'Bedford's put in for a post with a firm in Nigeria,' she said, half defiantly. 'He knows the assistant manager — met him at the Club here. There's a fair chance he'll get it.'

'Nigeria——'

'Yes,' she said tiredly. 'I know what you're thinking. It'll start all over again. And end the same way, too, I suppose. Their independence is coming up, isn't it, within a few years?'

Then she laughed.

'A few years——' she said. 'That's eternity. I try not to think more than six months ahead now.'

The desk was littered with samples of mammy-cloth, and James was completely absorbed in studying them.

'Sit down, Johnnie. I won't be a moment. I'd just like to finish these——'

He held up a patch of cloth, an orange elephant and a green palm. He shook his head and picked up the next, patterned in blue clocks on a chocolate background. Satisfied, he fingered the material, then placed it carefully with the others that had passed inspection.

'An African,' James said, 'would not be able to select these patterns, for the simple reason that he'd only know what he liked himself. From a commercial point of view, one's selection has to extend much further than that. It's a question of judging the general taste.'

'I expect you're right.'

'Of course I'm right. And they'll find it out one of these days, too. I've been studying pattern trends in tradecloth for many years. I fancy I know what these people want better than they know themselves.'

Reluctantly, he turned from the varicoloured scraps.

'What is it, Johnnie? You wanted to see me?'

Johnnie looked away from the creased simian face.

'Yes. I suppose I should have told you before. That day you asked me to speak to Cameron — I didn't accomplish anything you intended. Not anything.'

James sighed.

'I didn't really think you would. I'm afraid he isn't a man who can be persuaded or convinced.'

'No, but——'

'I don't want to hear the details,' James said. 'I'm sure no one else could have done any better. Probably it wouldn't have made much difference in the long run, anyway.'

He glanced up.

'You've heard about Bedford, I suppose? It was to be expected, of course, that he'd be the first to go. I never had a very high opinion of his work, yet now I feel — well, I shall miss him. Strange.'

Then James sat up straight in the hard high-backed chair that he had brought to this country with him and had used ever since, an uncomfortable chair, darkened with years but still unmistakably oak, not 'ofram' or African mahogany.

'You mustn't think I'm despondent,' he said. 'I believe

239

there's every chance that the Board will come to its senses despite Cameron. As a matter of fact, I've written to one or two people about it, and I expect to hear from them quite soon. I know some of the directors very well. Nicholas Moore, for example. Why, I've known Nicholas for twenty-odd years. I think he'll understand my point of view.'

Johnnie turned to go.

'I'm sure he will. I'm sure he'll understand.'

As he left, he noticed that James had picked up one of the fragments of mammy-cloth once more. The Squire was turning it over and over in his hands, and his unseeing eyes were fixed on the printed clocks.

'Come with me,' Aya begged, 'come to the meeting, Nathaniel.'

'Why doesn't Charity go with you? She always used to go.'

'She's busy.'

'Well, so am I.'

He had been trying all day to get this one thing done. He was writing to Adjei to say that he wanted the post of clerk to Nana Kwaku Afrisi. He had not known the letter would be so difficult to write. The sheet of paper still only said 'My dear uncle——'

Aya gave him a furious glance.

'All right,' she said. 'Don't come with me. I didn't want you to come, anyway. If my pains start, somebody will help me home.'

And so of course he had to go.

It was an evangelist church, one of many, for this city which had absorbed into itself so many gods always seemed to have room for one more. The meetings were held outside, under a huge rough shelter of fresh palm boughs piled on pole frames. The benches were nearly filled by the time Nathaniel and Aya got there. They sat down, Aya waving and shouting greetings to everyone in sight. Nathaniel was stiff, embarrassed, conscious of the glances of Aya's friends. He had never been to a meeting with her before.

The preacher was an African. Bulbous and earnest, with protruding eyes, he prayed as though God were sitting next to him in an Accra municipal bus.

' — Lawd, you see these people — '

'Yes, yes!'

' — Lawd, you see these sinners — '

'He sees!'

' — Lawd, what we gonna do with 'em?'

'Save us, save us!'

If he could be saved, Nathaniel thought. If he could be saved as easily as that. But this meeting was a game. The preacher knew his part and the congregation knew their part and they knew what would happen this night. Nathaniel did not want to see it. He looked around at Aya, hoping she would not yet have entered in, that he would be able to persuade her to go.

'Yes, yes!' Aya was saying.

Nathaniel turned away.

The meeting provided for every man, every tongue. The prayers were alternately in Ga, Twi and English.

A man in a green shirt printed with purple orchids got up and said he had once smuggled cocoa into French Togoland, where it fetched a higher price. He had been driving his lorry one night through the Aburi mountains on his way back to Tafo to see his family. He had been drunk, he said, drunk on the money he got from his crooked work. It had started to rain, up there in the Aburi mountains, on that narrow winding road. And he, in his drunkenness, had driven the lorry too close to the edge, and the wheels had skidded and the lorry started to go over into the ravine. The lightning flashed all around him, he said, and he knew it was the anger of God, like his sister had told him many times before, and she was a Christian also of this Church, only he never paid heed to her. And his soul was afraid in that moment. But listen, brethren, do you know what happened then? 'No — what? What happened then, man?' That lorry caught on a big jagged rock, and the rock held it long enough for him to scramble out. And he fell out onto the road, and the lorry plunged down into the deep ravine. And he knew that God had saved him. And God had punished him. Yes, man, God had punished him and saved him.

Nathaniel looked down at his feet. His shoes badly needed polishing, he noticed. He tried not to listen. But he knew he was listening. Beside him, Aya swayed and moaned.

Nathaniel sweated and tried to think. But all he could think of was that boulder and that lorry and that man, saved.

— He saved me, He saved me. Who all could be saved?

— Not Nathaniel, oh no, not him. Not Nathaniel, over whom both gods had fought and both had lost.

— Nathaniel. That was his name. Before he went to the mission school, he had had an African name. He never thought of it now, even to himself. His name was Nathaniel. They had given him that name at the mission school. They always did. They went through in alphabetical order. If he had been the first boy to arrive that term, his name would have been Abraham. And after they had given him a different name, they began to give him a different soul. They talked of God the Father, God the Son, God the Holy Ghost. The God of Abraham, the God of Isaac, the God of

Jacob, the God of Moses, the God of Nathaniel. And the boy had listened, he with the new name had listened, bored at first, indifferent, then frightened, until finally he came to take it for granted. The new name took hold, and the new roots began to grow. But the old roots never quite died, and the two became intertwined.

— I was of both and I was of neither. I forgot one way when I was too young to remember everything of it by myself, without help. And I learned another way when I was too old for it ever to become second nature. Do not question me too closely about God the Holy Ghost, for the meaning is not clear to me. And do not ask me who Nyankopon is, for I have forgotten.

— Did my father think I could take the red wine of Communion and return then to offer red 'eto' to the gods? And did the mission fathers think that when I tasted the unleavened bread, the smell of the sacred 'summe' leaves scattered in the grove would ever quite be gone from my nostrils?

— Once, when the boy was in his second year at the mission school, some of his schoolmates said they would let him accompany them on an adventure. They went, all of them together, to the grove outside the town, where there was the hut of a powerful fetish. The other boys, brave laughing boys, had shown Nathaniel the black earthen pots beside the fetish hut, where the townsfolk left their offerings of money. Look — what a hoax! That was what the boys had said, laughing. The fetish priest has plenty of palm-wine on that. And Nathaniel said, bitterness in his heart, look — what a hoax! The fetish priest is well-fleshed and his sorrows are soothed away by palm-wine, on that money. So they stole it, that boy and the other boys, they stole the money from the earthen pot and divided it among them.

Some of the boys bought sweets, some bought palm-wine, and if it gave them nightmares, they never told. But Nathaniel buried his share under a casuarina tree in the compound of the mission school. He buried it, just in case. For six months it stayed there, before he found the bravado to dig it up and spend it. And when he did, the sweets were like a bitter leaf in his mouth.

— There was a line from a funeral song, long ago:

> ' *Thou speeding bird, tell father*
> *That he left me on the other side of the River*——'

— Oh, my father, why did you leave me here? And what shall I do?

— Our Father——

— my father — my father which art in Hell——

— You cannot tell me, either of you. There is no advice from you or You. Two silences.

In the gathering darkness the bodies swayed and moaned with the fever's beginning.

'He saved me. He saved me. I was in the brothel, in the jail, and He saved me. I was in the fiery furnace and He saved me. I was in the lion's den and He looked mercifully upon me.'

The palm leaves of the shelter were disarrayed by the wind, and the night was hot. The night was hot and still, and you could see the stars through the screen of palm branches, and the moon, thin as a golden necklace.

They were mostly women, the congregation. And when they sang, they sang of themselves, of despair and exultation. They sang in the warm night, and their cloths rustled in the half darkness. Their shoulders and big breasts lifted to the song, and their sandalled feet shuffled in the dust, in the dark.

Nathaniel listened.

> *My soul in the River — gonna sin no more,*
> *My soul in the River — gonna sin no more,*
> *My soul in the River — gonna sin no more,*
> *I'm gonna walk up Jordan shore——'*

And the preacher.

'What did the Lord say to Joshua? What did He say to Joshua? I'll tell you what He said. He said, "Be strong and of good courage. Yes, be strong and of good courage, for the Lord thy God is with thee." And the Lord said, "Don't be afraid. Neither be thou dismayed. Cross Jordan." That's what the Lord said. And Joshua, he crossed over.'

> *'Jordan, Jordan, Jordan shore,*
> *I'm gonna walk up Jordan shore,*
> *Live in the glory forevermore,*
> *I'm gonna walk up Jordan shore——'*

The drums caught the rhythm and gave it back. And the women swayed, swayed and sang. They sang in the hot still night, with the smell of charcoal smoke and palm oil and frying plantain heavy in the air. And Nathaniel listened.

He listened to the preacher.

'Do you think Joshua was afraid, brethren? Was that man afraid? Yes, he was afraid! Yes, he was afraid! Joshua had a big battle to fight and Joshua had a big river to cross. Yes, he was afraid. Nobody ever got to the promised land without a fight. Every man want salvation, and every man afraid, afraid to try for fear he fail. But the Lord say "Cross Jordan, Joshua". And the Lord say

"Be not afraid, Joshua. Cross over. Yes, man, cross over that river and win that battle."

' — Yes, man! Yes!'

'And Joshua say — "All right, God. I'll try." And he say "That's right, God, I'll try if You say so. Yes, sir, I'll try if You say so." And he tried. And when he got to that river, see what happened! Just see! Why, that river parted its waters. Yes, those waters rose up! And it says, those waters rose up in a heap far from the city that is beside Zaretan, and it says, those that came down towards the sea of the plain, even the salt sea, why, those waters failed. The Jordan was flooding its banks, because it was that time of year. And those big waters were cut off, this side, that side. And the children of Israel crossed over on dry ground.'

' — Tell it! They crossed on dry ground! Amen! Amen!'

The preacher raised his arms. He was a small man, and fat, but when he raised his arms he seemed to grow enormous, tall as the palms, and his arms reached out, reached out. The women swayed and their tears flowed down their singing faces.

'That's salvation, brother! That's salvation! A man's afraid. He's got fear and he trembles and he won't come forward. He's afraid to cross that river, that Jordan. And then he tries. And what happens? I'll tell you. Yes, I'll tell you! He finds it's easy, easy, easy! He finds it's easy, for the Lord parts the waters, and he walks over on dry land. You going to come over?'

' — Yes, yes!'

'You going to come over?'

' — Yes, yes!'

And they went forward, singing. And the preacher blessed them and prayed for them.

'Come over into salvation! You, man, you!'

They surged forward, swaying and singing. Forward to be blessed.

In the warm night they sang, their voices hot and hungry. And the drums beat, beat, beat. The drums pulsed this hope, as they had pulsed the hope and despair of a thousand years, here, in this place.

> *'Joshua crossed the River to the Promised Land,*
> *Joshua crossed the River to the Promised Land,*
> *Joshua crossed the River to the Promised Land,*
> *And The Lord gave the battle into his hand——'*

And then triumphant, feet stamping, hands clapping, bodies sweating, voices shouting, triumphant —

> *'Jordan, Jordan, Jordan shore,*
> *I'm gonna walk up Jordan shore,*
> *Live in the glory for evermore,*
> *I'm gonna walk up Jordan shore!'*

Nathaniel listened. His throat felt tight with wanting to sing, and he clenched his hands that wanted to clap.

Then he stopped holding back, and he sang. He threw back his head and sang into the warm night.

> *'Joshua crossed the River to the Promised Land——'*

— Oh, the River was many things. Now he knew it. The River was the warm slimy womb of all, lapping around the little fish, holding him so that he might not learn lungs. And the River was Jordan.

— The River was Jordan.

*'Jordan, Jordan, Jordan shore,
    I'm gonna walk up Jordan shore——'*

Nathaniel sang, his head thrown back, the look of him forgotten. He did not mind about his glasses, that they shone with his tears. He did not mind that his shoes needed polishing. The doubt and the shame, for the moment, were no more. Nathaniel sang, and his voice was deep and true.

— Who all can be saved? Oh, every man, every man, no matter what his trouble. I heard that You did not turn any away.

— The Kyerema had not known its name was Jordan. But perhaps, after all, when he set the boy's feet on that path, he knew it was goodbye. Maybe he knew his son would have a strange new river to cross.

— The land was there. And the land was theirs. And the people crossed over into their land. The land was there, waiting for them, waiting for them to walk up the shore of Jordan. And the Lord gave the battle into their hands.

*'Live in the glory for evermore,
    I'm gonna walk up Jordan shore!'*

Then it was over. For a second there was silence. And in that second, Nathaniel wondered what Joshua had done once the walls of Jericho fell down. What had he done with the city, when it was his?

Then time began again. He must be crazy. He was going back — had he forgotten? — to the Forest and the dark River.

What was Jericho to him? What was Jordan to him?

★ 14 ★

It was late in the night when Aya wakened Nathaniel. The pains had been coming for about two hours. At first she hadn't been sure, but now they were getting stronger.

Nathaniel looked at her face to see if she were frightened, and she turned her eyes away. He asked her.

'Not of the baby,' Aya said. 'I'm not frightened of the baby.'

'What, then?'

'The hospital,' she said. 'I don't want to go, Nathaniel.'

Then another pain came, and he watched her as she drew up her legs and moaned. When it was over, she turned to him angrily.

'Why do you make me go there?' she cried. 'You don't know! You don't know!'

Suddenly Nathaniel was appalled at what he had done. It was not he who had to bear the child. Why had he not let her have it here, with the people she knew and trusted around her? What was it to him? Progress or pride? For his pride she now had to pay with her fear. He could not let himself think of it. Even to him, now, the presence of Aya's mother would have been reassuring.

What if there was any trouble about Aya being admitted to hospital at this time of night?

'Where's Akosua?' he asked.

'She's making some tea,' Aya said. 'I wakened her before.'

249

They dressed and went into the other room. The children were rubbing their eyes and blinking like two ruffled owls. When they were fully awake, they squatted cross-legged on their sleeping-mats, and stared with the ruthless curiosity of the young, as though they hoped Aya's pains would soon reach screaming pitch and provide a dramatic entertainment.

Akosua, her cloth draped sparely around her gaunt body, came in with the tea and immediately began to question Aya sharply and minutely. Had there been blood yet? Was the child moving a little or a lot? The water had not broken? Were the pains small, like this — she half clenched her hand — or strong, like this — her thin fingers snapped in toward her palm in a vivid gesture of tension, and Nathaniel, horrified, looked away.

Aya said she did not know. Her voice faltered and she began to cry, softly, in jerky little breaths.

Akosua glared at Nathaniel.

'Have you turned to stone?' she demanded crossly. 'You'd better hurry if you want to take her to that — that place——'

She said it as though the hospital were the Pit of Hell. Aya sobbed.

Nathaniel, angry and terrified, stumbled out to the street. He felt certain he would be unable to find a taxi. But of course he did find one. There were always dozens of taxis in Accra, day and night.

Akosua said goodbye to Aya as though she never expected to see her again.

The hospital seemed quiet as death. At first they went in the wrong door, and finally the watch-night, an old man in a Muslim robe and dishevelled turban, showed them the way.

They walked across the verandah, their footsteps loud in the dark silence. In the reception room a single bulb burned, and a sleepy clerk sat at the desk with his head propped on his hands. He looked up blankly.

'Amegbe?' he repeated doubtfully after Nathaniel.

Nathaniel felt his last drops of confidence ebbing away. What would he do if the clerk said he couldn't find any record of anyone of that name? Would it work if he dashed him? And how much money would it take for the dash to be effective? Nathaniel realized he had only eight shillings and a few pennies left in his pocket after he had paid the taxi.

Aya gripped his arm, and looking at her, he saw her face was drawn with pain, but she would not cry out in front of the clerk.

The clerk saw it, too. Surprisingly, he brought a chair for her. And when he looked in the book, he found the name with no difficulty.

'Wait,' he said, 'only a minute. She is coming — the sister in charge of the ward.'

Nathaniel wondered why he had doubted the clerk. Why, he was a fine man, very polite and thoughtful. Look at the way he had brought a chair for Aya. Why didn't Africans trust each other more? His relief made Nathaniel feel weak.

The click-clack-click-clack of heels made him look up. The sister. She was an African. How incredibly white her uniform looked, how stiff and white and efficient. She was a slim, pretty girl, and for a moment Nathaniel felt hesitant about speaking to her. She was obviously a 'been-to', probably trained in England. Even her walk showed it — such rapid steps, so much hurry. No African-educated person ever walked like that. Nathaniel wondered if everything Victor said was true.

Peering for a moment out of his misery, Nathaniel discovered that she was smiling at him.

'Don't worry about your wife, Mr. Amegbe,' she was saying. 'She will be perfectly all right.'

She was bending over Aya, talking to her in a low voice.

'Please—' he burst out, 'please — be patient with her. She does not speak much English, you see, and she is rather frightened. She has never been in a hospital before——'

'It will be all right,' the sister said soothingly. 'She is among her own people here, really, you know.'

'No—' Nathaniel stammered, 'to her, her own people are her family.'

'I know,' the sister said. 'But you are not to worry. It will be all right.'

She spoke to Aya again, this time in Twi. Aya looked up and the fear in her eyes began to recede. She answered the question in a whisper, and then, as another pain came, she reached out for the sister's arm and held onto it. She reached out to this woman, Nathaniel realized, rather than to him.

Confidence returned. The sister did know. And it would be all right.

'Thank you!' he cried fervently.

The sister looked at him shrewdly, sympathetically.

'You did right,' she said, 'to bring her here to have the baby.'

'Do you think so?' His eyes searched her face. 'Do you really think so?'

'Yes,' she said firmly. 'Yes. Don't let anyone tell you differently. I know what it is like.'

A look of comprehension passed between them. Was it possible that this girl really did understand? Yes, yes she did. Victor had been wrong. Nathaniel felt a strange hunger to talk to her, to pour out all his indecision.

There was no time. But he had to say something.

'Our country needs people like you!' he cried impulsively.

That would sound foolish to her. How could he have let himself say it?

But the sister's smile had no mockery in it.

Nathaniel turned to Aya and said goodbye, but she had already turned to the world that was within her. Her eyes were vague, and she said goodbye absentmindedly. Then she followed the sister down the corridor, towards the ward.

Nathaniel phoned the hospital three times the next morning. Each time it was the same.

'Has Mrs. Amegbe had her baby yet?'

'Who?' a girl's voice drawled.

'Mrs. Amegbe,' Nathaniel said clearly.

There was a short pause.

'She is not here,' the voice said finally, in a bored tone.

'She is there,' Nathaniel resisted the impulse to shout. 'She went in last night.'

Another pause.

'I cannot find her card. She is not here.'

'She is there,' Nathaniel said. 'I beg you — go and ask if the baby is born.'

Another pause, very short this time.

'She has not given birth,' the voice said distinctly.

'Pardon?'

'She has not given birth,' the voice repeated angrily.

'But——' Nathaniel began.

'Visiting hours from four to six,' the voice concluded.

There was a click.

Nathaniel did not believe for an instant that the voice knew one way or another, or that anything could have persuaded her to go and find out.

He could not tell Akosua.

'Well,' she snapped, 'what is happening?'

'It is not born yet.'

'What did I say?' Akosua demanded. 'She did not want to go there. And now — look! A difficult birth — a difficult birth. How many hours? So many I dare not count——'

'It is just twelve o'clock,' Nathaniel said testily. 'It is less than twenty-four hours.'

'Oh, less than twenty-four? Fine, fine. Very easy. What do you know about it? When I had Abenaa, I was in labour only — what? — five hours. Twenty-four — don't talk to me about your twenty-four. What are they doing to her there?'

'Abenaa was your second child,' Nathaniel said, certain she was lying anyway.

'If she dies,' Akosua said hysterically, 'may her ghost never give you rest!'

'Akosua! Can't you stop it? Don't you think I'm worried, too?'

'You!' Akosua yelped. 'You! What do you know? If men had to bear the children, the world would die of your fear!'

Nathaniel walked out and slammed the door.

He had to come back, though, to eat his lunch. He was almost sorry the school was not in session, so he would have somewhere to go. Then he remembered he was not going back to the school next term anyway.

At two o'clock Aya's mother arrived, vast and tent-like in a new dark purple cloth.

Adua was overwrought. Not trusting Nathaniel, she had gone to the hospital herself, demanding to see her daughter. She had not been allowed in, and they would not even tell her if the child had been born or not.

Akosua was in command of herself by this time.

'Of course,' she said scornfully. 'They would not tell Nathaniel anything, either. What a fine place, where their doings are so shameful they must keep them secret——'

'They're not keeping them secret!' Nathaniel cried. 'In two hours I can go and see her.'

His head pounded and he wondered how much longer he could stand these two women.

'By that time,' Akosua said, 'who knows — it may be too late.'

Adua rose ponderously, like a cow-elephant shifting up from its knees. Her small eyes glinted cruelly in the sweat-glistening moon of flesh that was her face.

'How many times did I tell you?' she cried. 'Answer me only that one thing — how many times did I tell you not to take her there? She didn't want to go. But oh yes, oh yes, you knew——'

Soon it would be over, Nathaniel thought. Soon they would know that the child was born, and they would forget all this. But now, now——

'Wait,' he said stubbornly. 'Wait and see. It will be all right.'

The old woman waved her fat hands feebly.

'She is my only daughter,' she groaned. 'Aya! Aya! Who is it that has killed you?'

'She is not dead!' Nathaniel shouted. 'Who says she is dead? Can't you stop it, both of you! You and Akosua! All day long — I've had enough. Can't you stop acting like a pair of parrots cackling from the treetops?'

Adua's bulk rose up in front of him and she thrust her face close to his. She was waving her arms frantically now, and her heavy face was distorted with rage and anguish.

'Better that my daughter had never married at all, if she had to marry you!'

She slumped down on the floor and began sobbing.

'I am an old woman — I am an old woman — what is left to me — what is left?'

She called on her gods, loudly, hoarsely, without restraint, her huge body quivering on the floor.

Nathaniel thought he was going to be sick. Either that or pass out. Unless his body made him collapse, he would kick her, lying there on the floor like some great animal in its death throes.

He slammed his hand down hard on the table, his invariable gesture, the assertion that came with desperation.

'Enough!' he bellowed. 'Enough! Stop it! I am going now. I will wait outside the hospital until it is time.'

The mound of flesh trembled on the floor, and then, surprisingly, Adua arose.

'Nathaniel,' she whispered, 'I beg you——'

She was frightened. She was only frightened. It had not been malice against him. Just fear. Only that. And he had given her, for her consoling, the harshest words he dared.

'It will be all right,' he said. 'You will see.'

But by this time their fear had filled him, too, and when he reached the hospital he almost expected to be told that Aya was dead.

As he had anticipated, the girl at the reception desk told him visiting hours did not begin until four.

A blue-uniformed African nurse was in the room, consulting a large book with names written in it. She glanced at Nathaniel. Then she asked him his name.

'Amegbe——' she said finally, as though her mind were on something else. 'Yes. Let him go in now.'

Surprised, Nathaniel followed the receptionist.

'Room four,' she said, pointing down the corridor.

He did not know what to think. He paused at the door of

room four and peered in apprehensively. It was a big room. There were four empty beds in it. The others were screened off with blue plastic screens.

Aya was there. She was there. Nathaniel gasped. She was lying there neat and beautiful. She could not read, but she was looking at a magazine as though she had been used all her life to such things. She was wearing her new night-dress. It was white cotton with a blue ribbon through the lace around the neck. Her face was calm and she was smiling at him.

'Aya——' he stammered, 'what——? Are you all right?'

She laughed at his startled look.

'Don't you know?' she said. 'You told me you would find out.'

'They would not tell me,' he said. 'I tried, many times. Is it born?'

'Of course,' Aya said complacently. 'At eleven o'clock this morning. A boy, Nathaniel. Just like you said. A fine one. Seven and a half pounds.'

'Is that big?'

'Oh yes,' she said professionally. 'It is quite big.'

She laughed.

'He was big enough for me.'

Nathaniel remembered her.

'Are you all right? Was it all right?'

'Yes,' she said. 'It was bad, but it was all right, too. It's over. I didn't know what it would be like. I didn't know it would be like that. But it's over. My mother said a woman forgets as soon as she hears him cry. It's true.'

'A son——' Nathaniel said. 'A man——'

He kissed her.

'You did well,' he said.

He felt he should say something solemn. But he could not think of anything.

'You will be pleased with him,' Aya said. 'I knew he was mine as soon as I saw him. You could not mistake him, Nathaniel. Go and see him. They will let you.'

So he went. The nurse showed him the cot. Nathaniel could not see anything about this baby to connect it with himself. It was a brownish-pink fragment, wrapped around in a shawl, so that only its head showed. Its eyes were tightly closed.

Nathaniel was pleased and yet disappointed. He had expected to feel something great.

He took a quick glance at the next cot. It was a European baby and it had no hair. At least his son had hair, a tight black thatch of it, as a child should. Were all white babies born without hair? This baby looked very red and very bald. Nathaniel looked at his son again, this time with satisfaction. He was beginning to feel proud. That was right.

But something bothered him. He soon became aware of what it was. Once he had told himself that this child might grow up to be anything, to be Someone. A doctor, a barrister, an official of Ghana. But not now.

Now he knew what his son would be. He would be reared in the bush and he would grow up to be a planter of yams, a teller of old tales, a drinker of palm-wine.

— Because of your father, my son. Because I did not know what to do.

— Kyerema, here is your grandson. Take him. Is it not enough?

The family would be satisfied but the bitterness of it would never leave Nathaniel. He could not look at the child any longer. He went back to Aya.

'Isn't he fine?' she asked eagerly.

'Fine,' he agreed, exaggerating a little for her sake. 'A fine boy. Wonderful.'

He searched for something to say.

'He looks like you,' he added. 'I think he will be good-looking like you.'

She knew he was saying it only to please her, but she was pleased all the same. She reached out and held his hand.

'The nurses——' Nathaniel said, 'the hospital — what do you think now?'

'The woman who delivered him,' Aya said, 'she was an old woman — not really old, you know, but not young. A big woman, big, like my mother. She was kind, Nathaniel. She was — oh, she was like my mother to me——'

Nathaniel looked at her, hardly able to believe it.

'Then — everything has been fine?' he asked. 'You are not sorry now?'

Aya's expression changed. The warmth faded and the beauty of her face turned to petulance.

'I do not like the food,' she said in a whisper. 'And the doctor — he came around afterwards, Nathaniel, and I was ashamed——'

'It is always done, for the doctor to examine——' Nathaniel explained. 'A doctor is not like an ordinary man, not then. I have told you——'

He saw with surprise that she was close to tears, and he could not understand the sharp change, in a matter of seconds.

'I know,' she said, 'but I cannot help it. Oh — the nurses are kind, Nathaniel. But then there is the food — everything is cooked separately and they give it in little dry heaps on your plate. And most I don't know — how can I eat it if I don't know what it is? And it has no taste.'

'It won't be for many days,' he said soothingly.

'There is something else.'

'What?'

Aya looked doubtfully at the blue plastic screen around the bed on the other side of the room.

'Do you know who is lying there?' she hissed.

'Of course I don't know.'

'Mrs. Kestoe.'

'Her?'

'Yes,' Aya went on in a low voice. 'She has not had her baby yet.'

'Then what is she doing here? Something wrong?'

'Oh — no. Yes. Maybe. She came in yesterday afternoon. The pains had started, and then, last night, just before I came in, the pains stopped.'

'How can it be?'

'It happens so, sometimes,' Aya said wisely. 'Since then, nothing. It is too bad for her.'

'Oh yes,' he said insincerely. 'Too bad.'

'I am sorry for her,' Aya said guiltily, 'but I wish——'

He looked at her suspiciously.

'What is the matter?'

'Oh, Nathaniel,' she burst out, still speaking in a whisper, as though Miranda could understand Twi, 'she troubled me all the time. Last night, when the pains were bad, all through the night, she got up and came over here. The nurse was not with me for a long time. I was alone. I was afraid, yes, but I wanted to be left alone. She kept talking and talking, and asking if she could help me——'

Aya began to cry, silently.

'I did not want her to see me like that,' she went on, finally. 'I did not want to talk. I could not remember any English. Oh, Nathaniel! What does she want from me?'

As Nathaniel listened, he remembered. Everything. Were they meant to be grateful, he and Aya?

He rose.

'She won't trouble you again. She won't trouble either of us again. I am going to tell her——'

Aya held him.

'No——' she said. 'You don't understand. I — I told her to go away.'

He looked at her.

'You did?'

'Yes. I had to, Nathaniel! Did I do right?'

'Yes,' he said fiercely, 'you did right.'

Aya's face grew thoughtful.

'I heard her crying,' she said, 'afterwards. I did not think anything of it at the time — I was in pain, then. But later, when the baby was born, I wondered——'

'Never mind,' Nathaniel said coldly. 'We've had to take enough from them. Let it be the other way for a change.'

Aya was scrutinizing his face, sensing a change in him.

'Did I do right?' she asked again.

He turned away from her.

'I don't know,' he said. 'Why ask me?'

They left it at that. Nathaniel told her about her mother and Akosua, and Aya told him some more about the birth. The nurse stuck her head in the doorway — it was time for the patients to have a bath and then tea, and he could return at four if he wished.

Nathaniel had intended to tell Aya that they were going back to the village. But he did not tell her. It might excite her too much. He would wait until she got home. He knew he was putting it off, but he did not know why. Perhaps he was waiting for a sign from heaven.

Nathaniel stepped outside the plastic curtain that screened off Aya's bed. Only two beds were occupied in the ward. Behind the other screen he heard the faint rustle of magazine pages. He had only to speak to the white woman. Surely it would be easy to call out something, say hello, tell her he hoped the baby would be born soon. It would be easy. All he had to do was open his mouth and say the words. It would be the only chance to speak to her alone. Next time, her husband would be here.

Nathaniel stood by the door for a long moment. Finally he shrugged and walked out, but as he went down the corridor, he had a sense of disquiet, of something lost.

He thought of the woman lying there waiting for her child to be born, leafing through a magazine, crying because she had not been wanted. He wondered how she had felt when Aya said that. Not that he blamed Aya. How could he? The white woman was a stranger. It is not a stranger's place to observe our pain. But that woman had reached out her hand, and that hand had been struck away. Aya was soft-spoken and gentle, but she was strong and vehement, too. It was odd — he had worried that Aya might be hurt here, in this unfamiliar place, by the callousness of strangers. And it had been the other way round. He felt in a way proud of Aya. And yet he had an inexplicable pity for that other woman.

Nathaniel stopped walking. He half turned to go back. But when he looked over his shoulder he saw that the nurse with the trolley of bowls and dressings was already entering the room.

It was too late, for him.

Nevertheless, in some subtle way he was different, changed. Miranda's eagerness to know, her exaggerated politeness, her anxiety to please, her terrible kindness — none

of it had moved him at all. Only, now, the sudden knowledge that she could feel humiliation and anguish like
himself.

Miranda's labour began again at six that evening.
Johnnie was with her. At first, the contractions were light,
and Miranda talked to him quite normally, pausing to
grimace slightly with each muscle spasm.

Delilah, the African midwife, came on duty at eight.

'All right, Mrs. Kestoe?'

'About every fifteen minutes now,' Miranda said.

The big woman nodded.

'It will be a few hours yet.'

She shot a disapproving glance at Johnnie as she walked
away. He grinned.

'I think she deplores the presence of a male.'

'Perhaps so,' Miranda said, 'but I don't.'

Johnnie recalled his interview with the doctor.

'Not every man is a suitable subject for this kind of
experience,' the doctor had said. 'However, your wife
appears to want you with her very much, and if you feel the
same about it, fair enough. Only for God's sake don't bother
the nurses, or ask stupid questions, or go to pieces at the wrong
moment. If you do, they'll have to turf you out.'

Johnnie had promised and had even contrived to appear
fairly nonchalant. But when he brought Miranda to
hospital, he wondered how he could possibly stay. He had a
day's respite, when Miranda's labour stopped, and he had
hoped unreasonably that it would begin suddenly and be
over before he could get to the hospital again. But of course
it had not happened that way.

Miranda's contractions grew closer together, and soon she
did not want to talk. Her hand tightened on Johnnie's, until

he could feel his bones grating together. Then, as the pain released her, her fierce strength ebbed.

Johnnie made himself stop glancing continually at his watch. Miranda's face looked bleached and drawn, and her sleek hair was disarranged. Her breath came raspingly. Johnnie choked down the pity and disgust that threatened him. The writhing of her swollen body was almost more than he could stand. The time seemed forever, but it had been, in fact, less than six hours.

Finally, Johnnie could not stay alone with her any longer. He went out to the corridor and found the midwife.

When Delilah saw Miranda, she gave Johnnie an approving nod for the first time.

'You did right to call me. It will not be long. I will have her moved to the delivery room now.'

'Can't you — isn't there anything you can give her?'

'I will give her an injection — it will help for a little while, anyway.'

The plump brown face suddenly creased into a smile.

'Do not worry, Mr. Kestoe,' Delilah said. 'It is not as bad as it looks to you. Your wife is quite all right.'

The delivery room was like an operating theatre, all gleaming metal, with glaring overhead lights that drove bright splinters into the eyes.

Johnnie wanted to walk out, to get as far as possible from this weird antiseptic prison. But he could not. Now he had to remain. And there was nothing he could do. He felt helpless, trapped.

Miranda lay on the delivery table. In between contractions, she shuddered as though chilled to the bone. The contractions were very close now. Her body twisted and her back arched with each wave, but she did not seem conscious of these contortions.

It seemed to him that pain was pouring over her like a wild river, snatching her into its whirlpool. It tore at her muscles, bent her spine to snapping point, tossed her like a matchstick on its cruel and cunning surface. She had to bargain with it for each breath, and each breath won only racked her and seemed almost to split her lungs as though, drowning, she had breathed in water instead of air.

She caught at Johnnie's arms. Her grip tightened and she drew herself partly up, not seeming to realize she was doing it, as her body was caught in another spasm.

'Johnnie——' her voice was a whisper, 'you won't leave me?'

It was a moment before Johnnie could reply steadily.

'I won't leave you, Manda. I'm right here.'

Then, once more, she was unaware, unrecognizable.

'Won't it——' Johnnie heard his own strangled voice, 'won't it ever be over?'

'It is nearly over now,' Delilah said calmly. 'Soon the second stage will start. Then it will not be so bad.'

The waters broke. Johnnie looked at the fluid that gushed from her. He had imagined 'waters' meant just that. But this was yellow and thick like pus. How could a living creature issue from that poisonous flood?

Johnnie looked away. The half-formed thought had been in his mind all along. He was certain that his son would be born dead.

He saw now that Delilah and the two junior nurses had strapped Miranda to raised footholds at the end of the delivery table. The apparatus looked like part of a medieval rack.

Delilah was bending over Miranda, trying to get her to inhale gas and air, but Miranda pushed the breathing tube away roughly, as though she did not understand its purpose.

There was no rest for her now. Her body strained and pressed, arched and strained again. Johnnie forgot his own repugnance. Now he felt only fear for Miranda, fear that he would somehow lose her, that she would not return from this pilgrimage which had already taken her so far from him.

She was no longer human. The voice that came from her throat was an animal's coarse voice. Then a jagged scream, the last cry. Johnnie put his head down on his outspread hands. He closed his eyes. He was shivering, as though with shock. Whatever unspeakable thing had come forth, he did not want to see it.

Then, incredibly, Miranda's own voice.

'Johnnie — look.'

He lifted his head. At first he could scarcely believe what he saw. His son had not been born dead. As it happened, it was a girl, and she was quite alive.

The child had only been born for a second and she had not breathed yet, but the small shoulders stirred. Johnnie watched. The baby's spine was still curved around and her legs folded. There were smears of yellow slime and blood on her body. She looked damp and crumpled. One arm moved. Then she cried, a thin wailing.

Johnnie Kestoe watched his child enter the breathing life that would be hers until the moment of death.

The cord was tied and cut. Delilah wrapped the baby and took her to be weighed. Johnnie looked at his watch. Nearly two a.m.

Then the blood. The placenta came away, and a torrent of bright blood followed. The sight of it did not sicken Johnnie, and for a moment he wondered why. Then he knew. Always, before, he had thought of blood only in relation to death.

He turned to Miranda. She look⸰⸰⸰⸰⸰, but he knew she was all right. Neither spoke for a whie.

'We must've been sure it was going to be a boy,' Miranda said finally. 'I don't think we ever discussed girls' names.'

'Manda — would you mind very much if we called her Mary?'

He saw her eyes widen questioningly.

'It's just — well, that was my mother's name.'

He felt embarrassed, saying it. But Miranda did not seem to think it odd.

'Of course I won't mind,' she said. 'It's a good idea. I think your mother would have been pleased, Johnnie.'

Now it was his eyes that widened, with surprise. Then he understood and wanted to laugh. Of course. Miranda came from a world in which children were named after grandparents, a world in which grandparents danced delighted attendance upon children. Miranda thought the name was a sort of memorial to his mother.

He did not know exactly why he wanted to call his child by her name. Reasons could be dragged up, no doubt, like the roots of swamp weeds, but he did not want to see them. Only one thing he felt sure of — the name was given not for her sake but for his own. He did not think he could explain.

'Yes,' he said, 'she would have been pleased.'

★ 15 ★

ONCE, AT THE prayer meeting, and again when the child was born, Nathaniel had felt a terrible longing to stay after all, to stay here in this city where you could feel tomorrow being reached for; where you could believe it might happen so, and to you.

But he was not a man of that tomorrow. He did not know how to act in it. He was a plain man, not cut out for battles of the spirit. Now, when he tried to think back over the whole thing, it only gave him a headache.

Jacob Abraham Mensah had just arrived back from Ashanti. There was no longer any excuse for delay. Nathaniel went to tell the headmaster he was leaving.

Mensah beamed and offered Nathaniel a cigarette. Confused, he took it.

'Glad to see you, Amegbe,' the big man said. 'Good to be back. We shall all be glad to get back into harness, as they say, eh?'

His voice dropped to a loud whisper.

'Oh, by the way, Amegbe, before I forget. We mentioned some time ago that fine possibility to start — ah — an employment bureau here. What happened to those boys?'

Nathaniel fingered his glasses. He had not visualized being quizzed like this. The clown-giant still exerted an inexplicable power over him.

'They were no good,' he stumbled. 'Mr. Kestoe didn't give them a fair trial, it is true. But they were — unsuitable — anyway.'

Jacob Abraham's eyes narrowed.

'I see,' he said. 'How many did you send?'

'Two.'

'No more,' Jacob Abraham asked, 'when those two were not taken?'

'No.'

'Well, well, that won't do, Amegbe. You must send plenty. Let him take his pick. We have plenty of fine boys. And we do not want to lose this contact with a European employer, do we? It might work up, you know, into something quite nice. Through Mr. Kestoe we might meet other Europeans. I do not think you have organized it very properly. On a business basis. It must be on a business basis. I trust you agree? We will discuss it, what each of us is to do. You need guidance. You will go and see your white friend once more——'

Mensah had it all planned out, then, how he could get a cut out of the whole thing. But even that did not matter any more. Mensah's face became blurred to Nathaniel. He rose to his feet, gropingly, hardly knowing what he was doing.

'No!' he shouted. 'No! I will never go to see him again! Never, all my life! He only made fun of me, he only mocked me. The boys were no good for anything. What could they do? They'd only been given dreams here, only dreams, do you hear? Don't you know anything?'

Jacob Abraham sat back in his chair as though he had been struck. His deep hypnotic eyes rolled in fury and astonishment.

'Are you mad?' he roared. 'Yes, that's it. Mad! Crazy!'

'No,' Nathaniel said, and it was easier now, 'no, I'm not mad. I've worked here long enough. You put your feet on your carpets and you forget a school needs books, teachers. What do you care? The place is no good, you hear? And I'm no good here. I wanted to do something. But I can't. I don't know — but I can't, it doesn't happen. My family keeps troubling me for money, and I haven't got any money. They keep troubling me to go back to the village, and now I've had enough. I'm no good here. I don't know what to do. I don't know how to do something. I'm going back. That's what I came to tell you.'

He sat down again, clumsily, and took off his glasses. He put his palms to his eyes and found the tears were running down his face. He had said it now. Now it was final. He had spoken the words.

— Oh, River, you are not Jordan for me. Not for me. And you, Forest of a thousand gods, a thousand eyes, I am coming back. I will offer red 'eto' to the gods, and scatter the sacred 'summe' leaves. And some day I may forget this pain.

'My uncle is going to get me a job,' Nathaniel said dully. 'Clerk to a chief. It is in a town not far from my village.'

He could not look at Jacob Abraham. But the clown, now entirely giant, was silent, and in a few moments Nathaniel did look up.

Jacob Abraham was sitting perfectly still. His head seemed like the ebony heads the carvers sell to Europeans. It was heavy, solid, dead-looking. Nathaniel saw that the big man's eyes were shut.

Finally Mensah sighed. Nathaniel peered at him intently.

'You were the only one,' Jacob Abraham said. 'I thought you cared about Futura.'

Nathaniel could not understand. Then it occurred to him

that the man was being genuine. Jacob Abraham really did care about the school. Underneath the cheating and the self-deception, he wanted it to be something.

'No good, you say?' Mensah went on in the same oddly tired voice. 'I should be angry. But I always thought you were interested in the school——'

'I was,' Nathaniel said hopelessly. 'But it's no use——'

'I suppose,' Jacob Abraham said slowly, 'I suppose that you are determined to go?'

Nathaniel stared at him.

'Clerk to a chief, eh?' Jacob Abraham mused.

Then the ebony head came alive. The eyes glinted once more with inborn shrewdness.

'How much did he offer you?' he asked abruptly.

Startled, Nathaniel told him.

'Well, well,' Mensah had regained his effusive manner, 'if you stay, I'll give you twenty pounds a year more than that.'

'Why?' Nathaniel cried. 'You don't want me to stay, after what I said? Why?'

Jacob Abraham leaned forward across the desk.

'Shall I tell you?' His voice was amiable. 'Shall I tell you why I want you to stay? Because you are a sincere man, Amegbe. You have said hard things to me just now. And to my mind you are not as clever as you might be. But you are sincere and hard-working. That is not so easy to find. Yes, and you are honest.'

He gestured with one hand, and it became a gesture of helplessness. He frowned, and for a moment his face was puzzled.

'You must realize,' he said, 'I have made up my mind — we are going to achieve government standard for this school. Yes, I have made up my mind on that. Only — I am

not a young man, Amegbe. The ways of today are not —
sometimes they are not so much known to me. Perhaps you
young men — ways and means — you know about these
things——'

His voice trailed off. He did not want to say it. He wanted
Nathaniel to understand without having to hear it said.

And all at once Nathaniel did understand.

Jacob Abraham was a man of energy and persuasion, and
he dreamed of glory. For him, glory was to see Futura
Academy accepted in all the right circles, a respected
institution, himself the head and founder. But things were
being done in a new way these days. Perhaps he even
realized at last that higher teaching standards might
actually pay him in the long run. He needed someone to be
an interpreter for him, a barometer by which he could
gauge the changing weather of the spirit.

They looked at each other across the desk. Nathaniel felt
tense, excited. Jacob Abraham needed an honest man. It
was as simple as that.

All these years, Nathaniel had believed he was being kept
on here only on sufferance. But it was not that way, not any
more. Jacob Abraham needed him. Jacob Abraham needed
an honest man.

What if things had gone wrong once? They need not
again. Now he would have power here, power to change
things. And he would change, himself. At heart he was an
honest man.

It occurred to Nathaniel that if he returned the necklace
and the shirts, it would buy back his honesty. That was
what he would do. He would do it. And after this, he would
not be foolish again, he would not make any more foolish
mistakes. He would be the man he had been before. He
would come back to the school with new authority.

'I will stay,' Nathaniel said at last.

— Let the grey parrot scream from the 'odum' tree and let the strangler vines reach down to grasp at nothing. Forest, you will not have me yet. And let the River beat its brown waters on the banks. Let it mourn for its child that has shed its gills forever.

'I will stay,' he said again.

Jacob Abraham's head bobbed up and down with pleasure.

'Fine, fine, fine,' he said smoothly. 'We will work it out together. We will make people hear about Futura Academy. You will make suggestions, eh? You are in touch with these things. A new curriculum — yes, yes, that's it. You are a sincere man, Amegbe. Not too clever, in some ways, perhaps, but a sincere man — that is the thing. You will be Futura's "kra", eh? How is that?'

He laughed uproariously at his joke.

Nathaniel tried to laugh, too, but the laughter stuck in his throat. He was to be its 'kra', then, its soul, seeking perfection? Its guide in a new land, its ferryman across Jordan. All that, when he did not know the way himself?

'What does that leave you to be?' he asked.

Jacob Abraham chortled appreciatively.

'Yes,' he said, 'just what you are thinking.'

By the same sacrilegious comparison, Jacob Abraham would be the 'sunsum' of the school. Its personality, filled with self, greedy for life, but with an enormous vitality, an enormous will.

Perhaps the analogy was not so absurd after all. Nathaniel felt hope flowing back into him. They might just bring it off, the two of them. They might just manage it. They might, after all, make something of this old grey wreck of a place, this chipped, battered, decayed and twisted shell that dreamed it was a pearl. They would blunder and deceive themselves. But they might just do it.

'We must have faith!' Nathaniel cried, in impulsive joy. 'We will do something, do something. It will be all right — you will see!'

On his way home, Nathaniel stopped in at his church. It was cool and quiet inside, away from the sun and heat. No one else was there. Nathaniel walked the length of the church to the niche where the ebony Madonna stood.

She was there, serene with love, the Mother of all men, her painted blue cloak around her black-gleaming shoulders. She looked at him from her calm eyes, and they became for him no longer wood.

He stood beside her, awkwardly, wanting to kneel but afraid someone might see him there in broad daylight and wonder what trouble he had that made him kneel here, now by himself.

— Mother, Mother — forgive me. I am staying here. Forgive me, but I cannot go back. Never in my life. Let them understand.

— I have a new chance and I have a new name and I live in a new land with a new name. And I cannot go back. Let them understand. If I do something or if I do nothing, I must stay. A man must belong somewhere. If it is right or if it is not right, I must stay. The new roots may not grow straight, but they have grown too strong to be cut away. It is the dead who must die. Let them understand.

— In my Father's house are many mansions. A certain Drummer dwells in the House of Nyankopon, in that City of Many Mansions. I know it now. It is there that he dwells, honoured, now and always. It may be that I shall never see him again. But let him dwell there in peace. Let him understand. No — he will never understand. Let me accept it and leave him in peace.

— I cannot have both gods and I cannot have neither. A man must belong somewhere. Mother of men, hear me——

— My God is the God of my own soul, and my own speech is in my mouth, and my home is here, here, here, my home is here at last.

— Let me wash my soul.

— And let the fear go far from me.

After he left the church, the mood of exaltation wore off and reality returned.

He had to send the money to Kwaale. He had to. There was no excuse now. And Adua was insisting on a celebration of the birth of the child. She had asked more than twenty people already and she promised to provide chop. That left him with the drink to buy, palm-wine and gin. How was he going to do it?

Nathaniel began thinking once more about Kumi and Awuletey.

Could honesty be bought back with a piece of gold and a piece of cloth? It was the way a man felt that mattered. If you resolved to do right, what did it matter what went before?

How could he return them, anyway? Kumi and Awuletey would not be impressed. They would only think he had gone crazy. They did not expect the gifts back. They had long ago shrugged it off — the luck of the draw. What would he say to them? He would be too embarrassed to say anything to them. They would think he had lost his mind.

He knew if the boys had got the jobs, he would never have considered returning the gifts. Why should he now? A gift was, after all, a gift. Besides, one of the shirts had been worn.

Nathaniel decided to put the whole thing from his mind. He turned his thoughts to the plans he had for next term. He whistled 'Akpanga' softly to himself.

And soon the uneasiness passed.

At mid-day, the Club bar was empty except for Kwaku, the old steward, who stood behind the counter, his shrunken shoulders hunched inside the white-drill jacket as he polished doggedly a battered champagne bucket. Johnnie wondered how many people drank champagne these days.

'Use this one much, Kwaku?'

The old man shook his head.

'No, sah. On'y small-small, dis time. Dis one, he too cost. Long time pas', Eur'pean use dis one — oh, plenty-plenty.'

He chuckled softly, perhaps recalling those munificent years, and the 'dash' given by the drinkers of champagne to a young stewardboy, quick on his feet, strong, princely in white robe and turban and vivid cummerbund.

'No big man now, sah,' Kwaku said. 'All dey gone.'

He fetched Johnnie's beer. Then he picked up the yellow flannel and began polishing once more, polishing memories.

Johnnie paid for his drink and went out to the verandah. The branches of the giant niim tree waved slowly, hypnotically. This place was remote, cool, deceptive. The city, the shouting streets, the gabbling markets, the beggars and traders and clerks, the children like insects crawling and swarming, the clinging red dust, the heat of the sun — all seemed very far removed, but they were only a stone's throw away.

Johnnie drank, and the cold brown taste washed the hot morning from his mouth. He thought of the phone call he had received earlier. Cameron Sheppard had just arrived at the airport. He would be busy until noon, but he wanted Johnnie to meet him then.

Cameron would have to be told about the boys. And there was something else to be done as well. Johnnie wondered if anyone had ever before told Cameron Sheppard to go to hell.

Here he was now.

'Nice to see you again, Johnnie.'

Cameron wore a light suit of some wrinkleproof material, the type of suit sold by tropical outfitters in Bond Street. He had probably picked that shade of grey because it matched the sincere grey of his glasses' frame. Johnnie became conscious of his own clothes — limp sweat-pocked shirt with the sleeves rolled up; khaki trousers clumsily sewn by a local tailor and badly pressed by Whiskey with a charcoal iron.

'Two more, Kwaku,' he called, half angrily, and the old man appeared on the stoep, bearing in arthritic hands the tray of bottles and glasses.

'I expect you're wondering why I've come out again so soon,' Cameron said briskly. 'I'll go directly to the point, Johnnie. First of all, the pilot scheme we agreed upon. I realized afterwards, of course, that boys from secondary schools simply wouldn't do. If we had more time to train them, yes. But as it is, we've got to go further up. I mean the university here — that's where the real administrative potential exists. We've been trying to do things on the cheap. We can't think in those terms any more.'

Openmouthed, Johnnie gazed at the other man.

'From now on,' Cameron was saying, 'our thinking must be on a larger scale. That brings up the second and most important point. I've put the case before the Board——'

He paused. He poured out his beer and took a quick sip.

'It's all arranged,' Cameron said, and his voice was almost brusque in his mannerly attempt to be casual in triumph. 'James is going to be retired right away. That's one reason for my trip — I have to tell him. Bedford, of course, will be going — perhaps you've heard. I shall come out here and manage the Textile Branch myself, at least until after Independence. I managed Textiles in Lagos, you know, for quite some time before I got the partnership. It'll be a temporary measure — I shan't stay indefinitely. I'll tell you quite frankly, Johnnie, once things have been organized here, I've been promised a senior partnership when Mr. Bright retires next year. You can see, then, that I'll need an assistant, a man who can learn quickly, who can help with the Africanization programme, and to whom I can ultimately hand over.'

He broke off and smiled.

'Will you do it, Johnnie?' Cameron asked.

Johnnie gaped at him. Assistant manager, with the prospect of becoming manager within a year. It would be meteoric, compared with the Firm's past policies. But things happened quickly nowadays. The time of the twenty-year period of virtual apprenticeship was over.

Johnnie felt vaguely that he ought to observe a decent interval of deliberation. But it would be pointless to pretend there was any real question at all.

'Yes,' he said. 'Certainly I will.'

'Good,' Cameron said. 'I knew you would. Another thing, Johnnie. I'm not particularly worried about your short experience in Africa, but when you take over from me, you'll need a right-hand man, someone who knows the country inside out. I've found just the chap. An African. I knew him at the London School of Economics. I went back a few years ago, you know, and got my degree. He's an

odd sort of fellow, but rather brilliant in his way. Bit of
luck, really, my knowing him. That was where I was
this morning — seeing him. The way I visualize it, the three
of us will work in close co-operation over this Africanization
business. You, myself, and Victor.'

Johnnie blinked.

'Who? Who did you say?'

'Victor Edusei.'

Johnnie threw back his head and laughed. So this was
Victor's informant in London. No wonder the African had
been so amused, so smug, that first time.

'That's strange,' Cameron said. 'Victor did the same
thing. He said he wasn't much interested in textiles, but
nevertheless it was the only job in the country that would
tempt him. But he wouldn't say why. He told me you'd met.
What did you think of him?'

'I may as well admit it — I didn't like him.'

'Well, it was mutual, as no doubt you know. But I don't
give a damn whether you like each other or not. All I want
to know is — can you work together?'

Johnnie hesitated.

'I think so,' he said finally. 'We'll watch each other like
hawks, but perhaps that won't be such a bad idea. One
thing about him — he doesn't put on an act. At least you
know where you stand with a person like that.'

'Yes,' Cameron said. 'That's precisely what he had to
say about you.'

Johnnie drove back to the office alone. He parked his car
and walked along the street to Allkirk, Moore & Bright's old
building, the building that had stood since the year of the
last Ashanti War.

He walked past Mandiram's, and suddenly he stopped.

Cora was in there. She was dressed in yellow, and on her jaundiced face was an expression of hopeless longing. She stood at the brocade counter, and her hands quivered over a bolt of rich blue.

Johnnie looked quickly away. Then he crossed the street, so she would not see him.

That afternoon, Johnnie and Miranda left the baby in the care of Whiskey's young wife while they drove out to Sakumono beach. They walked along the sand, past a grove of palms, a sacred grove. A few old fishing boats rested on the shore near the palms. They were grey and cracked, husks of fishing boats, like shells cast off by sea creatures. Beside them, the women of the village waited with their headpans for the evening boats to ride the wild breakers, bringing the day's catch to shore.

Miranda walked close to the fetish huts, little hives of woven straw, concealing their power and their fear from the casual eye.

Johnnie watched her. She would never know what was inside the huts, what collection of bones or tangled hair or freak sea-spine comprised their godhead. They were tightly tied at the top of the hive, sealed off as their worshippers were sealed, defying curiosity.

The green ragged leaves of the coconut palms rustled and whispered, ancient untranslatable voices.

But there was another voice on the wind. In the nearby fishing village, a young man was singing a highlife, a new song.

NATHANIEL lifted his son up and took him onto the
stoep. In front of the house the city sprawled, lax-
limbed, like a giant fisherman tired after work, like
a giant cocoa-picker tired after work. The houses sprawled
yellow-brown along the shore, and it was not yet night. The
lamps were not lighted yet, and the night drums had only
begun. The women at their stalls were still selling hot kenkey
balls and peeled oranges. There was a smell of sweet food
frying on charcoal burners. The mammy-lorries honked their
horns, the city's voice.

And beyond the city, the plains. And beyond the plains,
the forest. And beyond the forest, the desert.

'Aya!' he cried. 'Shall we call him Joshua? That's a
good name, isn't it?'

'He has his names already,' she said, smiling.

'But Joshua — that's a good name.'

'All right,' she said, 'if you want it.'

Nathaniel held the baby up again, high in his arms.

'See —' he said, 'yours, Joshua.'

— Someone saw it. Someone crossed that River and won
that battle. Someone took that city and made it his.

'You'll know what to do with it, boy, won't you?' he said
softly, pleadingly. 'You'll know how to make it work. You'll
know how to make it all go well.'

The baby began to cry. Aya shouted that it was feeding time and did he want the baby to catch a chill out there anyway?

Nathaniel adjusted his glasses and walked indoors, the child held clumsily in his arms. He felt a little self-conscious, even in front of his wife, and wondered why he let himself be carried away.

Aya took the baby and put him to her breast. Nathaniel got out the new curriculum and picked up his pen. But he could not concentrate on the work.

He glanced at his son, and the name kept beating through his mind like all the drums of Ghana.

— Joshua, Joshua, Joshua. I beg you. Cross Jordan, Joshua.

THE END

Afterword

BY GEORGE WOODCOCK

Margaret Laurence completed the first full draft of *This Side Jordan*, a highly topical novel about Africans and Europeans in the Gold Coast, in 1957 – the year the colony gained independence as Ghana – and it was published in 1960. Thus we look at it now through two dense and different screens of events: Laurence's own later achievement in the cycle of Canadian novels that began with the publication of *The Stone Angel* in 1964; and the changes that have taken place in Africa since 1957 and have forced us to reconsider what Laurence herself described as "the predominantly optimistic outlook of many Africans and many western liberals in the late 1950s and early 1960s," an outlook she saw reflected in her books on Africa.

This Side Jordan was the first work – and in many ways a tentative one – of a major literary career, and also a book that, if we see it as merely topical, deals with events long superseded. But, unlike many such apprentice books reflecting a lost past, it is a novel that continues to be read in its own right and not merely because of Laurence's later and better-known books. And there are excellent reasons for its tenacious survival when so many novels inspired by the breakup of the British Empire are already forgotten. *This Side Jordan* remains important for two reasons: for its peculiar insights into the changes going on in the outlook of Africans during the 1950s and in their relation to the Europeans; and for its relationship to Laurence's other writings.

This Side Jordan was Laurence's first published book, though some of the short stories about Africa that were collected in *The Tomorrow-Tamer* (1963) had already appeared. With the latter collection, and *The Prophet's Camel Bell* (1963), arguably the best travel book ever written by a Canadian, it forms a closely knit group projecting the seven years of experience, in Somaliland and in Ghana – experience of strange places and of her own often unexpected reactions to them – that really started Laurence off as a writer. She had indeed been writing since her teens, but in Africa took place the happy conjunction of time to spare and an environment that from the beginning engaged her imagination. As she herself observed, "I was fortunate in going to Africa when I did – in my early twenties – because for some years I was so fascinated by the African scene that I was prevented from writing an autobiographical first novel."

Laurence used her African experiences and first impressions so intensively and with such empathetic imagination that, by the time in the early 1960s when she turned to her mythical Canadian community of Manawaka, she no longer had the sense of a need to write about the continent that had once so commandingly preoccupied her, and none of the major characters in her Canadian novels is shown as having been anywhere near Africa. Yet, though the experience of Africa itself seems to have become encapsulated in Laurence's memory, the links between *This Side Jordan* and the later novels are in a formal way very clear.

This Side Jordan not merely took the place of a thinly disguised fictional autobiography as its writer's opening book. It also showed itself as something more than a mere apprentice's exercise by the audacity with which it handled the vital conjunction in the mid-twentieth century of the African tribal consciousness and the European rational and individualized consciousness.

In appearance at least, *This Side Jordan* is a realistic third-person novel, a "well-made" book rather neatly arranged around an African couple, Nathaniel and Aya Amegbe, and an English couple, Johnnie and Miranda Kestoe. The place is the Gold Coast capital of Accra, and the time is the eve of independence; with a touch of rather obvious symbolism, Aya and Miranda have children in time to anticipate the birth of the new state.

The appearance of a deliberately integrated structure is deceptive, as the reader begins to anticipate when he finds his attention engaged by individual scenes – a market, a night club, a noisy religious procession – which are richly evoked and at times divert one's attention from the flow of the narrative to admire the local colour on the way. And in fact, as Laurence herself has stated, she wrote the novel in a series of episodes, beginning with the final scenes, and only after a great deal of writing did she see the novel as a whole and realize that there was a natural order to it.

Laurence had already, it seems, adopted the practice that she developed in her later novels of conceiving the characters first and allowing the action to take its shape from their *inter*-action. In fact, though the novel is told by an anonymous narrator, we actually see everything through the alternating viewpoints of the two leading male characters, and we observe the other people in the novel, however important they may be, through their eyes; the pattern of alternating chapters, devoted to African and European points of view respectively, is perhaps somewhat mechanical in effect, but nonetheless effective in a novel where the theme of opposing cultures is dominant and the issues, at that moment in colonial history, are clear and straightforward.

This Side Jordan departs from the orthodox third-person novel in developing the interior monologue in a way that anticipated Laurence's richly varied experimental renderings of awareness and memory in the books of the Manawaka cycle. Later on, in an address, "Gadgetry or Growing: Form and Voice in the Novel" (1969), Laurence expressed doubts about the effectiveness of what she had done in *This Side Jordan*.

> As far as voice is concerned, I think now that the novel contains too much of Nathaniel's inner monologues. I actually wonder how I ever had the nerve to attempt to go into the mind of an African man, and I suppose if I'd really known how difficult was the job I was attempting, I would never have tried it. I am not at all sorry I tried it, and in fact I believe from various comments made by African reviewers that at least some parts of the African chapters have a certain authenticity. But not, perhaps, as much as I once believed.

The African chapters not only have authenticity. They carry conviction in a surprising way when one considers that Laurence lived only five years in Ghana, and, while she was there, mingled mainly with Africans who were already largely Europeanized. The crucial passages in these interior monologues are those in which Nathaniel's tribal myths – those of his ancestors and his own early childhood – clash with the Christian myths and values imposed on him from the time he went to mission school as a small boy. In this sense Nathaniel is the type of the educated African at the end of the colonial era in the late 1950s.

What is especially interesting is that Laurence does not attempt to treat tribal beliefs as rationally comprehensible concepts; rather she materializes them as visions and voices in what seems to be a bicameral mind in the process of detachment from the world of myth.

One can get a sense of Laurence's intuitive originality by reading *The Origin of Consciousness in the Breakdown of the Bicameral Mind*, a controversial book in which Julian Jaynes traces the rise of rationality in the ancient world through the breakdown of the myth-making mentality, a change he attributes to the influence of massive external catastrophes impinging on ancient myth-dominated cultures. But Jaynes did not publish his book until 1978. Laurence was already putting forward similar ideas two decades before him in her portrayal of Nathaniel Amegbe struggling with the voices of myth and custom that echo in his mind as he makes his way through a world irrevocably changing under the influence of colonialism and its aftermath.

This Side Jordan is a brilliant imaginative grasping of what must indeed have been going on in terms of changing awareness in the minds of many Africans of this period. In terms of Laurence's work as a whole, it takes on importance as the first of her explorations of the various uses of the interior monologue as a means of giving fictional form to the way our minds work as they mingle memory and present perception in the great tapestry of the retrospective consciousness.

This Side Jordan was the best of a number of novels published during the 1960s by Canadians who had lived and served in West Africa, and it can still be read as a valuable fictional document of the times. But, more than that, Laurence carried out the unusual feat of writing a vividly topical novel that would turn, as time went on, into what seems now a valid work of historical fiction. This, I think, is because she wrote about people – both Europeans and Africans – who remembered the past vividly and lived the present fully, but who also looked to the future that has been unfolding in Africa since the book's publication. Some of them – mainly Africans – looked to the future with a naive optimism, and some were still too trapped in tradition to look anywhere but into the past; others, particularly the older European merchants, anticipated with dread the collapse of the paternalistic establishment they had created. Yet others, less naive, saw the future in more realistic terms, like the ruthlessly climbing young Englishman, Johnnie Kestoe, who sees in the rapidly changing course of events the setting for his own career, and Victor Edusei, the realistic and English-educated African journalist, who utters to Nathaniel a prophecy in which we see Laurence in the late 1950s foreseeing with remarkable accuracy the course that events in Ghana and so many other of the liberated African states would take once these countries gained their independence.

> You put your faith in Ghana, don't you? The new life.
> Well, that's fine, boy. That's fine for you. But as far as I'm concerned, it's a dead body lying unburied. You wait until after Independence. You'll see such oppression as you never believed possible. Only of course it'll be all right then – it'll be black men oppressing black men, and who could object to that? There'll be your Free-Dom for you – the right to be enslaved by your own kind.

Of course one does not count political foresight among the necessary virtues of a novelist. But, taken with Laurence's evident understanding of the role of myth and custom in primitive societies, its presence does indicate the kind of many-sided sensitivity to the total nature of a community that makes for successful social realist fiction. In this and other ways, *This Side Jordan* is not only the first chronologically of Laurence's novels but also a book that, despite all the vast differences in setting and action, anticipated almost all that Laurence eventually achieved in her Manawaka novels.